Murder Between the Worlds

A Between the Worlds Novel

By Morgan Daimler

ISBN-13: 978-1502837318
ISBN-10: 1502837315

This book is for everyone who reads the old fairy-stories and wonders, what if?

Dedicated to the Fairfield County Writers group, and especially my friend Cathy Kane, who inspired me to give this fiction novel writing a try. And to my "beta readers": Tricia, Maya, Maddy, and Cathy, who read the draft and gave me constructive criticism and encouragement.

Table of Contents

Guide to Characters Names and Pronunciations

Aliaine "Allie" McCarthy–Ah-lee-awnya–
Bleidd–Blayth
Syndra Lyons -
Elizabeth "Liz" McCarthy–
Jason Takada–
Jim Riordan–
Rick Walters -
Jessilaen–Jes-ih-layn
Brynneth–Bree-nehth
Zarethyn–Zair-eh-theen
Aeyliss–Ay-ee-lihs
Natarien–Nah-tah-ree-ehn
Ferinyth–Feh-rihn-eeth
Daeriun–Day-rih-uhn
Morighent–Mor-ih-hent

Elven Clans mentioned in the book:

Firinne–Fih-rih-neh
Leighis–Lee-his
Soileireacht–Sol-eh-recht

Prologue

Awareness came slowly, through a fog. Her first clear thought was that she was cold, followed immediately by the realization that she was lying flat on her back, naked, on what seemed to be a rock. The rough prickling of stone was uncomfortable on her back and she felt exposed laying out like that. Her mouth was dry and tasted strange. Her next thought was to wonder how drunk she'd gotten to end up like this and then to worry that someone had slipped something into one of her drinks. It had been a crazy party and she hadn't known most of the people there, anything could have happened. Groaning, she tried to roll over and only then realized she couldn't; her wrists and ankles were tied to something. Sudden panic pushed through the last of the haze and she forced her heavy eyes open.

The sky was a dark void above her, rimmed with the darker shapes of trees. She managed to move her head to the left, towards a slight shuffling sound, and was momentarily blinded by a sudden flare of light. Her mind felt as if it were working in slow motion as she realized it was a candle being lit. The flickering light illuminated a figure moving purposely around where she was lying, but the person was covered, head to toe, in what she thought was a long cloak. She couldn't even begin to guess whether it was a man or woman and her head pounded with the effort to keep her eyes open. The figure lit a second candle closer to her feet; she tried to speak, to beg to be freed, but all that came out was a muffled groaning sound. The figure paused for moment then moved to light a third candle. *Please*, she thought, desperately, pleadingly, *please let this be a dream. Let me really wake up now.*

But the cloaked figure moved on, relentlessly, to a fourth candle. She thought about her mother, warning her before she went out earlier to be careful. Telling her about the murders that had been in the newspapers, about the girls' bodies found in parking lots…she'd blown her mother off, of course. Nothing bad was going to happen to *her*. She started to cry, tears making her vision a pool of light and shadow.

As the fifth candle added its glow to the circle, the figure turned towards the girl bound to the rough altar-shaped rock in the center, and the silence of the deep night was broken by screams.

A long time later, as pre-dawn began to light the eastern sky the little clearing in the woods fell silent again.

****

"So tell us again how you found her," Detective Riordan pressed, trying to push without letting the suspect know he *was* a suspect. The whole thing was hinky as Hell, and he knew deep down he shouldn't even be talking to the guy. Elves were out of his jurisdiction.

The suspect was sitting at one of the cheap wooden desks in the room that the department had set aside for non-humans to write down witness statements when they needed to, since that was about as much as the treaty allowed. He was tall, over 6 and a half feet, and wore jeans and a black t-shirt. Riordan couldn't figure out why half the elves kept dressing in fancy imitations of medieval human dress, and the other half embraced modern human fashions. He'd have thought they'd have their own styles, but it seemed like it was all copies of human stuff. The guy hunched over the paperwork as if he didn't want to be watched and that was another weird thing; in Riordan's experience elves were usually all about getting attention.

The elf sighed, looking bored. "As I said before, I was walking from the coffee shop on East Road towards Oak.

"Down the back alley" Riordan said, wanting to make sure.

The elf gave him a long look. "Yes, heading down the alley. And I saw something that seemed, odd, out of place. I went to get a closer look..."he trailed off, then shrugged slightly.

Riordan tried not to sigh. This was another non-specific non-answer, just like every other tonight. Getting any details out of this guy was like pulling teeth. He'd practically memorized the *Law Enforcement Guide to Inter-cultural Interactions* but he still couldn't figure elves out. They never did what you expected them to do and they took everything you said as an insult while simultaneously being a touchy-feely nightmare. Even for an elf though this one was squirrelly as hell and Riordan didn't like it.

He tried a different tactic, "Pretty horrible thing, that poor girl getting raped and cut up like that."

The elf gave him another long condescending look, and said nothing.

A slight tap on the door distracted him, "Listen, you keep working on that witness statement, lots of detail, I'll be right back."

The detective tried to act nonchalant as he left the room, carefully closing the door behind him. As he'd expected his partner, Detective Rick Walters, was waiting in the hallway.

"You're not gonna like this, Jim."

Riordan sighed and rubbed his eyes. "I haven't liked anything so far tonight. Just get to the point."

"I contacted 'em like you asked and they pulled jurisdiction on us–sent a whole squad of their own. Said if our guy's the killer then it's their job to handle it."

Walters sounded really spun up. Not too surprising since this had been their case since day one and the idea of having some pointy-eared Fairy cops waltzing in now that they finally had a suspect was pretty galling, even if he'd expected it. The Treaty was explicit in defining who had jurisdiction over which suspects. Riordan groaned inwardly though knowing that his partner was going to have a hard time not saying or doing anything to insult the Elven cops. Walters was a great cop–one of the best detectives on the force, with an almost supernatural ability to solve tough crimes–but he had a real problem dealing with the various Fairy beings, especially the elves.

Riordan shook his head and headed down the hall as Walters kept talking, "The Captain's with them now, kissing ass…"

The two detectives rounded a corner and Riordan saw Captain Lewis standing with the four Elven Guards. It was hard to miss the elves; they stood out in the human squad room, making everything around them look cheap and bland. Of course it would be hard to go anywhere and miss a group standing at military attention, in formation, wearing swords.

At least they aren't in armor, Riordan thought, *it's bad enough seeing people running around wearing swords, but the armor they wear for high security stuff makes me feel like I've time warped back a couple hundred years. Not that black cargo pants and medieval tunics make much sense as a uniform either, but I guess it is distinctive. So is the matching long hair in matching braids. God, elves are weird.* Riordan felt a headache coming on and wondered if he had any Tylenol in his desk.

The Captain saw them walking across the room and waved them over, "Riordan! Walters! How's it going in there? Any progress?"

"Not yet Captain. He's still sticking with his story, saying he was going down the alley and found her."

"And you doubt this?" One of the elves, a tall blond, asked.

"Yeah, his whole story seems off to us. The guy just isn't very bothered by finding a dead girl. Didn't even want to stick around to talk to us. Something weird going on with him, for sure," Walters said, and Riordan prayed he'd watch his mouth. He and Walters had been partners for years; they were friends outside of work. Hell, he'd even asked Walters to be his daughter's godfather, but he knew his partner was a straight up bigot where elves were concerned and it made cases like these an even bigger pain in the ass to work than they already were.

Very familiar with Walters's track record with non-humans, and possibly thinking the same thing, Captain Lewis stepped in.

"Detectives, this is Captain Zarethyn and his squad from the Border Outpost. They're here to help us investigate the murders."

Help us my ass, take over is more like it, Riordan thought, but he smiled and extended a hand, which the tall elf shook. "I'm Jim Riordan and this is my partner Rick Walters."

The elves all nodded and their Captain gestured at his people, starting with the closest, a slightly shorter blond. "This is Commander Jessilaen," next a red haired woman, "Aeyliss, a gifted magical tracker…"

"What's a magical tracker?" Walters cut in, and Riordan winced slightly knowing it was rude, and elves hated rude. This lot was either really forgiving or on orders to be nice because they ignored the faux pas and answered politely.

"I can track most spells back to their source," the red head said, after a slight nod from her Captain, "under the right circumstances."

"And this," Zarethyn finished before Walters could ask anything else, gesturing at the last elf, who had dark hair and an annoyingly calm expression, "is Brynneth, our medic."

"Captain Zarethyn and his people are going to form a joint task force with you two to get to the bottom of whatever's been going on with these killings," Captain Lewis said, ignoring the outraged looks from both detectives. "All the victims may be human but if the killer isn't it's out of our jurisdiction. This way whether the killer's human or not we're covered and we'll have more people on the job working at solving this."

An uncomfortable silence followed as Riordan and Walters fumed and the elves ignored their obvious anger.

"Perhaps now would be a good time to share what you know so far, before we question the suspect?" the other blond, Jessilaen, finally said.

Walters bristled immediately, so Riordan spoke quickly. "This is the fourth body. They're all the same: young women between 15 and 23, raped, slashed repeatedly, methodically, then killed and dumped in parking lots. We hadn't had any strong leads until now. This guy is smart and he covers his tracks."

"Then why would he suddenly change his pattern and report a body himself?" the Elven Captain asked.

"Hard to say. Maybe he's getting cocky. Maybe he's playing with us. Maybe he even wants to get caught," Riordan explained.

"This guy has a record," Walters added, obviously happy about that.

The elves exchanged glances then their Captain spoke "How can he have a human criminal record?"

"Not a human one," Walters said, "with you guys. You kicked him out."

All the elves went very still. Zarethyn continued to speak for the group. "He is an Outcast?"

"Oh yeah," Walters smiled.

Riordan cut in. "According to his file back in the 1960's he was Outcast by the Guard." He looked up and was surprised to see the cold calculation in the elves eyes now.

"Let us go question your suspect," the Captain said, and suddenly Riordan felt bad for the guy, shifty and guilty as he seemed to be. He led the way to the small room and opened the door for the Guard to enter, as soon as they did the suspect leaped to his feet so quickly he knocked the chair over. It hit the floor with a loud bang. Riordan's hand twitched towards his gun unconsciously; it was not hard to remember how strong elves were or how fast they could move when they got jumpy like that.

The Guard didn't like it any better than Riordan did, moving to block the doorway. The suspect backed against the wall, his eyes shifting from one elf to the next. Riordan had a sinking feeling that the whole thing was about to go to shit, but irrelevantly found himself hoping they kept speaking English and didn't go off in their own language, which just sounded like a lot of indecipherable vowels and mumbling to him.

The Guard Captain spoke briskly, "We are here to clarify your role in this situation."

"My role?" the other elf said, clearly furious. "My role? Screw you."

The Captain's voice was cold, "Do not presume to speak to me that way-"

"I'll speak to you however I want. I'm not part of Fairy anymore, thanks to the Guard. I've already told the police everything I can so you can take your presumptuous questions and shove them right up your ass," the other elf said, still flat against the wall as if he expected a fight. Riordan was half afraid that was exactly what was going to happen.

"Keep a civil tongue, Outcast," the second in command said, his hand grasping the hilt of his sword.

"Or what? You'll strike me down for treating you with the respect you really deserve? Fuck you," the other elf shot back.

The second in command's eyes narrowed dangerously. "Perhaps I should cut your insolent tongue from your foolish mouth."

Riordan felt a surge of panic, envisioning the reams of paperwork in his future if the Elven Guard killed or maimed someone in his custody, but before he could decide how best to diffuse the situation, the Guard Captain spoke again, "Enough. Tell us plainly if you are involved in these murders."

The other elf looked like he wanted to spit at the Fairy cop. "Go fuck your own sword."

"You do not deny the accusation then?" the Captain said. The Outcast elf spit, although he missed hitting anyone. Two of the Guards started to step forward, but their Captain shouted, "Hold!" and they froze. He looked at the other elf like he was trying to see through him as the seconds ticked by. No one moved. Finally he turned and walked out, his squad following him. Riordan hurried after, trying to get out before the suspect could ask to go.

Walters, standing in the hallway, looked as shocked as Riordan felt, "What the hell just happened?"

"His refusal to answer questions is very suspicious," the Guard Captain said tensely.

"Maybe, but we can't hold him without evidence," Riordan said, his head pounding.

"What do you normally do in such situations?" the dark haired elf asked, sounding genuinely uncertain.

"Let the suspect go and try to get enough evidence to question him again or arrest him," Walters said.

"Then we must try to do this your way. It is unnatural for an elf to act this way, but as an Outcast he is beyond our reach, unless it is proved he is guilty" the second in command said, clearly still angry.

I bet you aren't used to getting told off like that, Riordan thought before saying, "Okay, we'll do this the human way."

Chapter 1 - Monday

Allie woke up with a jolt to a loud bang; she began reflexively yelling at the cat when a second bang followed the first. Feeling thoroughly annoyed with the world she glanced at the clock–2:16 a.m.–and struggled out of bed. Halfway to the bedroom door a third crash accompanied by the distinctive sound of breaking glass could be heard. She dragged a hand across her face and contemplated pulling on some pants before deciding that the oversized t-shirt she slept in was fine. Since none of the magical wards had been breached the odds were this was roommate related and not a break-in or anything worse.

She opened her door and peered out into the dark second floor hallway, thinking, not for the first time, that while her mixed heritage was often more of an annoyance than anything else, the ability to see well in low light situations certainly saved on electricity. Although the hallway was empty, the sound of shuffling and a muffled thump from the downstairs entryway indicated where the problem was. As Allie headed towards the stairs, feeling resigned, she heard the soft click of a door closing at the opposite end of the hall. It was mildly surprising that Liz was home at all since her job at the theatre usually kept her out until near-dawn, but not that she was choosing to stay out of whatever drama was unfolding downstairs. The house technically belonged to Liz, who took in roommates to cover the costs of maintaining the hulking old Victorian, but Allie's cousin had no magical abilities and limited self-defense skills, so she usually relied on the others to take care of security issues. Allie and Bleidd handled the magical end, and Syndra and Jason took care of physical threats. Living where they did, right in the very heart of one of the Borderlands between mortal Earth and Faery, there was a constant threat of some kind of disturbance at the house.

Many houses in the neighborhood had been abandoned decades ago as people moved closer to the Earth edge of town after the Sundering had ripped the fabric of reality and permanently fused the two worlds together. Of course the town had torn the abandoned homes down over the years, but it meant that the old Victorian that had once been surrounded by tightly packed neighbors now stood alone in the middle of a rough wood that was quickly reclaiming the empty lots. There were only three other houses on their street and none of them were exactly close, making the house a tempting target for thieves. And living by the wild wood meant that it wasn't uncommon for fairy creatures to wander in either, like the pixies that had invaded the garden a few weeks back, or the ghostly dog that had gotten into the house and taken hours to chase back out.

I should be grateful Syn's working tonight, Allie thought grudgingly looking for the bright side, *she'd be charging down the hall waving her gun and scaring everyone to death.* Allie knew that Syndra had become a police officer because she genuinely wanted to help people but she often teased the other woman about joining the police force just for an excuse to wear the gun. And handcuff people, although that second accusation was more accurate than teasing given Syn's personality and proclivities.

She moved down the stairs trying not to anticipate what she might see, but was still unsurprised to find Bleidd's tall, dark form sprawled out next to the broken remains of what had been a coat rack, side table, and hallway lamp. The clearly intoxicated elf was trying to get back to his feet without success and the tang of blood mixing with the waves of alcohol in the air told Allie he'd probably cut himself on the broken glass from the lamp. Certain it was unnecessary, her eyes nonetheless flickered quickly around the space by the door, but no one else was there. She had known there wouldn't be anyone; in all the years they'd been roommates Bleidd had never brought anyone, friend or lover, back to the house. Allie suppressed a sigh, tried not to think about how much effort it took him to get drunk in the first place, given his tolerance for alcohol, and moved to help him. She had no doubt this was one of his worse episodes based on his current inability to stand. Even drunk and collapsed in the wreckage of the furniture Bleidd was beautiful in the way that all the elves were. His long black hair had escaped the ponytail he usually wore it in and hung loose around his face. His attempt at non-descript dress–jeans and a black t-shirt– looked incongruous on his tall, lean frame, as if he were trying too hard to be someone he wasn't. There was an aura of Otherworldliness about him that guaranteed no one would ever mistake him for human, even without glimpsing the gracefully pointed ears.

His green eyes fixed on her as she crossed the last few feet between them. He smiled widely, oblivious to the wreckage around him, and greeted her in Elvish.

"Aliaine!" he said, drawing the pronunciation of her full name out into ah-lee-aw-ny-uh, as if each syllable was separate. "Are you heading out to work already?"

She was really tempted to answer him in English so she could avoid the headache of trying to conjugate in Elvish, but wasn't sure if he was sober enough to understand the native language.

"No, Blay-the," she said, intentionally drawing his name out as he had done hers, "it's still night." She spoke as patiently as she could under the circumstances and was rewarded with a befuddled look. He turned and peered intently at the nearest window as if he expected the darkness to disappear.

"Truly?" he asked and simultaneously reached out to grab her, trying again to stand, this time by using her to pull himself up. Caught off guard by the sudden movement, Allie staggered and almost joined him on the floor.

"Bleidd," She grunted, fighting to keep her balance as his weight shifted wildly. He was a foot taller than she was and almost 50 pounds heavier, "Bleidd, stop."

He let her go so quickly that she fell back into the wall with a thump. It was enormously tempting to leave him to sleep it off on the floor, but she considered him one of her few good friends, and she couldn't quite bring herself to leave him to his own drunken devices. He looked up at her, wide eyed, "Did I hurt you?"

"No, but I think you hurt yourself," she replied gently.

He looked quizzical for a moment, and then seemed to lose focus. "Where are your pants?"

She smacked his bloody hand away as he reached out towards her bare legs. *How drunk are you,* she thought, feeling really irritated, but she kept her voice calm when she answered.

"In my room. Come on. You've cut yourself; let's go see how bad it is."

His head dropped, his long dark hair falling across his face as he turned both hands palm up and studied them minutely. After a few seconds he looked up at her, surprised, "I cut my hand."

"Yes, I know, come on..."

He talked over her, "It doesn't hurt."

"My friend," She said, as if she were speaking to a small child, "You are extremely drunk."

"Are we friends?" His voice was sad, but she refused to be distracted now. When he was drunk enough he often sank into self-pitying reflections about being Outcast. She genuinely felt for him, being cut off from his own people and society, but she'd heard the same story too many times to get sucked into it again now.

"Yes, good friends," she said, sliding an arm under his shoulder and managing to get him more-or-less on his feet. She felt a sudden press of tangled emotions coming from him, and took a moment to strengthen her personal shields; the energetic barriers that protected her were her only line of defense against feeling the unwanted emotions of other people. Usually Allie was very good at ignoring her inborn ability, but sometimes, especially when she was touching someone, she couldn't totally block it out. She had long ago decided that being an empath was extremely inconvenient. "Come on, help me out here, you're too heavy for me to carry…"

By alternating coaxing and pushing she managed to get him down the hall and into the first floor bathroom, where she let him slide gracelessly to the floor. The house was old and nowhere did it show more than in the bathrooms with their claw footed tubs and hand carved cabinets. *Liz could probably live for a year on what she'd get selling the vintage fixtures.* Allie thought, not for the first time. Well, she could think about that later; right now she was crammed into the narrow room with a drunken elf bleeding on the pretty tile floor–also not for the first time. She flipped the light switch by the door, wanting better light to see by in case he had any glass in his hand, and the room was filled with weak yellow light from the single wall sconce. *Vintage*, she thought, *isn't all it's cracked up to be.*

He watched her silently as she quickly gathered the basic first aid supplies to deal with whatever damage he'd done to himself. She took his injured hand, turned it over, and after assuring herself the cut was glass-free was just about to clean it out, when he spoke.

"I found a dead body."

"What?" She froze, blinking at him. That was so far out of the realm of anything she thought he might say that she found herself speechless.

He cocked his head to the side, frowning, as if he was trying to decide if he'd misspoken, before repeating, "I found a dead body"

"You found a dead *body*?"

"Yes. A girl. A pretty girl. Dead." He shuddered, something passing over his face that Allie didn't want to think too hard about, "very dead."

Allie looked at him, feeling her mouth hanging open, but too shocked to do anything about it. She heard herself repeating, "A dead body?"

Bleidd kept talking as if he hadn't heard her. "I reported it of course," his voice grew bitter "and they questioned me. *Me*. Of course. Don't have any honor do I?"

His eyes fastened onto hers fiercely, almost desperately, "They questioned me about it. But I would never. Never. It was terrible what was done to her, they asked me about it, raped, mutilated…"

She tried to cut him off then, sensing that he was about to tell her in graphic detail about something that would never get out of her head again. "Of course you wouldn't," she interrupted briskly, getting back to cleaning his hand and swallowing hard. *It must be one of those murders, the girls being killed that Syn was talking about. What are they calling the guy? The parking lot killer, because that's where they find the bodies.*

"She was like you," he said softly.

"Like me? What do you mean?" she felt suddenly frightened by the idea of any connection to this dead girl, like a tingle of foreboding crawling down her spine.

"She wasn't all human," he said, starting to sound sleepy. "Not as much not-human as you but it was there, something in her that wasn't…" He yawned widely. "Wasn't… there was something of Fairy there."

Allie had finished cleaning his hand and was bandaging it now, her mind racing. "Did you tell the police this?"

"Police," he mumbled, the drink clearly catching up to him now, "not *police*. Elven Guard. Bastards. They won't listen to me. They should see it themselves… anyway…"

Well, Allie thought *that explains this particular spectacular bender.* The Elven Guard is the Fairy equivalent of police in the borderlands, but they are also the judge and jury by the law of Fairy. While the human police handled human crimes and suspects, the Guard handle any crimes or suspects involving non-humans, although the increasing number of mixed species people like Allie could end up in either jurisdiction and the occasional cross-species crime was a complicated matter. The important difference is that where the human police are only one part of the justice system, the Elven Guard *is* the system, at least for everyone who isn't a noble. It is the Guard that had Outcast Bleidd and she doubted he would ever forgive them for it, although she was also unsure that they would see what he saw in the dead girl. Bleidd had lived, as an Outcast, among humans for over 50 years, longer than any elf would have done by choice and Allie knew he had developed certain perceptions that others didn't seem to have. He was the only one that had ever known her for what she was on sight anyway.

She wanted to ask him more, but he was trying to curl up on the floor and she knew if she didn't get him up now there'd be no moving him until he sobered up. "Come on, "she said grabbing his other arm and pulling hard, "no sleeping on the floor. Get up."

He mumbled something incoherent but with an effort she managed to get him back on his feet. He wrapped his arms around her, continuing to mumble into her hair, but she ignored him, focusing on getting him to keep moving towards his room. She was just glad it was on the first floor. As she pushed open the door she felt the usual hesitance to enter his space, the side effect of the heavy wards he placed on the room. If he hadn't keyed the wards to let her pass them she would have been unable to get into the room without breaking the spell that held the energetic shields in place. Ignoring the urge to leave she managed to get him the last few feet over to his bed before he passed out, but just barely. For a moment she stood over his inert form in the dark room, trying to catch her breath and wondering why he kept doing this to himself. It was like a slow suicide and it bothered her to think that her friend was so deeply unhappy with his life that living this way was better than facing it. Allie frowned at the thought and then picked a blanket up off the floor to cover him with while he slept, since there was no way for her to get him properly into the bed. She could worry about how to break her friend's self-destructive habits later.

She stood looking down at the unconscious elf for another minute before sighing and heading back out to clean up the mess in the hall. She'd rather just go back to bed, but the odds were that Bleidd wouldn't wake before noon and it was easier to clean up his mess herself than listen to the other three roommates fighting over it. The lamp and table were broken beyond repair but the coat rack was mostly undamaged, having lost a few pegs off its wooden trunk but otherwise still being serviceable. She stood that back up by the door, dragged the assorted wreckage out to the garbage cans by the side of the house, and returned to begin the painstaking process of wiping up the blood and picking up the tiny shards of glass scattered across the floor. She had gotten most of it taken care of when she heard the sound of a key in the door and looking up realized that the hazy light of dawn was just breaking through the window.

She was standing up, feeling satisfied, as Syndra walked in, but her mood soured as soon as she saw the other woman's face. Syn's short blond hair was in its usual chubby ponytail and her uniform was spotless but her expression was so grim Allie expected her to break some horrible news. She didn't have to wait long.

"Where's Bleidd?" Syn asked without the teasing tone that normally colored her voice.

"In his room sleeping off a roaring drunk," Allie responded puzzled.

"You're sure?" Syn pressed.

"Sure?" she shot back, even more confused. "Of course I'm sure, I'm the one who put him there after he practically passed out in front of the door."

"He was really that drunk?" Syn's eyes were moving around the entryway, noting the missing furniture. "What time did he get here?"

"A little after 2. Well, that's when he got in, I have no idea how long it took him to get up the walk and in the door," Allie said, thinking of how totally out of it he'd been.

"He came straight home after the bar closed?"

Allie was getting annoyed now at all the questions, "I didn't ask, but I assume so. *The Tiger* closes at 2 and it's a 5 minute drive. Are you going to arrest him for drunk driving? What the hell's going on Syn?"

"What's going on? He's the prime suspect in all those murders is what's going on," Syn replied grimly.

"That's insane," Allie winced, horrified, "Why? Because he found that body?"

"How'd you know about that? Never mind, he told you right?" Syn pushed past her, tossing her uniform jacket at the battered coat rack and heading towards the kitchen, forcing Allie to jog after her, "It's a total fucking mess. They questioned him; they called me in after they cut him loose and questioned me. They'd been thinking it was just some run-of-the-mill nut job, some human nut job," Syn paused digging through the fridge for a beer. "But now they're looking at it not being a human. They called in the

Guard, formed a joint task force. It's a total fuck show and he's right in the middle of it."

"But why?" Allie asked, genuinely confused.

"His history's against him…"

"You can't be serious!" before Allie could build up any real outrage Syndra kept talking

"His criminal record, his attitude…"

"That's ridiculous! Why would he report the body if…"

"I'm not saying it's him. I'm telling you what they think!" Syn cut her off, her voice rising. "They hinted that maybe he was trying to throw them off track or some stupid shit. It didn't help anything that he basically told the Guard to go fuck themselves. They thought it was really fucking weird that he wouldn't answer any of their questions when elves are supposed to be straight up with each other. He wouldn't tell them anything, but they knew from his address I knew him, and that was fucking fun to explain. So they asked me all kinds of questions about where he goes, what he does."

Allie shook her head, as Syndra chugged half her beer in a few gulps before adding, "Al, I think I may have made it worse."

"Worse? How?" Allie felt her heart sinking at Syn's expression.

"I told them he's a fucking alcoholic. Don't give me that look, he's my friend too, but we both know if there's such a thing as Elven alcoholics he is one. I told them he goes to work and goes to the bar and that's about it, but they got all in a twist about that. Seemed to think it proved he was some kind of deviant or something."

Syndra looked miserable as she spoke and Allie shook her head again, not knowing what to say. All the roommates had become friends over the years, and Allie had no doubt that Syn would never purposely betray anyone in the house, but she was also a cop and her job came first. Syndra finished off the beer and threw the can into the garbage.

"But can't they just do testing, DNA testing, to clear him?"

Syn winced and shook her head. "This killer's really smart. He's like a ghost, no physical evidence worth a damn left behind. No DNA. He uses bleach to clean the bodies up."

Allie shook her head, "But surely there's something? I mean if they know the girls were raped–don't give me that look. Bleidd mentioned the police questioning him about it– isn't there some trace of something, er, genetic, somewhere?"

Syn looked like she'd swallowed a lemon and Allie had the feeling she wasn't going to like whatever was coming next. She was right.

"You aren't getting the fucking picture here. Al. He uses bleach *everywhere*. Injects it *into* the bodies. Nothing left to test. What samples they can get show that there was definitely rape, but the quality is so shitty we can't even tell what species the perp is. Everyone assumed human up 'til now, because that's, well I mean isn't it always a fucking human asshole? But after this shit, all bets are off."

For several minutes Allie was too horrified to speak and she watched as Syn grabbed and quickly drank a second beer. She almost wanted to join her. "How much trouble is he really in?"

"I don't know," Syn answered quietly, "Honestly. I can't get a read on the Guards at all, except that they don't like him, and the two detectives working the case have been on it for months now. Maybe they really think he did it…"

"Or maybe," Allie finished for her, "they just want the case closed."

"Yeah," Syn agreed, sounding frustrated. "Maybe."

"This is really bad, Syn."

"No shit Sherlock."

****

"I still think he's our guy," Walters insisted, stubbornly.

Riordan shook his head as the group of Elven Guard looked on. They'd debated for hours after letting the suspect go. Then they'd called in Officer Lyons when Riordan realized her address was the same as the guy they'd just interrogated, questioned her, and debated some more.

"We don't have enough to hold him."

"Then we need to get enough," Walters insisted.

"Does there seem to be a purpose to the murders?" the Elven Captain, Zarethyn, asked suddenly, breaking his silence.

"Purpose?" Walters snorted. "He's a freak. You heard what Lyons said, he drinks like a fish, he's got no life. He probably just likes to hurt little girls."

"If we are seeking a motive for the killer it would seem logical to start by looking at what possible reasons the girls might be targeted," The elf said calmly.

"Because being a crazy serial killer isn't enough of a reason?" Walters scoffed.

"May we examine the last body?" Zarethyn asked ignoring the human's attitude.

"Sure, "Riordan said, feeling tired, "She hasn't been transferred out to the state coroner's office yet. You might as well."

He led the group down into the station basement which had a small section that acted as a temporary morgue when needed. The bodies were only held until a hearse could get there to transfer them out to the state office to be autopsied, but Riordan was sure #4 wouldn't be much different from the first three. He walked over to the locker that held her body and paused for a moment of silent prayer before opening the morgue drawer and pulling the sliding table out.

"Do you want me to open the bag?"

The elf nodded, so Riordan made a note on the evidence tag and then unzipped the body bag. A strong bleach smell filled the room and he wrinkled his nose even though he'd been expecting it. Just like the others. To his surprise the red-haired female elf moved up to stand over the body holding her hands out about a foot above the dead girl.

"What's she doing?" Walters asked, clearly unhappy.

"Checking for spells," Zarethyn replied, unperturbed.

Before either detective could respond to that Aeyliss spoke, "Yes, there is magic here."

"She was spelled?" Riordan asked, feeling uneasy

"No, but she herself was part of a spell," the Elven woman replied.

"What does that mean?"

"It means," the other blond, Jessilaen, said grimly, "that your murderer is using these girls, their pain and their death, in some way. Either to power a spell directly or to raise energy for some larger purpose."

"So it is an elf then," Walters sounded smug and Riordan shot him a cautionary glance.

"Not necessarily," Aeyliss replied. "Humans can work magic as well, especially here in these lands. The traces of this spell are too corroded to be certain of its purpose or what type of magic it was, but I am certain those traces are there."

"So what do we do now?" Riordan asked feeling frustrated and wishing elves would just say things straight out.

"We need an expert in ritual magic," Zarethyn said quietly "Someone who may be able to recognize what the purpose of the ritual is or what style of magic utilizes these methods."

"Okay, so we'll find an occult expert and let you guys know what he says," Walters said, a little too casually.

The Elven Captain looked at him sharply, "I think it best if we conduct this investigation jointly; one of us may see something another might miss."

Walters scoffed openly, "So what all six of us are just going to walk around as a big group? That ain't subtle and it isn't going to convince people to help us. Seeing you four coming is going to freak most of our leads right out."

The elves looked perplexed. "Why should we need to convince anyone to help us? If they are innocent but have knowledge of this crime should they not want to help find the killer?"

Riordan winced "It doesn't work that way. People get scared, they get nervous…"

"Nonetheless," Zarethyn said, with an air of finality, "we are a joint task force. We will investigate together. Find an expert and we will all go and question him and see if answers can be found that might be the start of a trail to this killer"

Chapter 2 - Monday

Later that morning as she drove in to work Allie couldn't shake the general feeling of foreboding that had lingered since her conversation with Syndra. At first she drove on autopilot, the trees a blur next to the road, but as she left the house behind she found herself thinking of what the town must have been like 100 years earlier, before the Sundering. The event itself was still a mystery; no one knew why it had happened, only that one day reality had fractured; mortal Earth and Fairy had been permanently fused together. In some places Earth remained unchanged, in others Fairy dominated; where the two areas met there were the Borderlands, places that were neither wholly of Earth or Fairy. Ashwood was one of those places. It had been a small New England town before the Sundering, the kind of place that you would drive right through without ever realizing you'd been there. Most of the town had been farms–dairy, sheep, horses–and what passed for downtown covered barely a dozen blocks. After the worlds merged it became something more complex; the farms still took up much of the town but now they provided most of the food for the locals and downtown had taken on the air of a very small city. Since technology was effected by the seeping presence of magic in unpredictable ways and it was expensive to hire a magic worker to set up the protections constantly necessary to keep each electrical device running, most people got by with minimal household tech and used non-electrical means, like woodstoves, to heat their homes and cook with, saving their money to spend on technology like cell phones and computers. Iron also warped the effectiveness of magic and physically harmed most Fairy beings, making the iron stoves and cookware a line of defense for many people against the Fey creatures that wandered the land now. The old Victorian Allie and her roommates shared was unusual because it could boast most of the technological luxuries that mortal Earth had, since between them Allie and Bleidd were more than capable of handling the magical energy and spells needed to protect the electrical circuits.

The effect of the Borderland was strongest on the eastern side of town which opened up into Fairy through a wide swath of woodland that had once been a state forest. The elves, who were the rulers of the Otherworld although far from the only beings to exist there, had an outpost along the main road through the forest which acted now as the gateway fully into Fairy. On the other side of town the human government had a similar outpost that controlled travel into America. In between the two outposts the town of Ashwood sat as it had before, except that it was no longer totally on Earth.

The effect of the Borderland was weakest on the western side of town which was closest to the regular Earth end. The river formed a natural border here and the single bridge that crossed it was patrolled at all times since passage between American territory in the West and the realm of the local Fairy Queen to the east was strictly regulated. Next to the bridge was a small government outpost which acted like a border crossing, checking passports and residency passes and monitoring who entered and left the town. Even with the worlds twisted together like a patchwork quilt traveling from one to the other wasn't easy. Someone trying to simply walk out of one world and into the next would find themselves hopelessly lost but nonetheless firmly within the world they had started in, unless they had magic to guide them. Only by crossing through the open borderland areas, which had formed around the towns and cities trapped between worlds during the Sundering, could direct passage be found, and so those areas were carefully maintained by a joint effort of both governments.

Sometimes Allie wondered what had happened to all the people, in both worlds, in the areas that were missing from the new reality, but she didn't think anyone would ever know. Those places had simply ceased to exist in the reality that they now lived in. *Maybe there's a whole other world now, an inverse of this one,* Allie mused, *where all the Earth bits here are Fairy and all the Fairy bits here are Earth.* It was a strange thought, but also oddly comforting, to think that the missing pieces of the world hadn't been obliterated by the melding of the worlds. Allie had a hard time imagining what the world had been like before, without magic but also without Borderlands and with powerful, unified governments. *It must have been nice,* she thought, *to just be able to drive straight from one place to another, without going through check points or needing residency passes...* Of course it was still that way in large sections where one world dominated, but here in the Borderlands it was easy to forget that.

Downtown started just past the bridge and hovered on the edge where magic was weakest. The town's one real sit-down restaurant, the Tiger, was also the only bar and did a brisk business thanks to the booming tourist trade. It was quite trendy for tourists from both worlds to come to a Borderland town to get a taste of the other side without going all the way into the foreign world. There were three hotels, one of which specialized only in fairies and catered to both Otherworldly tourists and the different traders who came in to sell their goods which would then be resold out to Earthly markets or passed on into Fairy. Besides the hotels, Main Street was dotted with expensive boutiques, fast food restaurants, specialty stores and the sorts of places only tourists shopped in. The residents of the town mostly stayed with the smaller stores on the side streets, unless they had to go to town hall or the police station, which doubled as a small jail. The town had a strong streak of self-sufficiency which meant that they tried hard not to rely

on outsiders for anything they didn't have to. The police
station handled all minor criminals, at least the human
ones, and it wasn't often that someone had to be sent out
with the State Police Officer stationed in town to be dealt
with by the full court system. What had been a small walk-
in clinic before the Sundering was now a small hospital and
handled all but the most serious cases in-house. Past Main
Street and the cluster of side streets the town opened up
into a small warehouse district to the south and residential
areas to the north.

Allie's store, *Between The Worlds*, was a specialty
book store on Sherwood just off of Main Street. When her
grandmother had died Allie had inherited the store and Liz
had gotten the house, with the understanding that each
would help the other; old Elizabeth McCarthy had been a
big believer in family standing by each other, and she had
wanted to be sure that her two favorite grandchildren would
not forget that. Liz gave Allie a place to live and Allie
made sure the taxes on the house were always paid, as well
as keeping up with things magically.

Allie pulled into the small parking lot next to the
store and parked her car at the far end by the dilapidated
wooden fence that rimmed the property. The single-story
building itself was old brick with huge plate glass front
windows and a recessed door with cheerful little bells over
the top. Most people thought the bells were quaint; only a
few realized they were but one of the many magical
protections Allie had placed on the store. She was not an
especially powerful witch but she was very good with
simple magics and charms.

Walking through the Monday morning chill Allie
paused for a minute at the back door, pretending to search
for the right key as she concentrated on lowering the
building's wards to prepare for another day of business. It
might have been silly to put so much effort into the wards
when the odds of a beak in were so slim—certainly there

wasn't a huge amount of cash in the store and most burglars weren't going to waste time with books–but Allie took a certain pride in her magical skill and enjoyed the effort of protecting the store. Those who weren't deterred by the magical protections usually wouldn't risk the store's antiquated surveillance system, a remnant of her grandmother's time.

As she entered the back hallway Allie felt the familiar rush of welcoming that she always felt in this place. She had all but grown up here; rushing to get to the store after school as a child anticipating her grandmother's warm hug and stories, getting her first official job here as soon as she was old enough to work. She had read every single book in the store, some of them several times. Over the years since her grandmother's death a decade before, she had been slowly shifting the focus of the collection into more occult books. Her grandmother, although a skilled witch, had always been vehemently opposed to carrying any magical books that went beyond bare basics, but Allie had slowly built up a loyal customer base by stocking exactly the books her grandmother had forbidden. It was those customers and the regular flow of tourists looking for outré souvenirs that kept the store profitable.

Moving down the hall she picked up the mail she'd tossed on the shelf lining the back wall a few days before, quickly sorted out the bills from the junk, which today included yet another invite to the local coven's Ostara celebration, and checked the answering machine. There were three messages: two asking to reserve books and one hang up. Doors led off the short hall to a back room full of boxed books that needed to be catalogued before they could be put out, or waiting to be shipped out to fill online and phone orders, a small bathroom, and a tiny kitchenette. Allie stepped into the little kitchen and put some water on to boil for tea before heading out into the main room with its maze of floor-to-ceiling book shelves to find the two books to put on hold. It was looking like a long day and she pushed her worry about Bleidd out of her mind as she got to work.

****

The early spring weather had turned cold and cloudy, and after the morning rush to catch up with orders and get new books sorted and put away Allie found all her motivation drained. Someone walking in the front door would see the entire left side of the store lost in book shelves, but the right side was open to the back counter, with only a scattering of chairs and couches for the people who wanted to sit and read a bit before buying. Her grandmother had wanted the store to welcome everyone, to invite people in; Allie was constantly talking about changing it but could never quite bring herself to go through with it. As she was standing there wondering if there was a way to at least rearrange the seating area, she saw a familiar red head walking past the front window towards the door and felt her mood lifting. The little bells over the door echoed her feeling, ringing out cheerfully as the front door swung open.

"Morning Adain," she greeted one of her best customers warmly and was rewarded with a wide smile in return.

"Mornin' Allie. Have you gotten m' order in by any chance?" Aidan's lilting accent betrayed his Irish roots but Allie was one of the few people who knew that the handsome young man was actually a member of Fairy; he went to great pains to pass as human. Not exactly illegal, but certainly a dangerous game to play in a world that tended to assume nefarious motives for such deceptions. Allie understood his reasoning perfectly, which was why he trusted her with his secret, just as she trusted him. After all, if it got around that he was a leprechaun no one would ever believe it wasn't like in the modern fairy-stories and he'd be harassed endlessly by stupid people. And she knew he liked mortal Earth too much to give it up, despite the risks.

"Not yet–you know I'd have called–but I did get in another one that might interest you…"she led him over to the shelf where she kept all the books on warding and protective magic and pointed to the new arrivals. The little bells over the door rang again and she left him to flip through his options as she headed back to greet the newcomer, who turned out to be one of the town's resident ceremonial mages looking for an obscure book on ancient incense blends for invocations. The rest of the morning passed in a blur as the steady stream of customers kept her busy.

By late afternoon the rush had died, no one had come in to shop in several hours, she was feeling the lack of sleep and stress and was wondering if it was worth the risk of missing potential sales to close early. She leaned on the long sales counter watching traffic and listening to the only radio station that came in play what passed for pop music. She thought for the hundredth time that she needed to get a CD player, but it was so hard to keep them working even with magic that it never seemed worth the money.

She had just decided to close early and go get some sleep when a group walked past the front window and Allie felt herself tensing. She knew before the six people had entered the store that they weren't customers. *You should have closed early after all*, she thought with a sinking feeling.

The first two men were in plainclothes but they might as well have been wearing uniforms; their demeanor screamed cop. They walked in checking the store out with open suspicion. The first was tall and lean, his light brown hair just starting to recede, but with a jovial air about him that made her think he probably smiled often. The second was shorter and stocky, the kind of guy who hit the gym every day and didn't smile very much at all. His dark hair was in a military style crew cut and his suit was perfectly fit and pressed; he looked like someone who expected perfection from everyone around him and Allie guessed he was difficult to deal with. It was the other four though that made Allie's stomach clench with something close to real fear. The Elven Guard walked in a rough formation, two by two, and their faces gave away nothing at all. She could see why Syn had said they were hard to read. They were all tall and beautiful, typically Elven, and they wore the tunics and dark, heavy cargo pants that were the uniform of the Guard. Each had a short sword belted at the waist where their human counterpart wore a holstered gun. Although it was true elves could not bear iron any better than the other Fey Allie knew from Syn that most guns now were more plastic than metal and she suspected the Guards' insistence on swords was as much for intimidation as effectiveness. Each had a small badge clipped to their belt. Two were fair, one had dark hair and the last, the only woman, was red haired; each wore their hair long, which seemed to be the Elven style, but pulled back in a braid.

Allie swallowed hard as six sets of eyes fastened on her. She knew what they were seeing, but wasn't sure what any of them thought about her. Short, and with a generous figure that was poorly hidden by baggy jeans and a loose t-shirt, Allie had been told many times that she would be considered pretty if she put a little effort into her appearance; most people failed to realize that her effort was aimed at staying inconspicuous and not attracting attention. Her long, dark blonde hair was up in a ponytail that covered her ears without being obvious about it. She felt her personal shields strengthening when her body tensed as she subconsciously tried to keep whatever the cops were feeling away from her.

The group crossed the open lounge area and headed straight for the counter. Part of her wanted desperately to stay behind the illusion of safety it offered, but she forced herself to step out and meet them halfway. Normally she would have had a cheerful greeting for anyone entering the store but she found herself speechless before the massed authority these people represented. After a brief awkward silence the tall cop spoke, with a reassuring smile, "Good afternoon. Is the store owner around?"

Allie cleared her throat trying to sound calm, "That's me. I'm the owner."

Surprise flashed across his face before he fixed the smile back in place, "You? You don't look old enough to own this store."

She wasn't sure if he was being disingenuous or sincere, but thought that his friendly manner probably worked really well in his line of work. She decided to stay polite, "I inherited it from my grandmother."

His smile widened, but it was hard to feel reassured with the wall of silent judgment standing behind him. "We were hoping we could ask you some questions, if you have a minute?"

She nodded wordlessly and he went on, "I'm Detective Riordan, this is my partner Detective Walters, and this is Captain Zarethyn and his squad; they're a detachment of the Elven Guard. We're investigating the murders, the ones the papers have been calling the parking lot killings."

She'd expected something like that but Allie felt her mouth go dry at his words. Before she could find a way to tell him she already knew more than he realized the detective was going on, "Several people recommended you as an expert on the occult, although to be honest I was expecting someone a lot older."

A what? She thought, confused, but pushed that aside for the moment. Taking a deep breath she forced herself to speak up, "Detective, I have to tell you, full disclosure or whatever, that I think my roommate is your prime suspect..."

"What?" The shorter cop, Walters, snapped.

"...and Officer Lyons is also my roommate," Allie finished.

"Interesting," The Elven Captain murmured, breaking his silence. The other elves stood impassively, seemingly content to let the humans handle the questioning. Riordan seemed at a loss for words but his partner didn't.

"That's a bit too much of a coincidence isn't it? You all being roommates?" The way he said roommates dripped with innuendo and Allie felt herself getting defensive.

"It's not like that."

"Oh I'm sure it isn't," the detective said sarcastically, "two women, an elf..."

"There's five of us living in the house," Allie said before she could stop herself. She realized he was trying to upset her, to keep her off balance. *Freaking good cop/bad cop, really? Isn't that a cliché? I wonder if it's on purpose or if they were assigned together to balance each other out?* She thought, feeling tired. "We're friends, nothing else."

Riordan finally recovered and cut in, talking to her in the same friendly way as before, earning an annoyed look from his partner, "Of course. What have your roommates told you about the case?"

"Not much. Syndra said a joint team had been formed," she replied, trying to be honest without saying anything that might get Syn in trouble.

"And what about him?" Walters asked sharply, "What did he tell you?"

She met his grey eyes and was surprised by the genuine anger there. "That he found a body and was questioned about it. That he didn't do anything wrong."

"And you believe that?"

"Yes, I do," she said simply.

"You know he's an ex-con?" Walters asked, clearly hoping for a chance to tell her the gory details.

"Yeah, I know," her answer seemed to catch him off guard.

"Are you kidding me? And that doesn't bother you at all? Or maybe his pretty face makes it all okay?"

Riordan gave his partner a warning look and Allie realized all four of the elves were frowning. *He better be careful how hard he pushes that*, Allie thought, *but he must really be bothered by the idea of elves and humans getting together. Fabulous.* He obviously wasn't aware of her ancestry and she doubted it would go over well when he figured it out.

"We're just friends nothing more. There's no romantic relationship between me and him–or her," Allie added quickly seeing Walters mouth opening and guessing where the next innuendo would be aimed.

"Right." Cynicism dripped from the single word. The detective was staring at her hard now and she fought the urge to fidget under the scrutiny. He was clearly trying to fit the pieces together, and she doubted he would have made detective unless he was good at it.

"What's your name?"

"Rick," Riordan tried to get his partner's attention, but the other man waved him off.

"We want to make sure she's the right person don't we?" His words were innocent but Allie doubted his motives matched them.

"Allie McCarthy," she replied.

"She's the one that was recommended," Riordan tried again to sidetrack his partner, without success.

"Allie's your first name?" Walters pressed.

"It's what most people call me," she said, trying to dodge the direct question.

"Don't get cute, honey. What's your *legal* first name?" he looked strangely triumphant, as if he thought he was being very clever. She wanted to hit him.

"Aliaine"

Everyone else looked surprised, but Walters let slip a petty little smile. It made him look ugly and mean, and Allie started to hate him.

"So what are you? A half? A quarter? You hide it really well, I bet you pass as a real human all the time."

She made a monumental effort to control her face and not react to that insult, even as the other cop looked mortified and told him to shut up. The elves all went completely blank faced and she had no idea what they were thinking. When she spoke her voice didn't betray any of her feelings; this was hardly the first time someone had said something rude to her about her parentage, after all. "Is it illegal to have mixed ancestry?"

"Trying to avoid an honest answer?" Walters sneered in response, but his partner grabbed his arm and physically pulled him back, leaning over to talk directly into his ear. Allie could just barely hear him telling the other man to ease off a little and not press so hard; she felt annoyed that her original guess that they were playing roles to put her off balance seemed correct, but she doubted Walters was really playing. She also wasn't sure the elves were on the same page of the cop play book and she wondered how well the joint task force was working together. If this experience was any indication, not very well.

The Elven Captain, who turned out to be one of the blond elves, stepped forward into the tense silence. Inclining his head slightly in a polite nod as if none of that ugly exchange had just happened, he greeted her in Elvish, "Good afternoon, I am Zarethyn. Do you speak the language?"

He spoke slowly and his tone was friendly but she knew he was testing her. He would not be rude enough to repeat Walters question, however he could judge her ancestry fairly well just by how she answered this simple question. If she didn't speak Elvish at all, then it was a safe assumption that her own connection to the Fey was slight; having a fairy name after all wasn't that telling, no matter how damning the Detective tried to make it out to be. If she answered him in kind he could judge by her fluency and which dialect she used. The Fey were notoriously classist and the elves were the highest ranking beings of their world so the language they spoke was more formal and used slightly different pronouns than the dialect spoken by the lesser Fey. For one moment Allie was sorely tempted to respond in English and let him make of that what he would, but she resisted the urge. The elves were often deceptive and tricky to deal with but it was unwise to lie directly to one, particularly when that one was the Captain of a Guard detachment and she was fairly certain lying by omission wouldn't be seen as any different than speaking a lie directly.

"Good afternoon," she replied, struggling to keep her voice level and think of all the proper polite things to say. She hated Elven etiquette. "I speak the language. My name is Aliaine. I would greet your comrades but I do not know their names."

She hoped that last was alright. She was too tired to remember whether it was rude to ask for the introduction or whether it was expected. He smiled slightly, relaxing almost imperceptibly, and she decided it had been the right thing to say. He gestured at his three companions, starting with the other blond on his left, "This is my second in command, Jessilaen."

Jessilaen, who was a bit shorter and had lighter hair than the Captain, nodded, and she nodded back. Zarethyn gestured at the dark haired elf next, "Our field medic and healer, Brynneth."

More polite nodding, then the final elf, the red-headed one, was introduced, "Aeyliss, who is an excellent tracker."

She nodded at the fourth elf, trying not to look impressed. She had heard of the magical trackers who could follow almost any spell back to its source like a hound following a scent. It was a rare gift and highly valued. The elves must be taking these murders very seriously to have assigned such a resource to the case.

"We are trying to find the one who has been killing so many women here and we believe you may be able to help us," Zarethyn said, stepping closer and leaning in towards her. Elves had very rigid rules of social interaction, but they were ones that often confused humans; much more physically open and seemingly unaware of the concept of personal space yet easily insulted and very formal. They thought nothing of casual physical contact that would make most humans squirm with discomfort, but considered minor slights of politeness or divergence from expected social norms to be serious breaches that could result in a challenge to a physical or magical duel. Leaning in would have been intended as intimidation by a human but Allie knew he was simply trying to be friendly; like Detective Riordan's constant smiling it was meant to reassure. Nonetheless Allie felt overwhelmed by his presence but she didn't dare insult him by stepping back, and for a moment didn't know what to say.

"I think it might be better to speak the native language here, so that the police are not offended," she said, although she was more worried about Walters' suspicion than any offense he might take. The Elven Captain inclined his head slightly in the equivalent of a shrug.

"Of course," he replied in English stepping back slightly to include the police in the conversation. "You were recommended as someone knowledgeable in the occult."

"Isn't it a problem that I know one of the suspects?" Allie asked, earning a derisive snort from Walters who obviously agreed.

"Not to our view," Zarethyn replied seeming genuinely unconcerned, "Such motivation should ensure your best efforts to find the killer in order to help clear your friend's name. If he is truly innocent you can prove as much. If he is guilty you will not be able to hide his guilt and will still aid us in rooting out the truth. All the people we have spoken too thus far recommended you and you are connected to two other people involved in this case–there is some higher purpose at work behind your involvement and we would see where it leads."

The other elves nodded slightly, supporting their Captain's words, but the human police looked unhappy; Walters looked downright pissed, but neither argued. Allie wondered who was ultimately in charge here. She cleared her throat and then spoke hesitantly. "I'm not sure what I can do to help. I'm not really an expert in anything. I'm just a book store owner who reads a lot and a witch with some skill with charms and enchantments. Nothing terribly out of the ordinary."

"You keep giving a lot of reasons why we shouldn't want your help, "Walters said, earning a warning look from his partner, "It sounds like you just really don't want to help us."

"If I can help I will, I'm just not sure I can," she said, feeling awkward saying it. The little bell over the door jangled and she looked up to see two older women, members of one of the local covens, stepping in. The local magical groups, covens, groves and lodges had become a strong customer base for her because they knew she carried a wide array of hard to find books as well as the usual popular ones and was always willing to special order. Borderland towns tended to attract a higher number of magic workers and psychics, drawn to the Otherworldly atmosphere that made their magic more effective, as well as people who had no innate magical abilities but were drawn to the idea of seeing fairies. Many people looked down on magically inclined-humans and assumed they were all just Fairy groupies, but Allie knew it wasn't that simple and treated them all kindly. The rare few that really were only interested in a close personal encounter with a non-human she directed to the *Seventh Star*, a small, notorious club across town. Her approach had earned her the respect of the locals, something that she considered a hard won victory.

Both women paused on the threshold taking in the strange scene by the counter: the two cops, the four Elven Guard, Allie standing awkwardly facing the six police. One woman started to step in, but the other clutched her arm and practically dragged her back out the door. Allie swore silently. Not only had she lost a potential sale but word would get around that she'd had the police and Guard in the store questioning her. Within a few hours the story would spread through the different groups in town, and like the children's game of "Telephone" by the end it would not resemble the actual event anymore. By tomorrow they'd probably be saying her store had been raided by a half dozen government agencies and a small army from Fairy. She was really starting to hate this entire day.

Oblivious to her dismay, Detective Riordan had regained his composure and his signature smile, "Basically we need to know what you might know about ritual murders."

"Ritual murders? You mean, like human sacrifice in an occult context?" she felt herself making a face, "It's really not very likely. I mean sometimes in the older accounts you see cultures that did it–were the girls' hearts missing?" Several people shook their heads no and Allie went on, "Then not that. Usually when you hear about ritual murders it's not actually any real tradition or group, it's just an individual crazy acting out some fantasy."

Walters was watching her closely and his face had become unreadable. She found it unsettling and lost her train of thought. *Can't the jerk just say whatever he's thinking instead of looking at me like he can't decide whether to hit me with his squad car or agree with me?* she thought uncomfortably.

"Are you certain?" One of the elves asked. Jessilaen, Allie remembered after a moment. He was also looking at her closely, but it didn't make her skin crawl the way Walters scrutiny did. It was almost a relief to turn and focus on the Elven Guard.

"Well…I can't be certain, no. There are a few groups that do use death to raise energy, but not usually human death. Animals mostly, from what I understand. And I don't know very much at all about that end of things, just what I've read and a few anecdotal things."

"How would you tell if it was such a ritual?" he pressed.

Allie took a deep breath, thinking about the question. "I don't know. It would depend on the ultimate point of the ritual, I guess. If it was just to gather the energy of the death, to harness it…"

Her voice trailed off as something Bleidd had said in the bathroom suddenly flickered through her mind. Something must have shown on her face because both of the closest elves, Zarethyn and Jessilaen, stepped towards her. Looking quizzical the Elven Captain stepped back slightly and the other elf moved forward putting his hands on her shoulders. She looked up, meeting his eyes without feeling uncomfortable at the physical proximity, which was the Elven equivalent of a pat on the hand or encouraging nod. Allie bit her lip, thinking fast. "He said the girls had been raped and mutilated."

"Who?"

"Bleidd"

"Gee, I wonder why he told you that?" Walters sneered, his voice implying unpleasant things. Allie couldn't stop herself from glaring at him but recoiled a bit at the open animosity on his face. The burly detective's gaze was fixed on the Elven Guard's hands on her shoulders, in a way that made her feel suddenly exposed. She shifted her weight away from Jessilaen but stopped short of stepping back. The Guard's head turned towards the cop and for the first time she saw something like real anger break through the impassivity that had been the Guards' trademark since they had first come in. She spoke quickly trying to diffuse what seemed to be an inevitably nasty situation. "He told me because he was telling me that you had questioned him, and he said what was done to that girl was horrible. He didn't get into any detail about it."

The shutters came back down over Walters face as his partner stepped up in front of him, partially blocking him from her view. Riordan spoke slowly but with obvious interest "Is that significant? The girls being raped and cut up? All of our investigation so far has pointed to that not being a typical occult thing."

"It isn't. But there's something about that– something familiar about that somehow," Allie frowned. "It's like when you're trying to remember a word and it's on the tip of your tongue, you know? I feel like I've heard about something like that or read about it before, but I can't quite think of where."

"What would be the purpose?" the red haired elf, Aeyliss asked, her voice as calm as if they were discussing the weather rather than the systematic torture of young women.

"Well, it's all about raising energy. There's different schools of thought about which methods are more effective–most people stick with the pleasant ones..." At the word pleasant Walters muttered under his breath; Allie was almost certain he said "I bet" but she ignored him. "e dancing, chanting, that sort of thing."

"And sex magic?" Riordan added.

"Well, yes. That's not a popular one though because it's difficult to do"

"Really?" the detective sounded skeptical.

"Yeah. The point isn't to have sex for fun but to focus during the, um, activity, on channeling the energy," Allie was sure she was blushing now and she more than half expected Walters to add another snarky comment, but he said nothing. All six investigators waited for her to continue and she floundered. Jessilaen's hands squeezed her shoulders gently and she felt a wave of gratitude as she shifted her focus back to him.

"I've never personally heard of anyone using rape as sex magic, but–it's theoretically possible. I think. And the mutilation, could, again theoretically, be used to raise magical energy."

"And that gets 'em more than just killing the girls?" Riordan asked, his voice serious and no trace of a smile now.

"I don't know." Allie answered honestly. "Death magic isn't exactly something many people talk or write about and most of what is out there is from religious rituals that are hundreds of years or more old. If you have someone who has adapted something or is working on a new theory..." she shrugged.

"But you think you have read of something similar to this?" Jessilaen asked softly

"I don't know," Allie repeated. "Like I said there's something almost familiar about it, but I can't quite place it."

The elves were exchanging looks that made Allie think they wished she didn't speak their language. After a moment Jessilaen stepped back and for an instant Allie had the unsettling desire to follow him. The four elves moved over to stand by the bookshelves and talked quietly among themselves. The two police came over to her, Riordan back to his reassuring smile, Walters stony faced. Riordan held out a business card, "Thanks for your time. If you think of anything else that might help this is my direct number. My email's on the card too."

She took the card and nodded, feeling a rush of relief that this bizarre interview seemed to be wrapping up. Both police hesitated a moment and then turned and headed for the door. She expected the elves to follow, but instead they stepped back over to her. She racked her brain trying to remember the correct etiquette for leave taking but the 4 hours of sleep and long stressful day were catching up to her and she felt blank. The Guard Captain nodded politely again and then extended his own business card, a small slip of cardstock filled with magic. Her fingers tingled as she took it and she tried not to think about what spells were woven into it. When he spoke it was in Elvish again, "We appreciate your time in answering our questions. If you think of where you might have seen such a ritual as this before please contact us. If we have any additional questions or need of your assistance we will be back to discuss this further."

She nodded, unable to think of a single thing to say and hoping that he wasn't too offended by her silence. As they turned to leave Jessilaen hesitated then turned back. He reached past her to take one of the store's business cards off the counter and then took her hand, slipping another business card in with the two she already held. "If you have any questions or need anything, call," he said simply.

The group left the store with Allie still standing there. Finally she shook herself out of the daze they had left her in and looked down at the cards clutched in her hand. Detective Riordan's card looked plain and terribly official. The Elven Captain's card was double sided, one side in English the other in Elven runes, both with the same basic information: rank, name, contact number, and the border outpost was listed as his address.

That was interesting. Allie had not known until then that the Guard operated out of there, although she could understand the logic. The Outpost was the mid-point between the border of the Queen's Fairy Holding and Ashwood and while it primarily acted as a border crossing it would be the most obvious staging point for the Guard to act within both realms. Curious she looked at the third card which turned out to be Jessilaen's. It listed his rank as commander, gave a different contact number from Zarethyn, but the same address. She had no idea why he had given her the card, unless the elves felt that she might be hesitant to contact the Guard Captain.

Shaking her head slightly she moved to lock the front door before anything else could happen. She was thoroughly done with this entire day.

****

Detective Rick Walters pulled his car into an open space in the gym parking lot and cut the motor, but he didn't get out. He pocketed his keys and sat behind the wheel, frowning, listening to the old motor tick as it cooled down. Walters was a common sight at the gym so no one looked twice at him sitting in his car.

That mixed blood bitch could ruin everything, He thought to himself, glaring at the dashboard. *Why couldn't*

Jim listen to me and go to a different expert? Walters had tried hard to convince his partner and the elves to go to someone else, but he couldn't be too obvious about it without making them suspicious, and since almost everyone they'd spoken to recommended her, in the end he'd had to go along with the consensus. At first it had seemed like it would still work out okay but then she'd almost remembered something; it was maddening, standing there waiting to see what she knew. Maybe nothing after all, but if she really did know about the ritual, if she remembered anything, or–worst of all–if she found a copy of the book before he could get his hands on it, then she could destroy months of work.

He shook his head. *No. No, I won't let it come to that.* He picked up his personal cell phone, the one that no one in the department knew he had, and dialed a number from memory. A distracted voice answered on the second ring, low and angry, "Why are you calling?"

"We went to the book store *Between The Worlds* for the investigation." He answered, his own tone harsh.

"You did what? Why? I told you…"

He cut the speaker off. "Wasn't my call. That was where everyone said to go and Jim and the elves decided it was the best option. It was mostly a dead end–we're going to start talking to some of the ceremonial mages in town next–but I'm worried."

"Don't be. We can handle it." The person said briskly. It was hard to hear with the background noise. He wanted to ask the other person to speak up but he knew it was useless.

"We need to find the book." He gritted his teeth.

"We don't need the book. You reconstructed the ritual and it's working perfectly the way you're doing it." His contact sounded annoyed now, and he chaffed at being spoken to like a child.

"There's more in that book than just the bits I know of. And if that mixed blood bi…"

"Don't worry about her." It was the other speaker's turn to cut him off mid-word, "We need to focus on the bigger threat. You said that elf can track magic. That's a much bigger problem."

"Yeah. That's a bigger problem, but what am I supposed to do about it?"

"Remove the problem." The speaker sounded bored now.

As if it's that simple, Walters thought, grimacing. "Are you kidding me? How the hell am I supposed to do that?"

"You'll think of something. We have time–they said she can't track the spell until they understand what it is, and without the book that will take time. So work out a solution. Think on your feet." The speaker's confidence in his ability to solve the problem made him feel flattered and frustrated in turn. He hadn't liked killing the girls at first, but he'd understood it was a necessary thing, something that had to be done for the greater good; however he really wanted to kill the bookshop owner. It seemed unfair after everything he'd done for the cause that he couldn't do the one thing he wanted to do now.

"I still think that mixed blood girl is trouble. If she knows anything…" he pressed, knowing the odds were slim of being allowed to go after her.

"Leave her alone. She's a distraction. Keep them focused on the elf as a suspect, work on taking out that tracker, and if we need to we'll come up with a way to throw them off track. But don't lose focus now–we're too close to our goal." The voice was firm and he felt his own resolve hardening again, "Now I have to go. Remember– stay focused."

The phone went dead in his hand. He nodded to himself. *Yeah, stay focused. Everything's fine. Everything's been going perfect up until now. Just keep the momentum. Do what has to be done to succeed. Keep the ultimate goal in mind, and don't get distracted.* Feeling better he got out of the car and went in to the gym to work out, thinking about how one would kill a stronger, faster, better armed enemy... without getting caught.

Chapter 3 - Wednesday ~ Thursday

After getting through a single day that felt like a week, the next few days seemed anti-climactic in their normality. Allie managed to get through 48 hours without any additional crises and to successfully avoid all 4 of her roommates which was no easy task. Usually the 5 friends enjoyed spending time together, often sharing communal meals and watching movies together in the evenings when they were home. Allie knew how lucky she was to have actual friendships with the people she lived with, but she dreaded having to explain her conversation with the task force. She had no doubt that Bleidd would be furious, Syndra would want the entire discussion repeated ad nauseam so that she could analyze it to death, and Liz and Jason would be worried.

As she'd expected business at the store had fallen off to almost nothing. Most of her customer base had a healthy caution around police and the idea that she was being investigated had freaked people right out, although to be fair she wasn't sure that knowing she was helping with an investigation would have been any better. She found herself hoping that the rumor mill found something new to talk about soon and people forgot whatever story was going around about *Between The Worlds*. Realistically she could only go so long without sales before it was going to start hurting.

After work Wednesday she decided to visit an old friend so she stopped at the town's Chinese restaurant on the way home to grab food to share. It was never a bad idea to show up to visit a creature of Fairy bearing a gift, and she knew this one had a weakness for sweet and sour chicken and pork egg rolls. *Dynasty Moon* was run by a pair of Hulijing, Chinese fox spirits, and it was widely agreed that they made the best take-out in town. They were pricey though, and Allie couldn't eat there very often, but she felt like splurging a little, despite her worries over her anemic bank account.

After picking up her order she headed home in a better mood. She parked her little car in its usual spot and hiked around the house towards the woods behind the backyard with the bag of takeout in one hand. The wards on the perimeter of the property extended to cover the expanse of yard from the curb to the stone walls that bordered the other three sides of the lawn, but the property itself actually went back almost a dozen acres. It just wasn't worth the energy and effort to keep wards up on the entire area all the time, so they didn't bother. Reaching the stone wall that marked the back edge of the yard Allie climbed over easily, feeling the customary tingle as she crossed from the warded to unwarded side. Her shoes crunched in last year's leaves and she whistled cheerfully, ducking low branches and weaving through the underbrush. There was no path to follow but Allie knew the way.

After several hundred feet she could see the open sky through the trees and the ground beneath her feet was noticeably softer. A dozen feet more and she was standing on the banks of the pond. The water stretched, black and still, as large as a football field, with the occasional clump of trees or half submerged log jutting up from the surface. She carefully sent out a tendril of focused magic to caress the surface nearest where she stood, like knocking on a door, and then waited. Within a few moments the still surface rippled, the dark, dripping head of a large horse emerging. Where the horse's eyes should have been were dark concave hollows and he turned his head to stare at her from one of these eyeless sockets for a moment before the head disappeared beneath the water again. A moment later the surface heaved and broke as the entire fairy horse emerged, walking onto the shore to her left. The kelpie stood there, water dripping from his mane and tail, and Allie smiled widely, proffering the bag "Good afternoon

Ciaran, I thought you might be in the mood for some excellent Chinese take-out."

The huge form rippled and shifted like the surface of the water a minute before and as she watched the horse's dark form changed into that of an equally dark haired man. Seemingly oblivious to the late spring chill and totally unabashed by his nudity Ciaran sniffed the air appreciatively." Is that sweet and sour chicken?"

"And two pork egg rolls." Allie agreed.

The kelpie smiled widely, "Nice to see you again Allie."

"And you." Allie had met the kelpie when she was wandering the woods as a child and although he normally could be quite a dangerous creature he seemed to have developed a rough sympathy for the lonely child over the years that eventually grew into a friendship. He often wandered the woods in the form of a large black dog, but he always hunted in his horse form; she had learned over the years that his humanoid form was a sign of trust with her, although she didn't doubt he would also use it to seduce the unwary if it served his purposes. Allie had been very clear with the other people living in the house that no one else was to go back into the woods; she doubted their friendship would keep him from eating one of her roommates, and while it was unlikely that he would risk the consequences of such an action, she didn't want to take the chance. These days the Elven Guard maintained order by ensuring none of the creatures of Fairy were allowed to harm humans. But in the old days Ciaran had fed on murderers and oath-breakers. Even as a child Allie had wondered if he occasionally still took human victims along with his animal prey and was just clever enough not to get caught, but she had never quite dared to ask.

"How have you been doing?"

"Not bad. Winter's always a slow time though, nothing much to do, no good hunting." He shrugged as she handed him the bag.

"Well I hope this helps a little, and you know anytime you want to borrow a book or five to read I'll be happy to lend them."

"That would be kind. I haven't read anything new in ages. I'm not picky, anything will do as long as it's a good story." He pulled out the package of eggrolls and eagerly began devouring them in a way that she would have found disturbing if she'd let herself think about.

"Sure thing. I'll try to get out here in the next week or two if I can, with some for you." Allie made a mental note to go through and pick out a selection of books for him to try. She certainly had more than enough to share.

"Allie, be careful with yourself." Ciaran said unexpectedly.

She cocked her head to the side "I'm always as careful as I can be Ciar. Unless you know something I don't?"

He shook his head. "Not really, but there are rumors going around among the lesser Fey. Everyone's agitated and with the Elven Guard out searching in the Borderland for someone, we should all be extra cautious. There is death in the air, and it would…pain me…to see harm come to you."

"Well you'd certainly be seeing a lot fewer egg rolls," Allie quipped, stalling for time.

She was touched that Ciaran cared enough to pass on any warning, since it was certainly not in his nature, and she was not at all surprised that the Guard were upsetting the Fey in the Borderland, many of whom lived in the Bordertown precisely to try to avoid the elves' control.

"The Elven Guard has already spoken to me about their investigation. They want me to help them find out why these murders are being committed."

The kelpie looked thoughtful as he chewed his chicken, eating it with his bare hands, "If you can help them, you should. That would put the Guard in your debt and that is not an insignificant thing. But be very careful Allie, very careful. It's a dangerous game to play."

She nodded "I will certainly take your excellent advice as always. Now, do you have time for a game of chess?"

Later, as she walked back through the woods to the house she found herself hoping that her part in this particular dangerous game was already over.

****

When a knock on her door woke her up early Thursday morning she felt an irrational rush of fear, expecting the worst. She rolled out of bed and pulled on her jeans from the day before, fastening them as she crossed to the door, shivering in the unusually chilly room. As a second knock sounded she yanked the door open with more force than she'd intended and caught Jason with his hand raised in mid-knock. His dark eyes widened, and he stammered, "Um, wow, sorry Allie. Hate to wake you but the breakers keep tripping, and, ummm, Bleidd isn't here."

He shrugged apologetically, his black hair falling across his eyes, while she felt an equally irrational rush of relief. "It's okay Jase."

She glanced over her shoulder and saw that indeed her clock was flashing, indicating a loss of power. One of the set-spells that protected the electrical wiring, or more likely the one on the fuse box, must have failed or been disrupted. Not an emergency but a tedious thing to fix. A quick look out the window at the pale morning light let her guess it was probably still early, maybe around 7 a.m.

Depending what shift he was working Jason was usually an early riser who made the coffee for the whole house and sometimes full, complex, breakfasts if he had time before heading out to work at the Fire Department. Since he was the only one in the house who could cook well, the idea of a possible breakfast besides cereal was a strong motivator. She yawned as Jason continued to look worried. "Seriously Takada, chill. It's no big deal. I'll fix it."

She stepped out into the hall with him, not bothering to dress beyond the t-shirt she slept in and jeans. If it was a quick enough fix she could go back to sleep as soon as it was done. Or maybe after it was fixed and she'd eat. "I'll head down to the basement of doom as long as you promise to make coffee and a decent breakfast for me."

Jason smiled widely, "Hey, for the joys of electric power and your fabulous magical effort you get coffee and an omelet."

"Bless you, Jason, bless you." They both laughed as she jogged down the stairs and through the kitchen to the basement door. She flipped the switch at the top of the stairs without expecting anything and then moved easily into the darkness.

The basement was a dreary musty place, full of old boxes, unwanted junk and an abundance of spiders. No one ever went down there without a reason, but unfortunately it was also the electrical center of the house. At the bottom of the old wooden staircase was a small utility room which housed the furnace, hot water heater, and the house's main fuse panel.

Allie entered the little room and opened the fuse panel door. The slight tingle of magic that should have tickled her fingers was unmistakably absent and she sighed. The spells she had set over the system to insulate the electrical wiring from the magical atmosphere had been broken, possibly by something as simple as a mouse or insect crossing their boundary. She–or Bleidd–could create more powerful permanent spells to protect the wiring but that sort of major enchantment was at the very limits of her abilities and would exhaust her for weeks. It never seemed worth it when it only took an hour at most to set up the lesser spells. And Bleidd had never been willing to risk the effort either, although his reasons were his own.

Chanting softly she quickly framed a basic spell and flipped the fuses back on. Instantly the hum of the furnace kicked in and light flooded the doorway behind her from the bare bulb that hung out in the main basement. She heard Jason's appreciative voice in the kitchen and didn't doubt that the smell of coffee would soon be wafting down the stairs. That spell would act as a Band-Aid for the moment as she got to work resetting the stronger enchantments that normally kept things running.

She had reframed the larger spell and was chanting and tracing the physical symbols of the spell over the panel when she heard Jason calling down the stairs again. She ignored him, unable to stop without losing the effort and energy she'd already put in. Moments later she was aware of the sound of the stairs creaking, and she felt the hair raising up on the back of her neck; the steps were too light to be Jason and she was almost certain it was more than one person. Still, if she stopped now she'd lose all her work so far and have to start over. She pushed the thoughts away and focused on finishing the spell work. As soon as the last syllable left her lips and she felt the spell settle fully into place she pulled her attention back outwards. The light from the door was lessened and she knew before she turned that it was being blocked by someone, or more than one someone, standing there. She took a deep breath and then turned to face her audience.

Two of the Elven Guard who had been at her store earlier in the week stood there looking at her. One was fair haired, the other dark. She wondered how they could have found her here and then realized that of course they knew where she lived because they knew where Bleidd and Syndra lived and she had told them herself who her roommates were. The two Guards looked incongruous in the grimy basement, like exotic art in a cheap motel. Allie was suddenly, acutely aware that she was standing there in dirty jeans, in a t-shirt she had been sleeping in every night for the last week, without a bra, barefoot, and with unbrushed hair. Both elves watched her calmly as she wished she could disappear through the cracked concrete floor.

After an uncomfortable silence the fair haired elf, Jessilaen, spoke, "Good morning, Aliaine."

She swallowed hard, "Allie. Everyone calls me Allie.' And then, belatedly she added, "And good morning to you Jessilaen and, uh," *Oh dear Gods what was his name?* "Brynneth."

The Guard commander smiled warmly, "You may call me Jess if you prefer."

She felt an almost hysterical urge to tell him that among humans Jess was usually a female name but she didn't quite dare. Elves were notoriously particular about their names, rarely offering nicknames. She knew that offering one to her, although probably a response to her insistence on being called Allie, was a rare gift. From the look on the other elf's face he had not expected it either. She nodded, unsure of the proper way to respond. Jess stepped into the tiny room, leaning forward to examine her spell, and she felt suddenly off balance by his close proximity and her own state of undress. She crossed her arms across her chest as subtly as she could, feeling mortified all over again.

"This is good work," he said approvingly. The other elf stepped into the room as well leaving no space for anything else and also leaned over to study her work.

"Clever to use minimal energy to achieve the desired result," Brynneth said.

"You do it differently?" she asked, genuinely curious despite her discomfort.

"We use layers of major spells," he replied.

She found herself nodding. "Yes, that would be a better system, more redundant."

"Indeed, but harder to set up and requiring more effort to maintain. There is a certain elegance in such a simple solution," Brynneth said, reaching out to trace his fingers an inch above the surface of her magic, feeling the strength and flow of it without breaking the pattern.

Jessilaen echoed his companion's sentiment, "Simple and elegant. This was your idea?"

She shifted slightly feeling the wall against her back. "Yes, actually. I'm not very powerful so I try to make the most of what I can do."

"Interesting," Jess said, both elves looking at her thoughtfully, "Many would simply use as much force as they could master, rather than trying to finesse the desired result."

"Mmmmm," she tried to sound non-committal while simultaneously wondering why they were being so complimentary. Elves were strictly honest but perfectly capable of misleading you without ever lying. She found herself wondering what they wanted from her that they were trying so hard to be nice. She started edging towards the door. "Well, I'm finished down here and I think I smell coffee up there. Would you like some?"

Both elves accepted the offer and followed her up the stairs. She wasn't usually a vain person but she couldn't stop thinking about how she looked; as soon as they were out of the basement she turned to Jason who was standing by the stove and looking a bit shell shocked. He was fine with Bleidd but easily intimidated by strange elves, who could be overwhelming without trying. She knew her next words were going to freak him out so she spoke quickly.

"Jason, I'm going to go get changed. This is Jessilaen and Brynneth. They'd like some coffee. Could you show them where the mugs are?"

Jason gave her a wide eyed look of sheer panic as she fled the room but she'd apologize later. She flew up the stairs and into her bedroom. The t-shirt and jeans were tossed into the laundry bin and clean clothes were pulled out of the dresser in record time. Fresh jeans, a bra, and a plain grey t-shirt made her feel more like herself, and after she dragged a brush through her hair she felt ready to face whatever questions the Guard had come here to ask. She walked quickly back down to the kitchen, not quite running, and found both the Guard standing next to the counter drinking coffee while Jason babbled, something he only did when he was extremely nervous.

"And then, well, it was hard to know what to do, but Allie told us to stay down–oh! Hi Allie!" Jason crossed the room in a few long steps and thrust a coffee cup and plate into her hands, "Here's yours, your food I mean, I have to go, sorry. I mean, sorry that I have to go not–you know. Anyway."

He gave her one last miserable look and disappeared. Allie bit her lip, wondering how long it would take him to get on his cell phone and start calling the others. Resigning herself she turned back to the elves in the kitchen who were still standing and drinking their coffee as if this was all perfectly normal. Then again if this was how most humans acted around them, maybe, from their point of view, it was. She went over and set her plate and mug down on the table before sitting down in the comfortable old wooden chair closest to the hallway.

"Would you like to sit down?"

The guards looked at each other for an instant and then moved to sit at the table. *This is too bizarre* Allie thought taking a sip of her coffee before starting to pick at her breakfast *It's like a Norman Rockwell painting gone horribly wrong.*

Jess set his cup down, but he didn't start asking her about the murders as she'd expected. Instead he said something that made her feel as unbalanced as if she were back in the basement "You look very pretty with your hair down loose like that."

Normal Elven manners dictated returning a personal compliment for a compliment, but she had no idea what to say to that. She had the sneaking suspicion that he was coming on to her but the context of getting hit on by someone in an official position was weird and she was a bit afraid of misinterpreting his intent and embarrassing herself. Elves were very straightforward when they were interested in someone and this seemed oddly subtle. Maybe he was hitting on her, or maybe he was trying to imitate human friendliness, something elves often found annoyingly hard to read. Elves were not generally subtle; their likes and dislikes were usually clearly expressed, if they were expressed at all. For an instant she was tempted to try to use her empathy to read him, but she quickly rejected the idea. After a pause that was too long she managed, "Thank you, um, your hair is very nice too."

It was an uninspired response at best. The dark haired elf smirked into his cup but Jessilaen ignored her blunder, continuing with another unexpected question, "Is he your lover?"

She blinked, unsure at first who he meant, "Who? Jason?"

Jess nodded, looking pointedly down at her food, and she belatedly remembered that among elves there were strict customs about preparing and serving food between people. Unless being served to guests or by someone in a servile or lower ranking position it indicated an intimate relationship, either family or sexual. Since her Japanese-

American roommate didn't look likely to be related to her by blood, Jess was assuming a sexual relationship. She was remembering now some of the reasons she hated the etiquette so much. *It is way too early in the morning for this crap* she thought before replying "No he isn't, just a good friend." Seeing the skepticism on his face she blurted out, "He's gay."

Both elves looked puzzled, so she added, "He prefers men."

They still looked unsure and Allie wanted to kick herself. Elves might have strict social etiquette about who could fix whose food but they were extremely sexually open, to the point that many humans thought them perverse. Allie tended to forget that aspect because it was not something she had much direct experience with or concern over. Struggling to be more precise, she said, "He only prefers to sleep with men."

They glanced at each other exchanging what she was almost positive was a "humans are so strange" look, but Jess nodded and seemed satisfied with her answer. "Have you had any luck in remembering where you might have seen a ritual that includes elements similar to the crimes we are investigating?"

Finally back on topic! She thought feeling a strange mixture of relief and disappointment. Relief that they were finally asking her the questions she had expected. Disappointment that she may have misread his interest in her which made her feel foolish on top of everything else. He was certainly attractive and she was drawn to him, but not only was getting involved with someone in his position a bad idea but she doubted his interest in her went beyond superficial physical attraction. The last thing she needed was to complicate her life with a one night stand, especially with one of the Elven Guard. Best to keep it strictly business. She shook her head. "I'm sorry, no. I'm sure I have seen it somewhere, but I just can't think where."

Several minutes passed as she ate and they drank their coffee, before she risked asking a question she needed the answer to, "Is there a pattern to the, um, the cutting?"

Brynneth, who had spent the last several days studying the police case files, nodded, "It's done very methodically. Regular parallel lines, shallow, across the torso, arms, and legs."

Allie flinched thinking of it while simultaneously trying not to think too hard about it but kept talking, "No patterns though? No designs?"

"No, "he said shaking his head, "Simple straight lines."

"All while the girl is still alive?"

"Yes."

She swallowed hard, starting to wish she hadn't eaten. "Is the blood loss what kills them?"

"No," Brynneth said, gently, "their throats are slit."

Allie nodded, thinking. "Is there a pattern to the timing of it?"

Both elves looked at her uncertainly. She tried to clarify. "Is it always on a full or dark moon? Something like that?"

The two looked at each other. Finally Brynneth shook his head slightly and Jessilaen turned back to her, saying, "Not that we are aware of. Not all the bodies were found immediately."

"Is there a way to see if there is a pattern? Based on when they are found and how long they seem to have been, you know, dead?" she pressed, suddenly feeling this was important. If they could find a pattern to the timing that might be the key.

Brynneth nodded "I will see to it myself."

She felt like they were starting to get somewhere at last but before she could think of the next logical step a loud bang reverberated through the house as the front door was thrown open. Allie jumped to her feet, knowing who it most likely was, even as the two Guards stood and started to draw their swords.

"No wait!" she said, getting them to pause just before Bleidd stormed in with Syndra right behind him. Bleidd looked ready to start throwing punches and she felt rising panic knowing how that would end. "Bleidd, wait…"

"It's not enough that I have to deal with the indignity…" he began, his voice rising on each word. At that point everyone began talking at once.

"What the fuck is going on?" Syndra shouted over Bleidd's complaint, cutting him off.

"This is no business of *yours,* Outcast." Jessilaen said forcefully, looking as if he would be perfectly happy if it came to blows.

"Officer Lyons…" Brynneth began.

"STOP!" Allie yelled louder than all of them. The silence was deafening. She felt her hands shaking but she kept talking as they all turned and stared at her. She started with her two roommates, "You guys just chill for a second. They're asking me questions about ritual aspects to the murders. Nothing to do with you guys."

Bleidd's face closed down completely and Syn looked skeptical but she pressed on, turning to the two Guard who were clearly still agitated, "I don't think I can tell you anything else right now. If I think of anything though, I'll call, I promise."

It was a reckless thing, to promise anyone of Fairy anything and she winced internally as soon as the words slipped out, but there was no taking them back. Brynneth nodded tightly his eyes still on Bleidd. "Then we should go."

"I'll walk you out," she offered, ignoring Bleidd's sharp intake of breath. She gave Syn a pointed look as she started towards the front door and mouthed the words "house meeting" over her shoulder. As they moved out into the hallway she heard her roommates' voices rising in the kitchen and hoped Syndra could keep Bleidd from doing anything stupid like chasing after them.

As soon as they were out the door she closed it behind them and took a deep breath. "I am sorry about that," she said sincerely, switching to Elvish

"Do not apologize, the fault was not yours," Jess said, with Brynneth agreeing. Jess nodded almost imperceptibly towards the car and the other elf bowed slightly to Allie by way of a farewell and set off across the yard. She had expected Jess to follow immediately but instead he reached out and stroked her hair. She could feel her eyes widening. "You look more beautiful without the other garment on, it's too restrictive."

She felt herself blushing, realizing he meant the bra "It is a part of human dress, human female dress."

"Elves do not wear such things. I like you better without it." He said softly, and before she could think of how to respond to that he leaned in and kissed her. Not a chaste first kiss, but a passionate kiss that left her gasping when he finally pulled away. So her earlier guess was correct; this was the direct approach she had expected. She just wasn't sure how to react to it. He spoke in that same soft voice, "I would very much like to court you."

Which means what? Allie thought, but hesitated to be honest about her ignorance. She had anticipated a direct proposition, something along the lines of being asked when and where they could meet for a tryst. Elves celebrated the sensual, including sex, as something to be enjoyed often and thoroughly. Allie had been trying to decide the best way to nicely turn him down without making herself sound prudish, since random sex was not something that interested her, but she had no idea what courting, in an Elven context, meant. Instead she hedged. "And if I agree?"

"We will see if we suit each other," he replied simply. *Like dating?* She wondered. She hadn't thought elves did that sort of thing, but it was obvious she was ignorant of some aspects of the culture.

"You barely know me," she whispered unable to deny that she felt drawn to him, had felt drawn to him since she had met him. And she could feel his emotions pressing through her shields, a heady mix of lust and something sweeter.

"I would like to remedy that, if you will allow it," he said softly.

She thought of all the reasons this was a mistake, not the least of which was the domestic turmoil it would unleash in her previously peaceful home. She thought of the likelihood that he was just looking for a new novel experience or something different and interesting. Of the misery of having her heart broken by someone who probably saw her as an interesting diversion to keep himself occupied with until the next new thing came along. And realized that part of her didn't care about anything but the feel of his mouth against hers. "Yes, I would like that; to be courted."

He smiled and kissed her again, pausing as he straightened up to inhale the scent of her hair before stepping away. "Then since we are courting I will be back as soon as I can."

She stood watching until the Guards' car pulled away. It was impossible not to recognize the vehicles the Guard used no matter how much effort went in to making them look like ordinary cars; they were manufactured special without any iron and layered with so much magic they veritably glowed. Usually the sight of one arriving created dismay, but Allie found herself feeling something very similar watching this one drive away. She wondered if this was how her father had felt around her mother, and found the thought extremely unsettling.

It wasn't until she turned to go back into the house that she realized that she had just made the greatest possible mistake anyone could make with Fairy; she had agreed to something without understanding fully what she was agreeing to.

****

The house meeting was a tense affair that didn't accomplish much except to alienate Allie from the other 4 roommates. Allie had managed to put Bleidd and Syndra off until Jason and Liz returned home insisting that she didn't want to have to repeat everything but that only gave them time to get more upset about it. By the time the other two got there Bleidd in particular had worked himself into a fine rage.

He started talking as soon as Liz walked in the door, turning on Allie, "How could you speak to them? What did you tell them? Why would you even let them in the house at all?"

"Let her answer one question before you ask another," Liz objected, frowning.

Allie found herself searching for the best way to explain and blurted out the truth, "It wasn't like that. They came and talked to me at the store the other day…"

"What?" Bleidd took a step towards her and Jason intervened.

"Al, why didn't you tell us?" Syndra asked, sounding hurt.

"I was going to…" Allie said.

"Which day? When did they seek you out first?" Bleidd snapped.

Allie felt her mouth go dry. Everyone was looking at her, waiting. Finally she mumbled, "Monday."

"Monday!" Syn looked appalled. Liz just shook her head not even trying to defend her cousin.

"I'm sorry!" she said sincerely, but no one seemed to care.

"Oh Allie," Jason said, "You should have said something."

She had been avoiding looking at Bleidd but when he said nothing she couldn't help glancing his way. He was glaring at her, his green eyes furious, and she swallowed hard. His voice was cold "You look like an adult but you act like a child, thoughtlessly. What did it take to buy your cooperation? Money? Empty promises? Or some flattering words? And never mind that you aid my enemies in framing me for crimes I'm innocent of."

What he said stung and Allie snapped back "That is not true! I'm trying to help you, to prove you didn't do anything. Nobody's paying me anything..."

"Oh, you should get paid," Syn cut in. "Don't let yourself get taken advantage of. If they expect you to be some kind of on-call expert..."

"Expert in what exactly?" Liz asked, frowning again, "No offense Allie but what could you possibly be an expert in that can help the police with these murders?"

Allie floundered, feeling ganged up on, "I'm not– they just had some questions about ritual murders and ways to raise energy that might apply here, and people recommended me because of the store. I told them I'm not an expert. And I'm not on-call."

"Then why did they show up here, at our home today, if they've already questioned you?" Bleidd asked sharply.

"Yeah, at the fucking ass crack of dawn no less," Syn added. "There's something not right about the whole thing."

Allie flushed, trying not to think about the feel of Jess's mouth against hers or her agreement to do something she didn't fully understand. No way was she mentioning his personal interest in her while everyone was already so angry and suspicious. "They wanted to see if I had thought of anything else that might help."

Syn looked skeptical and unfortunately Jason chose that moment to start contributing to the conversation "If you ask me I think that blond Elf has the hots for you."

Allie looked at him, horrified, which made him nervous so he kept talking, "I saw how he was looking at you. When you went to go change he watched you the whole time you were walking away and I know that look, like he wanted to go with you and…"

"Jason!" Allie cut in desperate to get him to shut up.

"Holy shit," Syndra swore, obviously remembering her rush to walk the two Guards out and her delay in returning "You have got to be fucking kidding me."

"Unbelievable! That is how little I mean to you that you betray me for the promise of a pretty face? Or are you such a fool that you believe he has any interest in you besides using you to get a foot in this house?" Bleidd was so angry now he was yelling in Elvish and she felt a mix of guilt and her own anger.

She found herself yelling back in kind "Why, because it's so impossible to believe anyone might find me attractive without an ulterior motive?"

He opened his mouth to respond and then turned and all but ran from the room instead. After a stunned moment Liz and Jason went after him, making it clear with their actions whose side they were on. Syndra stood indecisively shaking her head.

"Al, honestly, what were you thinking?" she asked her friend "I don't know what that last bit in Elvish was about, but seriously, he has a right to be mad. You should have told us Monday. And getting involved with a cop–elf cop or otherwise–who's investigating your friend for murder is just fucking asinine."

"I have to go or I'm going to be late opening the store," Allie said blinking back tears and feeling thoroughly misunderstood.

Syndra gave her a long look before saying "I guess you should do what you have to do then."

Chapter 4 - Friday

Allie spent most of Friday in a dark mood, glaring out the store's windows, resenting the bright sunny spring weather and not doing anything useful. She had worn an old hooded sweatshirt and jeans, refusing to even make an effort to cheer herself up by dressing nicely. Business was still slow giving her ample time to brood. She wished she could go back in time and undo everything.

Late in the day her thoughts were interrupted by two figures in heavy cloaks with the hoods pulled up walking in front of the store. Although the sight wasn't out of place in a town with a mixed population something about the two caught her attention. They pushed open the door to the store but the little bell above it remained silent; Allie felt her skin prickling as the ward set in the bells broke. Whoever these two were, they meant trouble. She watched them apprehensively as they pretended to browse but surreptitiously watched her watching them.

After a few minutes of this they both headed in her direction and she realized they were elves. If their entrance had broken the wards that could mean only one thing, and her mind raced, trying to think of the best way to handle this, if she could handle it at all.

"Hello," the closest of the two greeted her pleasantly, stopping a dozen feet away, "Perhaps you can help us? We are looking for a certain book."

"Good afternoon," she replied struggling to sound calm, "We have a wide selection of books. Which one are you looking for?"

He smiled, but his eyes were coldly assessing, "This one is special. Rare. One of a kind actually."

It was awkward talking with so much distance between them, but she hesitated to come out from behind the counter. "Do you know the title?"

"I know that it's here and that you know about it," he replied, still pleasant. The other elf stood near the book shelves, his fingers tracing the spines of the nearest books. Allie had no doubt he was magically searching for something, but she had no idea what.

She shook her head slightly, "I don't know what you mean."

His smile made it plain that he didn't believe her. "Is there a special section for rare books?"

"Yes, back left section of the store."

"Can you show us?"

She hesitated a moment and then edged out into the open area. There was a small space between the end of the counter and the wall which controlled access to the back. One of the large couches her grandmother had set up for people to sit and read in sat at a right angle to the wall six feet back from the counter, creating a small open space for people to stand when they were checking out; towards the bookshelf side of the store it opened up into a wider space. She walked to the rare book section with the second elf following behind her and showed him, wordlessly, where the shelves where before retreating. When she returned she found the talkative one leaning against the counter, blocking the narrow opening to the back. "So you are Elizabeth McCarthy's granddaughter," he said.

The words caught her totally off guard. "Yes."

"Interesting," he smiled and it wasn't pleasant, but then he seemed to switch gears. "This would be much easier if you would simply give us the book."

He leaned forward and she edged back and around wanting to get to the dubious safety behind the counter. He followed her, crowding her against the couch back and still blocking her way. "I don't know what book you are talking about."

"We can pay you. More money than you can imagine," he said, as alarms went off in her head. She wished now that she had stayed in the open area.

"I really don't know what you are looking for," she said, knowing it was true and wishing she could hand him what he wanted so he would leave.

"Or maybe," he said, reaching out to stroke her cheek, "if money doesn't interest you, you'd like a different form of compensation?"

She could feel his magic pushing at her, carried on the physical contact. Glamour was a potent thing and using it for seduction was illegal, the magical equivalent of a date rape drug. If she didn't have personal shields and a resistance to Elven magic she'd be panting at his feet right now with no idea why she suddenly wanted him. Her head jerked back reflexively, and before she could think of a more diplomatic reply she blurted out "No."

His eyes narrowed and he gathered his magic and pushed at her, hard. She stood fast. "No one," he said, his voice deceptively gentle, "turns me down. I have had more women than I can count. You should be grateful that I would even consider you."

Allie knew she was treading on very dangerous ground, that she should refuse him carefully without hurting his pride or insulting him. But she was genuinely frightened and before she could think it through she heard herself saying, "I'm sure you can find a willing girl down at the *Star*."

As soon as the words were out of her mouth she was certain that telling him to go find a bedmate at the club where the Fairy groupies hung out wouldn't go over well, but his reaction was worse than she anticipated. Faster than her eyes could follow his arm jerked back and he punched her. Her nose broke beneath the blow, blood spraying, and as she started to crumple from the pain he grabbed both her upper arms and slammed her into the wall. Then he kissed her, pressing his lips against her bloody mouth. She felt her stomach turning, both from his action and from the roil of emotions she could feel from him: a blend of lust, anger, and satisfaction. She struggled futilely against his iron grip. He pulled his face back slightly from hers, licking her blood off his lips. His eyes narrowed, a calculating expression on his face. Using one hand to hold her against the wall his other hand reached up and pushed her hair back from her right ear. "Well, well, what have we here? A little mixed blood girl masquerading as a human. How delicious you are little half-breed."

His hand in her hair clenched, forcing her head back painfully. She struggled against him as he pressed his body into hers pinning her to the wall. He ran his tongue up her throat, licking the trail of blood that dripped down into the fabric of her sweatshirt. She hit out at him with her free hand, barely connecting with his side; he smiled and said, "If you like it rough that's fine, I prefer a girl with some fight in her."

Allie panicked at the promise in his eyes and reflexively brought her knee up as hard as she could. She missed her target, but hit his thigh hard. He stopped smiling, pulling away from her, and punched her again, his fist catching the left side of her face. Multicolored lights sparkled in front of her eyes and she felt herself falling. She landed in the narrow wooden aisle between the wall and the end of the counter, with his weight settling above her pinning her down. She struggled to get her arms up but before she could do more than shove weakly at him he wedged his forearm under her chin, pushing her head back and pressing down on her throat. Her hands clawed at his arm as she tried to breathe but he was stronger than she and her efforts were useless. He shifted his weight to one side and his free hand pulled at the waistband of her jeans, yanking with increasing force until she heard fabric tear. Someone was speaking, but the sound was meaningless as her vision started to go dark and her lungs burned for oxygen. And then, without warning, the weight lifted and she took a deep breath. She tried to roll over but his hand returned, pinning her down; she almost didn't care as she lay there gasping in huge lungful's of air.

"You fool," a voice said angrily in Elvish somewhere above and to her left, "This is a public building."

"Did you find the book?" he snapped back. The haze had cleared and she realized that he was half kneeling above her, the second elf's hand grasping his shoulder. She stared at the long pale fingers digging into the heavy fabric of the cloak, and realized that the second one had pulled the first off of her.

"No, and we have no more time to delay here." The second elf never spared a glance at her, as if she didn't exist. Her head ached fiercely and she could feel the blood dripping across her face from her nose.

"I'm not ready to leave yet." He started to turn towards her, but the second elf jerked him back.

"Are you mad? And if someone walks in what will you do? Forget her and let us leave quickly and hope we don't draw any attention." For the first time his eyes settled on her, cold and measuring, "Leave her for now. We can come back later and search again for the book."

The words stirred a fresh sense of panic but her body refused to move. As if in a dream she found herself lying helplessly while the first elf considered his companion's words. After far too long he nodded once and the second elf let him go, disappearing towards the door.

Her tormentor leaned forward until his mouth was almost touching her ear. "I will be back little mixed blood girl, and next time we will not be interrupted. I will take my pleasure from your body and listen to you scream until your throat is raw."

As he spoke his hand snaked up underneath her sweatshirt, grabbing her breast and squeezing until she cried out and writhed away from him. A dark satisfied look filled his face and then he was gone, leaving her lying alone on the floor.

She had no idea how long she lay there, gasping, listening to the sound of her own heartbeat roaring in her ears. The sudden realization that they could return at any moment finally spurred her to action and she forced her battered body to move, half crawling to the door and locking it. She reached up to the light switch on the wall and turned off the lights, feeling slightly safer in the locked, dark store. Then she thought about how lucky she was that *he* hadn't thought to simply lock the door and she felt herself starting to shake. She tried to stand and a wave of dizziness drove her back to her knees, forcing her to crawl back to the relative safety behind the counter.

She needed help but she didn't know what to do. *If I call 911 there will be lights, sirens,* she thought, *and strangers. I'll have to explain to strangers.* She shook her head but stopped when the motion made her stomach turn. She needed someone she could trust, someone she could honestly talk to about the wider implications of what had just happened, of who those two were, and more importantly what they represented. Unfortunately the only person she could think of calling was barely speaking to her right now.

Finally she reached for the phone and reluctantly dialed.

****

"Unbelievably stubborn, ridiculous, fucking pigheaded," Syn's words matched the cadence of her steps as she paced across the small exam room. Allie had tuned her out, knowing that the other woman had to run out of adjectives eventually and that the stream of invective was Syn's way of expressing worry. Instead of listening she kept her eyes closed and focused on the pattern of Syn's steps on the industrial linoleum of the walk-in clinic that served as a small community hospital for the town and pressed the ice pack against her throbbing face. Syn had been at the gym when Allie had called and she was still dressed in her workout gear, a black tank top and spandex shorts; her sneakers squeaked every time she turned making Allie wince. Allie wanted to ask her to stop but Syn had done her a huge favor, getting her to the clinic, sitting with her, handling everything. She knew her friend didn't understand why she was refusing everything except basic medical care, and there was no way to explain it to her that she'd understand right now.

When the door opened Allie fully expected it to be the nurse returning to try to convince her, again, to let them conduct a more thorough exam so she was surprised to hear an almost familiar voice asking "Has the doctor been in yet?"

Her left eye was swollen shut but she forced her right eye open, ignoring the stabbing pain that went through her head. Crowding in to the small room were the same 6 people who had walked into her store at the beginning of the week, heralding the start of all of this chaos. It was Detective Riordan who had spoken; he looked genuinely concerned. His partner, Walters, was stony faced. The four elves looked grave and Jessilaen was moving past the rest towards the side of the hospital bed. She took this all in with an odd sense of detachment before turning to look at Syndra, who was radiating guilt.

"Don't give me that look, Al" Syn mumbled, before regaining her aggressive tone. "What the fuck did you expect me to do? I'm a cop and you're helping them investigate a serial killer and then you get attacked? Of course I had to call them."

Allie shook her head slightly as Jess's hand settled on her shoulder. She stared down at the dried blood on her jeans to avoid looking at anyone.

"Why is she still in those clothes?" Riordan pressed, managing to sound sympathetic and businesslike at the same time. "We'll need them bagged as evidence and the doctor's report–"

"No," Allie interrupted, her voice a painful croak. She felt Jess's fingers tighten on her shoulder.

"No?" Riordan repeated, sounding baffled. He turned to look at Syndra, who was glaring at Allie.

"She's refusing to let the doctor examine her," Syndra said, "She wouldn't let them do anything except a basic exam and that ice pack."

"Maybe because this is all just a waste of time," Walters said. "Maybe she wasn't really attacked."

"Are you kidding me?" Syn said, angry but obviously trying not to lash out at the senior officer. The four elves remained dead silent, their attention fixed on the detective.

"Walters," his partner said, a warning note in his voice.

"Hey, I'm just saying the girl doesn't want us involved. She didn't call 911. She didn't call us herself. She's refusing care. We don't know how she got hurt or what happened and I don't think we should jump to conclusions. She doesn't want our help; I'm sure she's got her reasons," he turned towards Allie, "You pressing charges?"

She hesitated, and then said softly, "No."

"What!" Syndra's shout echoed in the small room. "No fucking way. No–fucking–way. You are damn sure pressing charges..."

"Officer Lyons..." Riordan tried to cut in.

"You get jumped in your own fucking store, you get your ass kicked, you..."

Knowing what she was about to say Allie forced herself to speak, despite the pain. "Enough! Stop telling me what I'm going to do. Just drop it."

Syn's mouth opened and closed wordlessly, her cheeks flushing. Allie had never seen the other woman so angry before. Riordan tried again to intervene and diffuse the situation. "Ms. McCarthy, take some time and think about this. If you're afraid of some sort of retribution from whoever did this we can protect you. Why don't you let the doctor see how bad the injuries are?"

Syn found her voice, "Why don't you let them do a fucking rape kit?"

Allie reacted instantly flinging the ice pack as hard as she could and yelling "I was not." the ice pack hit Syndra squarely in the chest rocking her back but Allie's words were stopped by a wave of nausea that doubled her over and had her clutching the plastic trash can the nurse had given her in case she threw up. Walters chose that moment to mutter, loud enough to be heard "some girls like it rough" and all Hell broke loose as both Syndra and Jessilaen lunged at the burly detective. Riordan managed to hold Syndra back and the other three elves restrained Jess although none of them looked happy about it. It took several minutes for order to be restored during which Allie decided if she did throw up she was aiming for Detective Walters' shoes.

The doctor walked in to the tense silence that followed and stood looking from one person to the next clearing his throat nervously. Finally he suggested that the group move out to the hall and let Allie get some rest. After a quick consultation, Jess and Brynneth said they would stay with her. She expected Syn to insist on staying as well, but her friend was the first one out the door.

****

"So Doc, how bad is she hurt?" Riordan was all business with the ER doctor, not wasting time with pleasantries.

"Well, she isn't cooperating but her nose is broken and she almost certainly has a concussion, based on the vomiting and headache. She shouldn't be left alone for the next few days with the head injury. That'll need to be monitored, but that can be done at home." Doctor Brown cleared his throat again, "With the bruising on her throat there could be some swelling and pain for the next few days…"

"Bruising on her throat? Is that why her voice sounds like that? I thought it was because of the nose."

"No, it looks like, if I had to guess, I'd say she was either choked or hit hard across the throat."

"Was she raped?" Riordan asked bluntly.

The doctor looked uncomfortable. "She won't consent to an exam or tell us what happened."

"Off the record here Doc," Riordan said.

Brown hesitated, obviously debating what to say. "I can't tell you what I don't know," he finally said, "But if she *was* cooperating I'd order a rape kit and a full exam."

Riordan looked grim, but nodded, "Thanks Doc."

"There's really no reason to keep her here at this point, unless you can convince her to accept further treatment." The doctor headed back towards the front desk, leaving the group of police and Guard standing in the hall.

Syndra turned to Detective Riordan. "Are you going to be here for a little while?"

"What's up Lyons?"

"I just thought of something. Allie's store has a video surveillance system. Give me–20 minutes and I can get the video at the store downloaded onto a thumb drive and get back here."

Riordan nodded. "Walters go with her, and you two behave," he added as they glared at each other. "And get a unit started over there to work the scene maybe we'll get lucky and find some solid physical evidence."

"Detective," Captain Zarethyn interrupted, "didn't Aliaine say she did not wish this pursued as a criminal case?"

Riordan gave the elf a long look "Yeah she did, but firstly I think it's a bit beyond coincidence that we're investigating girls getting raped and murdered and our occult expert gets attacked and maybe sexually assaulted a few days after we talk to her. And secondly it wouldn't be the first time I saw a girl get raped and not want to press charges and then change her mind after she gets over the initial shock. So we're going to get started on this and see where it goes."

The elf inclined his head in the equivalent of a shrug, deferring to his human counterpart, even though his own inclination was to respect the girl's wishes. He did not understand the way that humans would turn a blind eye to some crimes yet insist on investigating others even when the victims didn't want them to. It seemed a baffling and ineffectual system to the Elven Captain. Riordan watched the two human police walking away and Zarethyn caught Aeyliss' eye and nodded slightly towards the remaining detective. The red haired elf inclined her head fractionally in response then said "Detective, is there somewhere in this building to get food?"

"What?" Riordan said, distracted, "Yeah, there's a small cafeteria."

"Could you show me? I would like to hear more of your thoughts on a possible connection between this incident and our case as well."

Riordan hesitated "I should question her more… but she is pretty upset. Yeah, come on, I'll show you."

Zarethyn waited until the two had disappeared from sight before returning to the tiny hospital room. Allie was sitting exactly as he had left her, clutching the cheap garbage bin. Jessilaen and Brynneth stood next to her; Jessilaen obviously concerned.

"Everyone else is gone?" Allie broke the silence, speaking Elvish to be certain they wouldn't be overheard by a nurse or wandering patient.

"Yes," the Guard Captain said "for the moment. The police believe this is connected to the murders."

Allie winced "I hope not. They were Dark Court."

Zarethyn inhaled sharply, but she kept talking, "They came in looking for a book. They said I knew what book they wanted, but I have no idea what they were talking about. I said something I shouldn't have, something rude, and that's when the hitting happened."

"You are certain they were Dark Court?" he pressed not wanting to believe it.

"Yes. Two elves. They broke the ward on my front door–it's set for the Dark Court."

"Why do you have a ward for that?" Brynneth asked.

"Because," she answered softly, "I know that they are real, no matter how convinced every other human is that they aren't, and I know how dangerous they are."

"This is why you wouldn't tell the police anything?" Zarethyn asked, speaking into the stunned silence that followed her revelation.

When Fairy and Earth merged and the two cultures were forced to deal with each other there had been some violent clashes at first until the current system was established. Part of what held the fragile peace was an effort on the elves part to convince humanity that Elven society was not inherently dangerous to humans, but this was only partially true. Fairy had long been divided into two courts, the bright and dark. The Bright Court currently held sway but the Dark Court was still a powerful force. They chaffed at the restrictions placed on them that didn't allow them to cause havoc or death among mortals. Decades of concerted effort had led most humans to dismiss the Dark Court as legend born of misunderstanding and fear, but the Elven Guard knew how real the threat was, and the potential damage that could be caused if the Dark Court succeeded in creating any harm to the human public that could be traced back to them. Zarethyn admired the girl's discretion in not mentioning who had assaulted her to anyone else.

"They probably wouldn't have believed me anyway, but if they did they'd stop investigating everything else. They'd never believe it wasn't these two. And it would create panic, people would be seeing Dark Court in every Fairy creature," she said, wincing as her throat ached.

"And you do not believe they are involved?"

"I don't know. I don't know why they were here or if it's related. It seems unlikely though," she answered honestly. "If it's alright, I'd like to get some rest now."

Zarethyn signaled for the others to leave the room. Jessilaen leaned over stroking her unbruised cheek "I will be outside if you need anything."

She reached up, surprising him by grabbing his hand briefly and squeezing it before lying down and closing her eyes.

Back out in the hallway again the three elves were grim. "Can she be right?" Zarethyn asked, still not wanting to believe it.

"We have no reason to doubt her," Jessilaen responded quickly, predictably defending her. Zarethyn was unsure why Jessilaen had become so attached to the girl so quickly, or why he was so insistent in pursuing her, but if his connection to the girl could be helpful to their investigation, the Captain saw no reason to discourage it.

Brynneth nodded, "I find it hard to believe the Dark Court could be here, but her injuries are too severe to have been dealt by a human."

"She allowed you to examine her?"

"No, but I observed her while we were in the room. Even at a distance it is obvious they were single blows from a fist. I doubt a human's ability to do such damage with one strike."

Zarethyn nodded, trusting the healer's opinion as an expert one. Before they could continue he saw Officer Lyons and Detective Walters rounding the corner down the hall. Walters called out to the group "You guys are gonna wanna see this."

****

After sending Syndra to find Riordan and Aeyliss, and commandeering the nearest computer, the group of 7 crammed into the doctor's office. The thumb drive video was pulled up and the screen divided into four sections: one displayed the front of a parking lot and part of the street, the second was obviously the sidewalk in front of the store, one appeared to be a back hallway lined with doors and a shelf and the final square showed the interior of the store from the front looking towards the back counter where Allie could be seen leaning and looking out.

As the group watched two cloaked figures appeared on the sidewalk video and entered the store. At the counter Allie straightened but when the two strangers entered the shot all that could be seen was their backs. In the heavy cloaks, with the hoods up, it was impossible to tell if they were male or female never mind what species they were or any distinguishing features. Riordan swore, "Do they ever turn towards the camera?"

"Not really," Walters said, tensely. "At the very end as they're leaving you get a glimpse, but not much."

Riordan swore again. The elves watched intently. The two walked forward, one moving towards the counter, one staying by the bookshelves. Allie came out from behind the counter and walked out of the shot to the left followed by one of the cloaked figures. Moments later she returned and the remaining figure blocked her way. They appeared to be talking as she tried to edge around to get behind the counter. The figure had turned towards the camera enough to tell that it was male, but the hood and camera angle completely blocked the face. He reached out towards her face; she moved away and then suddenly he swung. Even on the tiny screen the level of violence was clear as he threw her against the wall at the very edge of the camera's field. Between the limits of the camera's range and the obscuring effect of the cloak it was hard to tell exactly what happened then, until he pulled his arm back and punched her again. She fell to the floor, disappearing behind the bulk of the counter and he followed; the only thing visible was lower legs and feet thrashing. Suddenly the other figure ran across the screen leaning over the tangle of bodies. Seconds ticked by before the cloaked figure ran back across the screen towards the door; as Walters had said it was almost impossible to see any clear details. Moments later the other figure stood up more slowly and then jogged after his companion. Both disappeared out the door and across the sidewalk camera at a fast walk.

Riordan swore for a third time as Walters stopped the video feed. Syndra stood facing the wall, arms crossed, refusing to watch again. All the elves radiated anger.

"Detective Riordan," Zarethyn said his voice flat, "Brynneth is a healer and medic. Let him try to convince the girl to accept our help."

"Yeah," Riordan said "Do whatever you can."

****

Brynneth and Jessilaen came back into the room and found Allie sitting up again, hunched forward. Brynneth approached her slowly, Jess trailing behind, but it was Jess who spoke, "Allie, we have watched the video."

"What video?" she said, her voice a croak.

"The security video from your store," he said gently.

Her good eye opened slowly and she focused on the two elves. "From my store?"

"Yes."

She closed her eye and her head fell forward again "I'm sure it's–misleading."

"Allie."

"I was not raped," her voice trembled when she said it.

"Alright," he agreed. "Let Brynneth heal you."

"I don't..." she started and then stopped. "Listen, it wasn't like that."

"Aliaine," Brynneth began.

"He kept asking about the book. He offered me money and when I said I didn't know what book he wanted

82

he said–he propositioned me–said maybe I wanted other compensation. Tried to use glamour. I said no and he was pissed. He said no one refuses him…"

"Allie," Jess said, reaching out to take her hand, but she kept talking.

"So I told him to go find a willing girl somewhere else. And then he hit me and then we started fighting and then," -now that she'd started talking about it she couldn't make herself stop– "and then I was on the ground and he had me pinned down and he had his arm up at my throat and I couldn't breathe. And it's a little blurry after that but I wasn't–it definitely didn't get that far. The other one came over and pulled him off and said it was too dangerous in a public place and…"

She cut herself off suddenly. Both elves looked at her and then each other. "And?" Jess prompted gently.

Allie shook her head. "Nothing," she mumbled.

"Allie, please," he tried to get her to look him in the eyes but she avoided his gaze. "Please you must be honest with us. The Dark Court is infinitely dangerous. If they are seeking a foothold here we must know why and what it is they are seeking. Anything they said to you may be important."

She hesitated for a long time, and then finally said, "He said that they would come back to find the book–and the other one said he would–finish with me later."

Jessilaen's eyes narrowed dangerously but his voice stayed calm. "I will not allow anyone to harm you."

"Why do you care? You barely know me," she mumbled feeling miserable.

He shook his head not sure how to explain. "Have you never known as soon as you met someone that person was special?"

"That only happens in books and sentimental movies," she replied.

"No, that happens all the time. I do not understand why humans do not choose to trust their own hearts."

"Probably because human hearts are fickle."

"Elven hearts are not," he said simply, making her wonder which kind of heart she had.

"Elves are constantly hooking up with random people and then moving on to the next," she replied without thinking and then bit her lip.

"Life is full of physical joys to be experienced, but that is not the same thing as joys of the heart," he told her softly. She looked away, afraid that she knew exactly what he meant and wishing that she didn't.

"Aliaine," Brynneth said into the silence that followed. "Please let me heal you."

She was exhausted and thinking about Jess's words made her head hurt even more. It was a bad idea to be in debt to anyone of Fairy, and she had no way to pay for any healing work. But everything hurt, and she knew the physical healing would also help with her mental healing. She looked at Brynneth and nodded as much as her painful head would allow, capitulating suddenly and totally. His relief was obvious. "I will need to place my hands on your chest, above the collarbone. You may fall asleep during the healing so you should lie back, if you can. This won't be a major spell, just channeled energy. Have you been healed before?"

"Yes, I know how it works, and that it won't make everything disappear; it just speeds up the process, I should get more sleep the next few days, drink lots of water, that sort of thing."

Brynneth couldn't stop himself from smiling at her slightly exasperated tone.

She shifted back against the hospital pillows until she was semi-reclining and tried to relax. He lowered the wooden side rail on the bed and sat down next to her, leaning over slightly to place his hands in the correct positions to channel the healing energy. He closed his eyes to focus on the healing and as the energy poured into her she did indeed fall asleep.

Jessilaen stood tensely on the other side of the bed watching as the minutes ticked by and the bruising and swelling across her face slowly faded from painfully new to something that looked days old. He felt helpless in the face of her stubborn self-sufficiency and worse knew that his heart was already lost to her, even though he had begun to fear that she did not feel the same way or even understand what it meant to feel it. Elves had few unmixed emotions; what they felt they felt strongly and unwaveringly, which was why emotional attachment was discouraged. Intense emotions could be dangerous when you lived nearly forever with the same group of people. Love could turn to hate, anger and jealousy could motivate violence, and loss could cause despair that would spiral a person down into suicidal depression. Physical relationships rarely involved deep emotional attachment and it was uncommon for anything more than friendship to form between individuals outside of family units. His companions, and especially Brynneth who was Jess's true friend, were baffled by his decision to court Aliaine, to intentionally seek the emotions his kind normally avoided, and he did not know how to explain to them that he could not change how he felt about her. He felt as if he was being carried along at the mercy of emotions he could not control.

After longer than he had expected, Brynneth slowly opened his eyes and lifted his hands; Allie slept deeply. Jess was sure she would not wake but he spoke softly anyway, "How is she Bryn?"

"She will mend, but it was a near thing. A bit more pressure on her throat would have crushed her windpipe, even if the lack of oxygen didn't kill her," Brynneth shook his head slightly. "I do not understand the Dark Court and their love of such wanton violence."

Jess struggled not to betray his own rage, knowing that such extreme anger for her sake was exactly why emotions were best avoided. He thought though that he understood the Dark Court perfectly well since right then he very much wanted to do terrible things to the one who had hurt Allie. "You need to tell Zarethyn the details she told us and he will want to hear what you found. I will stay with her."

Brynneth looked at him sharply, "Jess I know you care for this girl but don't set your heart on the impossible."

Jessilaen frowned at his friend as Brynneth continued, more gently, "She does not seem to return your affection."

Jess shook his head, knowing that the others all felt Allie's choice to call her friend, and not him, after she was attacked was irrefutable proof of her rejection. "She accepted my court and has not denied me."

Bryn looked skeptical but before he could argue the point Zarethyn eased into the room, quickly taking in Allie's sleeping form and improved appearance. "We have little time before the human police will join us."

Brynneth nodded and gave his report without further prompting, "I have healed as much as I can without using any major spells; she will be more comfortable and in no danger. As the human doctor said her nose was broken and she was concussed. She also had a great deal of bruising on her throat from an injury that was nearly fatal. She was not raped but it was a near thing–a few moments more perhaps. When we returned to the room and told her we had seen the video from the store, she elaborated on the attack; the Dark Court seeks a book, as she had said, but they told her they plan to return to continue looking for it."

"And to finish what they started with her," Jessilaen added. Their Captain looked at him and then back at Brynneth, who nodded.

"Yes," Brynneth agreed, "she seems to be in great danger whether or not the book they seek is found."

"This girl seems to be the key to many things," Zarethyn said thoughtfully.

"Captain, "Jessilaen began, but the other elf held up one hand stopping him.

"In this situation it would seem our best strategy to achieve several goals is to protect the girl. We need to know what she knows about the murders, and we need to capture, if we can, these agents of the Dark Court and discover their ultimate purpose here."

Chapter 5 - Saturday

Consciousness returned slowly and at first she wasn't sure where she was or what was going on. After a moment she realized she was in her own bed, with its familiar feel and scent, although that seemed wrong somehow. She was fully dressed and she wasn't alone. Someone lay behind her, a warm presence at her back, an arm resting across her waist. The presence felt protective and there was something comforting about whoever it was being there. She started to move and the movement made her face ache dully, triggering memories of the day before. She swallowed hard, trembling, and the person behind her shifted; the hand that had been at her waist lifted as the person sat up.

"Shhhhh," Jessilaen whispered, "Everything is all right. You are safe."

Her heart leaped at the sound of his voice even as she wondered what he was doing in her bed with her. She struggled to sit up, feeling oddly disoriented, but realized that she could see out of her left eye again. Reaching up she tentatively felt her face and nose; still tender and slightly puffy but much better than yesterday. "What's going on? How did we get here?"

"You fell asleep during the healing and after the clinic discharged you we brought you back to your home."

"You brought me back here? I don't remember that." Allie felt disproportionately annoyed that she didn't remember. There was something very unnerving about going to sleep in one bed and waking up in another–with someone.

"You were sleeping," he said, resting his chin on her shoulder. And then added, "I carried you. Your friend, Officer Lyons, showed us your room, and Brynneth felt that someone should stay with you, lest you wake and have any dizziness or try to move too quickly and injure yourself."

She wasn't sure how to feel about any of that, or about his physical closeness. Too much had happened in too short a time and she didn't know how to feel about any of it. Instead she blurted out, "I need to go to the bathroom," and struggled to stand.

He moved quickly, trying to help her even as she stubbornly pushed him away. She stumbled, started to fall and found herself in his arms. A flood of tangled emotions welled up and she pushed him away again, walking unsteadily towards the door. He followed behind, ready to catch her if she fell again. Her jeans had started to slide off her hips and she stopped to pull them back up. She tried to refasten them only realize that they wouldn't stay fastened because they were ripped. That brought up memories of the events of the day before. *This was a brand new pair of jeans*, she thought and then found herself blinking back tears. Irrationally she started pulling off her clothes from yesterday, suddenly appalled by the dried blood.

"Allie?" Jess's voice was hesitant.

She started crying. "Everything's bloody," she sobbed. "My new jeans, my sweatshirt, my hair."

She flung her sweatshirt across the room and tried to kick off her jeans but tripped and fell. He caught her, pulling her in against his body and holding her as she cried. She could feel his concern, warm and comforting, and it was frightening how much she liked it. She turned in his arms, pulling back to look him in the eyes, "I hate feeling this way."

He stroked her hair, making soothing noises and she cried harder. "You were badly hurt. It's perfectly understandable to be upset about it."

Her body was shaking. She felt angry and helpless and she had no idea why he was being so good to her when she was a sobbing, nearly hysterical mess. She had been nothing to him but trouble.

"Why are you so kind to me? Why don't you just leave me alone?" The words came out angrier than she intended.

He stiffened; hurt by what seemed to be blatant rejection, he struggled to stay calm. "Do you want me to leave?"

"I want to understand what you want from me," she said taking a deep breath and trying to get her own emotions under control, becoming aware that some of what she was feeling was coming from him. She tried to strengthen her shields.

"I don't want anything from you," he said sadly, "I only want to be with you. I asked you if you would let me court you, but you keep pushing me away. If you have changed your mind..."

"Changed my mind about what?" she asked, wiping away tears. It was easier not to think about being hurt when she had something else to focus on.

"About being courted."

"We haven't had any time for that with everything else going on"

Now he was genuinely confused, "I don't understand."

"Don't understand what?"

He hesitated. He was starting to realize that her apparent rejection of him might not be what it seemed, but he wasn't sure how to clarify. Finally he said, "What do you think courting means?"

"Well, it's like dating isn't it?" she spoke slowly

He shook his head feeling foolish, "I do not know what dating is."

They both fell silent for a moment. Allie turned to face him and spoke, "Jessilaen–Jess–I need you to understand something. It's not something I talk about very much or tell most people."

He tilted his head to the side, to indicate that she had his full attention, and she continued, choosing her words carefully. "My mother is Elven–and she is Dark Court." She stopped and waited for his reaction but he gave none so she kept going "I was born in a Borderland but grew up with her in Fairy until–until I was…"

Crap, she thought, *what was the Elven equivalent of pre-pubescent?* "Just before my first Rite of Challenge. And then her clan and another clan went to war. My mother's clan won, but she was nearly killed. It made her realize that if anything happened to her–it would be bad for me. Because I had no one else there who would defend me but her, and I was–weak in their eyes. They have a word for it, cross-born, for a child who is in the Dark but isn't of the Dark. They say you were *born to the Light* and believe me, it's not considered a good thing. Everyone knew I was. She had kept in touch with my father and she took me to him and said I had to live with him…"

At that he interrupted, sounding shocked "Your mother handed you over to someone you didn't know?"

"He was my father. And I was safe with him. He did love me and he was very good to me, but–a few years later he died, in a car accident. And I came here to live with my grandmother."

Jess looked thoughtful, "That must have been a very difficult time for you."

"It was, but that's not the reason I'm telling you about it. I speak the language and I know the culture, but it's from a child's viewpoint. I know the manners and the nuances of many things, but other things, adult things– those I don't know well, or at all." She made a face and shrugged.

He nodded, "I think I understand."

He took both her hands gently and said "When two people are attracted to each other it is understood they will express it physically. Elven culture sees the joys of the flesh as a celebration. But when two people are emotionally attracted to each other, which is much less common, they may choose to court each other to see if the emotion has real depth to it. When two people agree to court they are agreeing to explore the depths of whatever emotion may be there. They hold nothing back from each other. If there is real emotion there, it can create a very strong bond, something most elves strive to avoid."

She felt her mind reeling, "I see. Sort of. That's–not what I thought it was."

He felt a raw surge of emotion that almost overwhelmed his self-control. After a moment to compose himself he said as carefully as he could, "I understand. I will not hold you to an agreement that you made in ignorance."

"No, wait," she felt him pulling back and her own hands tightened, holding his. "I don't want to not–sorry that's horrible grammar, damn Elvish!–I do want to continue, to keep courting or being courted or however it works on my end. You are the only good thing that's happened to me this week, even if I don't understand why I'm feeling what I'm feeling. I'm sorry if I've made you feel bad and honestly, even knowing now more of what it is I'll do my best but I don't trust people easily. I don't rely on others. And I don't know how to flip a switch and be a different person."

He pulled her close, resting his forehead against hers and trying to still the hurricane he was feeling. This was the true danger of the strength of Elven emotions, and he dared not lose control of them now. He breathed deeply. "I do not want you to be a different person. I only want you to be yourself."

Of her own accord she let his hands go and wrapped her arms around him, leaning her head against his chest. He felt his heart leap and carefully moved his arms around her shoulders. "Well," she said softly into his shirt "you are going to have to tell me when I'm being stupid. And that's probably going to be often. And if I hurt your feelings or assume anything or basically act like an idiot."

He smiled over her head, "I can do that. In turn you will have to tell me what you are feeling and when I am pushing you too far. You are right that I forget you do not know Elven ways and I am likely to continue assuming that you know more than you do."

She pulled back laughing slightly "I guess we both need a lot of work then, and I hate to ruin this moment, but I really need to pee."

He smiled in turn "You should probably get dressed first."

He gave her an appraising look, gently touching the partially healed bruise on her right arm where the Dark Elf had grabbed her when he'd thrown her into the wall.

"Although even bruised you are beautiful."

She blushed and looked away, not sure what to say, even though she knew she should complement him in return. Instead of responding she grabbed a pair of sweatpants and t-shirt from a pile of clean clothes waiting to be put away and struggled to dress. As she was walking slowly towards the hallway she stopped, causing him to nearly walk into her "Jess?"

"What is it? Are you dizzy?" he asked, genuinely worried.

"No. Well, not really. I just–does it bother you? About my mother?" she asked shyly.

"No," he answered seriously. "You are not your mother, and I have no doubt that you are a good person. "

She turned slightly, looking at him over her shoulder "Thank you. That–means a lot to me"

At the bathroom door she turned and said, "Okay, this I do by myself."

He started to argue "Brynneth said..."

"I don't care," she put her foot down. "I don't care if we just had a deep emotional moment. I don't care if he made you promise not to let me out of your sight. I go to the bathroom alone. If I need anything I'll yell, I promise. And if you hear any suspicious thumps, you have my permission to break the door down."

He agreed, reluctantly, but clearly intended to stand right outside the door as she went in. *Great,* she thought, *because using the toilet with someone listening in the hall isn't creepy at all.*

She took care of her hygiene needs as quickly and quietly as she could, making a face as the toilet flushed loudly. She brushed her teeth and her hair, trying not to look at her bruised face in the mirror; it was a painful reminder that although she felt much better she still looked like she'd gotten her butt kicked. Which she had, of course. As she was finishing with her hair she heard noises out in the hall and felt a rush of annoyance. *For an elf he's not very patient if he can't give me 5 minutes in here*, she thought.

Nonetheless she hurried up, washing the last of the dried blood out from under her fingernails before going out into the hallway. When she opened the door she was surprised to find Syndra standing there looking uncomfortable.

"Bathroom's all yours," she said reflexively. Syndra shifted slightly, her eyes cutting over to where Jess still hovered next to the door.

"Can we talk?"

"Sure," Allie replied, tensing. She wasn't in the mood for another lecture.

"Alone?" Syndra still hadn't looked directly at her. Allie hesitated, glancing at Jess who was frowning. She bit her lip before deciding.

"Jess?" she said and when she was sure she had his attention, "I'm starving, could you–please–get me something to eat?"

He paused, obviously torn between refusing to leave her and being flattered that she'd asked him to get her food, something that would not-so-subtly declare to anyone familiar with Elven society that they were a couple. More than a bit premature, since they had slept together in only the most literal sense, but she doubted Jess would care in this case. As soon as she thought about the full implications of that and what it would naturally lead others to assume she realized that Bleidd would probably not take it well. She wanted to kick herself, but it was too late to take it back now. Instead she added, "Syn can help me back to my room and I'll wait there for you."

Syndra gave her a strange look, but that last statement seemed to make his mind up for him and he nodded slightly and headed down the hall without a word. As soon as she was sure he was heading down the stairs she started back to her room; after a moment Syn followed. Allie sat back on her bed and Syn stood awkwardly by the door.

"What's up?" Allie asked, her voice sounding oddly flat even to her own ears.

"I wanted to say I'm sorry," Syndra said, sounding subdued.

Allie couldn't hide her surprise. "Sorry? Why?"

"Because you called me when you needed help and I..."

"Syn, don't," Allie started but her friend interrupted.

"Just let me say what I need to say," Syndra took a deep breath and went on. "I was mad at you for not telling me before about the task force thing and then you called and I came to the store and you were hurt. I said I'd help but I didn't tell you I'd called them in, I didn't warn you..."

Allie was shaking her head, but Syn held up her hand and pressed on. "I didn't warn you they were coming. I was mad, but not at you. I was mad at whoever hurt you but I think I kind of took it out on you. You're like my best friend Al, and I know I'm a cop and I've handled stuff like this before but never with someone I know. Never a friend. I get there and your bleeding all over the place and you won't tell me what happened. We get to the clinic and you won't let them help you. I can see," she took a deep breath, looking away "I can see that your jeans are ripped and you won't let them take your clothes or examine you–you think I've never worked a rape case before?"

"Syn, I wasn't..."

"I should have known better. I'm your friend. I should have..." Syndra broke off, shaking her head.

"Syn, really, I wasn't. It was close. He was, that was what he was trying to do, but he didn't. Really." Both women fell silent, and then Allie added "I'm sorry I threw that ice pack at you."

Syndra laughed, "Don't be. I deserved it."

"No, you were trying to help me, and I just didn't want to hear anyone saying that word. It was childish. You know, I guess I almost died–could have died anyway, yesterday."

"Allie, please don't," Syn said, obviously upset.

"No let me talk. You had your turn. I could have died and I was sitting in that hospital bed while you all were watching me on video or whatever..."

"Allie"

This time Allie ignored her and kept talking "And all I could think was, if he'd killed me in the store I'd have died with all my friends mad at me. No one was speaking to me…"

"Oh, fuck Al," Syn had started to cry, something she never did.

"And it just, it made me feel so sad, you know? To think that I'd screwed up and that I was letting stubbornness keep me from reaching out to you. We've been friends a long time Syndra. You're like my really bossy gun-toting sister." Syndra laughed at that, breaking the somber mood. "And I don't want us to fight over stupid things. And I really don't want to die with us not speaking over something dumb."

"Yeah. It's a good thing you didn't go and fucking die on me Allie. I'd never have forgiven you or, more importantly, myself, and I'd end up a lush like Bleidd." Both women laughed.

"So," Allie asked slowly, "are we good?"

"Of course we're good," Syn said simply. Then "So are you and tall, blond and elfin an item now?"

"Yeah," Allie said simply.

"Don't get mad at me for saying this, but you should know, I heard them talking–well the whole task force actually–and they have you under protective custody. That's why he's here. They think whoever attacked you is going to try again and might be connected to the murders."

"Well, at least that should help clear Bleidd," she said, realizing that the Guard must have listened to her about the Dark Court.

"I'm serious Al. I'm just saying, whatever he's telling you, just keep in mind he's here in an official capacity, okay?" Syn sounded unhappy and Allie thought she was probably waiting for more yelling to ruin their fragile reunion.

"Yeah, I will," she said instead. "How is Bleidd taking our new house guest?"

Syn winced, "Not well. It's not just your special friend by the way, one of the other three is always here too; they take shifts."

At that moment Jessilaen reappeared carrying a bowl in one hand and a glass of juice in the other. Syndra gave Allie a pointed look as she headed out the door, "I've gotta get some food myself, or at least some coffee, but I think I'll eat downstairs."

Allie sighed. A week ago Syndra would have stayed, or gotten food and come back up with it. A few months ago when Allie had been sick with the flu Syndra had all but camped out in her room for three days, making sure she was well stocked with ginger ale and tissues. Obviously Jessilaen's presence was changing everything and Allie didn't like it.

The source of the domestic turmoil seemed oblivious to his effect on the humans around him; he came over and sat next to her on the bed, offering what turned out to be a glass of orange juice and bowl of oatmeal. Allie managed not to make a face over the oatmeal, which she detested but would do her best to eat anyway, and thanked him, wondering to herself how upset everyone else was with her about the Elven invasion.

****

As soon as Syndra reached the first floor hallway Liz grabbed her and dragged her into the living room. Syn complained, more from surprise than real annoyance.

"Hey! I need some coffee. I'm working on like 5 hours of sleep here and I have to work tonight."

"How is she?" Liz asked, whispering.

"You don't have to whisper Lizzie. And she's your cousin. If you want to know how she is, go ask her yourself."

Syndra watched emotions play across the older woman's face and was suddenly struck by how different the two cousins looked. Syn was 26; she often forgot that Allie wasn't her own age or a little younger, when in fact she and Liz were both in their late 30's. Liz certainly looked her age, despite her efforts not to, and this morning without her usual artful make-up and trendy clothes Liz showed every day of her 38 years. Her shoulder length brown hair hung limply and she didn't look like she'd slept. Syn's expression softened as she took in her roommate's red, puffy eyes and pale face.

"She'll be fine. She's pretty banged up but nothing that won't heal. I'm sure she'd like to see you."

Liz shook her head, "No, I don't want to intrude."

"Intrude? Lizzie, you're her cousin. You're like her only living family. You wouldn't be intruding."

"No," Liz shook her head again looking uneasy "He's up there with her, isn't he?"

"The Elven Guard? Jess-something? Yeah he is, so what? Trust me, they aren't doing anything you need to be afraid of interrupting."

"Syndra!" Liz sounded genuinely outraged.

"Lighten up Liz. I guess they're kind of dating now so we're all going to have to get used to him hanging around. And personally I think she could have done worse and she needs to get a social life. Working and hanging out with us all the time doesn't count," Syndra tried to keep her tone light and ignore her own misgivings about Allie's choices.

Liz swallowed hard, "But he's–he's not good for her."

"Why? Because he's a cop?" Syn frowned and Liz gave her an annoyed look.

"Of course not. Because he's, well, I mean, do you really think he has any long term interest in her? Really?"

"Besides wanting to get into her pants? I have no idea, but you know maybe getting laid would do her some good." Syndra was only half kidding but Liz recoiled looking truly appalled.

"Lizzie, you have Fred. I have, well a couple good friends. Fuck, even Jason has an on-again-off-again boyfriend. Why shouldn't Allie have someone? And who else is she going to date in this shitty town?"

"How about a nice human guy?"

"Did you seriously just say that?" it was Syndra's turn to feel appalled. "You want to go tell your half-Elven cousin to stick to *your* own species?"

From the guilty look on her face, Syn realized that was exactly what Liz wanted to do and she shook her head. She never would have guessed Liz felt that way. Living with Bleidd for so long she'd never shown any signs of being anti-elf. *Or maybe*, Syndra thought cynically, *she doesn't mind it as long as it's not in her family, which makes no sense because Allie's already there.* To cover the awkward moment and possibly sensing that she'd gone too far, Liz said defensively, "What about Bleidd? They'd be great together."

Yeah Syn thought, *too bad Bleidd was too fucking stuck in beating himself up for something that happened before she was even born and waited too long. Which you know. Which is why you're suggesting someone who hasn't dated anyone in the entire time you've known him. Way to cover your ass there Lizzie.* Since that wasn't a fight she wanted to pick tonight she said, "They've been friends for more than a decade. If anything was going to happen there it would have by now."

Liz shrugged. "Well I don't trust this guy or the others. I don't want them in my house. The poor cat's been in hiding since they got here and I don't like feeling uncomfortable in my own home."

"They're afraid whoever hurt Allie might try again." Syn stopped short when Liz paled and sat down suddenly in the closest chair.

"What?" Liz looked really scared, "Why? I thought it was just, some sort of robbery or something."

Syn frowned, "What'd the cops who called tell you?"

"That she was at the clinic. That someone had attacked her at the store and she was hurt but nothing critical. That you were with her. Not much else," Liz looked at Syndra, wide eyed. "What's going on?"

"A couple guys came into the store yesterday looking for something and one of them jumped her, beat her up pretty bad," Syn hesitated for a second, but decided whether or not Allie liked it Liz needed to know "tried to rape her."

Liz shook her head wordlessly and Syn continued "The cops are concerned they might come back to finish what they started, so they have her in protective custody. Which is why there's always someone with her."

"What were they looking for?" Liz asked, obviously subdued.

"A book, I think," Syn said, looking away.

"Why would anyone do that to someone over a book?"

"I don't know, Lizzie, I don't know."

✳✳✳✳✳✳✳✳✳✳✳✳✳✳✳✳✳✳✳✳✳✳

Allie passed most the day in her room, alone. Jessilaen had been called back to the Outpost, she suspected to give his full report. Since she really didn't want to deal with any of the other three Guards–including Brynneth who she was grudgingly starting to like–she had finally promised to stay in her room until Jess could get back. It was extremely annoying to be made to feel like a prisoner in her own home, but she didn't like the idea of sitting and making polite conversation with the other elves either. She had a sinking feeling that she'd get an earful from her roommates later about the disruption to their routine that her situation was causing, especially from Liz, who had always been uncomfortable around elves. Even Bleidd, although Allie wasn't sure anyone else noticed. Between that thought and the knowledge that the store would have to stay closed for the day–indeed, it would need hours of clean up that she didn't want to think about before being reopened–she found it easier to stay in her room and ignore the outside world.

At first she tried cleaning up her room, embarrassed to realize that Jessilaen had seen it in all its usual disorganized glory. Despite Brynneth's excellent healing work she felt stiff and achy and quickly lost her desire to move more than she had to. Jess was just going to have to accept that she came with a certain inevitable level of attendant mess. After that she tried watching television, but she couldn't find a comfortable position to sit in to see the little TV set on her dresser. Reading was also out after she found herself re-reading the same lines over and over, unable to focus. At one point the house cat, who technically belonged to Liz but shared her time equally among the roommates, appeared and kept Allie company. Although gifted with a queenly name, Riona was a high-strung, skittish, pain in the butt and Allie was not especially fond of the orange tabby who regularly got into her room and knocked things over. Today, though, she found the cat's presence soothing, and she was glad that all the disruption in the house didn't have the poor thing cowering under a bed. Eventually Ri wandered out, leaving Allie without even that tenuous distraction. She wanted to think about anything except what had happened to her the day before, so naturally her mind kept flashing memories from the attack, leaving her feeling tense and near tears.

In the end she spent most of her time alternating between napping and staring out the window trying desperately to think of where she had seen any kind of ritual that was similar to the murders. It was a frustrating process; she normally had a fairly good memory but trying to go over decades of reading and casual conversations in her head and match anything to the scant clues she had to work with seemed futile. Yet the more she realized it was impossible, the harder she tried to think of where she had recognized it from. Somewhere in the back of her mind was the grim certainty that if she didn't fit the pieces together fast enough someone else was going to die because the police and the Guard were relying on her to give them a lead.

She was sitting on an overturned milk crate that usually held books staring out the window watching the light shift to the west and the shadows start to lengthen when she heard a soft knock at her door. She rubbed her tired eyes without thinking and then winced at the flash of pain on the left side of her face. She wasn't sure who it was, but she hadn't actually promised Jess not to let anyone else in, just that she wouldn't go out, and if it was anyone trying to kill her she doubted they'd knock first so she said, "Come in," and lowered her wards slightly.

She rested her chin on the window sill, watching as the tiny gnome that lived at the edge of their garden trundled across the dry grass towards the huge oak he lived in. It was odd to think that humans couldn't see him in his bright red and white clothes when he was so clear to her eyes. The door creaked open slowly behind her and she listened as someone walked part way into the room and stopped. She waited, but whoever it was stood there without speaking. Finally she gave in to her own curiosity and turned slightly until she could see Bleidd's reflection in the glass. She knew what it must have cost him to come up here and she wanted to say something funny or clever to break the tension; instead she said, "Hey."

He was silent for a long time and they stayed like that, staring at each other in the glass, until she couldn't stand it any longer "I don't want you to be angry with me Bleidd. We've been friends for too long to stop speaking now because of a misunderstanding."

"Angry with *you*?" his voice was mystified. "Allie, I swear, sometimes you are impossible. I came here expecting you to yell at *me*, throw things, tell me what a false friend I was, and you're worried about my feelings?"

"You're talking nonsense. I don't throw things," the image of the ice packing hitting Syndra's chest flitted through her mind but Allie pushed it away. "And you had every right to be angry with me for not being honest with you."

"You have never lied to me"

"A lie by omission is still a lie," she said softly. Another uncomfortable silence fell. Allie looked back out the window, feeling listless.

"Syndra found me last night–well early this morning actually–and she told me you had been hurt," he said, his voice tight. "I was quite drunk, as usual. Too drunk to be of any use to anyone. As usual. I woke this morning and find the Guard here, staying here. And I was angry at first. I thought it was all part of a larger plan to have an excuse to spy on me."

He stopped for a moment, looking down. "I have been–hiding in my room like a sulking child and I finally realized something important. I am being very self-centered Allie. I am looking at all of this as if it was about me, but it isn't. It never has been about me, except in a peripheral way, and I shouldn't have waited so long to come up here and speak to you. I should have come up right away, and the Guard be damned, but I was afraid you would tell me to leave. I rather think I deserve for you to tell me that actually. I said many things the other day out of anger that I should not have said, and I realized that I have gotten too accustomed to being able to–assume your good nature will allow for my bad behavior."

She sighed, "I don't know what you want me to say to that."

"You needn't say anything. I just wanted you to know that I realized I was wrong, that I badly over-reacted to… everything. You have always been a good friend to me, even when I least deserved it." He sounded as tired as she felt but she had a hard time trusting this sudden turn. Bleidd was a lot of things, and she truly believed he was a good person, but deep personal introspection wasn't his forte.

"You should know," she hesitated slightly, and then decided it was better to get it over with quickly "that I'm seeing Jessilaen."

The silence stretched out to a point where she started to brace herself for something spectacular. But when he finally spoke he sounded calm. "Why are you telling me this?"

"Because you warned me not to trust the Guard. That they would try to manipulate me. And I think you have a right to know that whether it's wise or foolish, he wants to be with me and I said yes." She fought to keep her voice even as she spoke. Bleidd had been her friend for more than a decade, there had even been a time early on when she had a crush on him, but he had never reciprocated in anyway and they had eventually fallen into a solid friendship. She didn't want to see it ruined now.

"You are right that I don't think you should trust them," he said slowly. "But he would be a fool not to see the value in you."

She felt her head starting to ache again, "What does that mean?"

"Allie..."

"No, for once just speak plainly. I'm tired of trying to decode everything today. Don't trust them, but understand that they have a good reason to want to use me? Is that it?" She could feel herself getting angry and stopped, taking a deep breath.

"No, Allie, of course not. I mean that I understand why he would be so quick to reach out to you, personally. You are very special..."

"Don't," she held up her hand resting her head against the glass. "Just don't. I'm so completely not in the mood to be fed a line about being the nicest wallflower at the dance after you made it clear no one would bother." She trailed off feeling the tears she'd fought off all day coming back and threatening to overwhelm her again. She hadn't meant to bring up his words from the other day after he'd made the effort to reconcile but they hung in the air between them now.

"I'm sorry I said that. It was petty and mean." He sounded like he meant it and Allie was truly shocked because Bleidd never apologized. Never flat out anyway; his apologies were always round about and hinted at rather than spoken plainly, something she knew well having received many of them over the years after drunken fits. She turned and looked at him, forgetting that he hadn't seen her since she'd been hurt.

"Oh Allie," he breathed, truly dismayed. He crossed the room in a few quick steps kneeling down next to her and taking her face gently in his hands. She swallowed hard and tried not to look at the raw emotion on his face, something she didn't usually see unless he was drunk.

"It's okay, its already healed a lot compared to yesterday," she said, trying to sound casual.

He traced his fingers over the fading bruises on her nose and cheek and then down to her throat his eyes darkening. "Whoever did this to you, I will find them, and I will kill them."

"No," she said forcefully, grabbing his hand, "No. Promise me you won't even try, Bleidd. I mean it. They will kill you and I will never forgive myself."

He shook his head, that dark, dangerous look still in his eye, "You underestimate me."

"No I don't but…"she hesitated, unsure how much to tell him. Only when she was sure he was almost certain to go out tonight and get into trouble trying to avenge her did she finish. "…they were elves, Dark Court elves. They would kill you."

He looked at her sharply, but that wildness was gone from his eyes as suddenly as it had appeared. "What happened?"

"Promise me you won't look for revenge for me, Bleidd."

He hesitated but finally, reluctantly, agreed "I swear by the endless sea, the firm earth, and the sky covering all that I will not intentionally seek to avenge your injuries. Now tell me what happened."

"They came in to the store looking for a book. Said I knew what they wanted but I have no idea what book it could be," she shook her head swallowing hard. She could feel the tears threatening again and realized she didn't want to talk about it or think about it anymore. She sniffled, struggling not to cry.

He lifted her chin gently, "It's okay Allie."

"No, "she said feeling the tears spilling over. "It's not. It's not okay. If I had the damn book I'd have given it to them, but I didn't know what they were talking about, and they kept saying I did."

He stood up, pulling her with him into a loose hug and she wept against his t-shirt. "And that was why they hit you? To get you to tell them where this book they sought was?"

She sobbed harder and shook her head. "No, that was my fault."

"Your fault?" he said incredulously.

"He, he said–he tried to use glamour on me," she swallowed hard, "and when it didn't work he said no one refuses him, and I told him to go to the *Star*…"

She sobbed harder now and he rubbed her back. Motion in the window's reflective surface caught his eye and he looked up and saw one of the Elven Guard–he assumed Allie's new lover–standing motionless in the doorway. Before he could decide how to react her arms had tightened around his torso and she kept talking, "And he hit me, and kissed me and threw me down. I couldn't breathe, he was choking me, and he tore my jeans. I was so scared."

"Shhhh. You're safe now Allie," He whispered, deciding to ignore the Guard until the other elf forced the issue.

"No, I'm not. You don't understand –" she looked up, her battered face tear stained, and caught sight of the figure in the doorway. Her arms tightened and then she pulled away, wiping her tears furiously. The newcomer walked slowly over to where they stood and Bleidd braced himself to be ordered out. He wasn't entirely sure how he'd react to that and he knew that getting into a fist fight with Allie's new love interest, while personally satisfying, would surely upset her a great deal and she was already far too emotionally fragile. He recognized the other elf from his own interrogation as the second in command, someone he remembered with intense dislike. But the Guard did not give any orders, rather he stepped up to where Allie stood until he was almost shoulder to shoulder with Bleidd and said "You did nothing to deserve any of this."

She shook her head sharply, "I knew it was stupid to insult him. I knew he'd react badly and I did it anyway. I'm weak. I can't defend myself."

"Allie," Bleidd said feeling exasperated, but somewhat grateful that Jessilaen wasn't trying to push him out. "No one has a right to force you."

She broke in, her voice bitter, "There is no rape in the Dark Court."

"What?" Jessilaen said, and Bleidd found himself sharing the other elf's confusion.

"In the Dark Court, you either enforce your own will, or you have other people's will enforced on you," she said. "That's why my Mother made me leave. She knew I wasn't strong enough. And she was right."

"That is barbaric," Jessilaen said simply.

Allie shook her head. "It's the law. The human world works because human society is held together by laws, right? The Bright Court works on structures of rank and societal positioning, and relies on laws to support everything. It's the same in the Dark Court, except the law there is based on structures of power; those who have power out rank those who have less, and on down the line. In the Bright Court if you're attracted to someone and make a pass at them and they say no, oh well, you go on to the next, right? In the Dark Court when someone who outranks you tells you they want to screw you, you bend over, period. No arguments or questions."

Jessilaen shook his head and asked sadly. "What kind of childhood did you have?"

"It doesn't apply to children, children are protected by their parents," Allie said dismissively. "But once you are an adult–you either have the strength and political connections to protect yourself or you don't. As far as that Dark Elf was concerned, as a mixed blood I have no inherent rank and no right to refuse him. And I am too weak to enforce my own will."

"Allie, you are a very strong person. Just because you aren't a skilled physical fighter doesn't mean you are weak." Bleidd said, wishing that he could embrace her again.

Jessilaen added, "And you can learn martial skills; those are merely a matter of practice and time."

"I–I need to take a shower" Allie said, pushing past both of them towards the bathroom.

Reflexively the two elves looked at each other, momentarily forgetting their past animosity.

"Does she always retreat to the bathroom when she's upset?" the Guard quipped, and Bleidd had to stop himself from smiling in response.

"So you believe these Dark Court elves will seek her out again?" he said as neutrally as he could manage.

"They told her as much," Jessilaen replied grimly. Then, giving Bleidd a measuring look, "How long have you been in love with her?"

Bleidd felt himself stiffening defensively as the other elf continued, "Your feelings for her are obvious."

"Not to her," he replied, "but it doesn't matter. You are just a temporary distraction–you'll be gone soon enough and everything will be back as it was before."

"She accepted my court–or didn't she tell you?" Jessilaen said, pointedly.

Bleidd kept his face blank with an effort, not wanting to betray that he hadn't already known that. "She doesn't even know what that means. It may suit you to take advantage of the ignorance of a young girl to your own purpose."

"She's an adult" Jessilaen said, although his voice now was less sure

"She's half Elven; don't presume it's so easy to judge her age. Trust me, I made the mistake myself once of assuming a girl who appeared to be an adult actually was one, to my own grief." He couldn't keep the bitterness out of his voice when he spoke.

"You are trying to mislead me so that I will withdraw my court and leave the field to you alone," Jessilaen said with more confidence.

Bleidd shook his head. "You are no competition. What can you offer her, but a world that will always reject her or see her as an oddity?"

Jessilaen recoiled, clearly angry, "I can offer her more than you. What have you? Not even a name of your own or any honor."

Bleidd shrugged, "I don't need any name but the one I have here with her. She knows that the value of my honor is in my actions, not in the opinions of people who don't even know me. You are a fool if you think she cares about such things."

"And you see such value in drinking yourself into a stupor every night that you think a woman would choose a lifetime of that? Where were you last night when she needed help? Why did she not reach out to you except that she knew it would be pointless?" Jessilaen's voice was low and dangerous.

The two elves glared at each other for several minutes, each trying to get the other to look away first. Finally Bleidd took a deep breath and spoke slowly. "Perhaps we are both great fools."

Jessilaen was caught off guard by this comment and cocked his head to the side listening as Bleidd continued, "We both care for her in some way. And she is not only very upset right now but also in grave danger. If you are right, then those who hurt her yesterday will be back. Whether they return or not, helping with this murder investigation by itself may put her at risk. I would rather put my own pride aside for the moment and see her safe than know that she died because you and I were squabbling like children over a toy."

The Elven Guard commander gave the Outcast elf a long appraising look, "You truly are innocent of these crimes."

"I have many flaws, Guard, some of them egregious. But my hands are clean of the blood of those poor girls," Bleidd said seriously.

"Why did you not simply say as much when we questioned you?" Jessilaen asked, confused by the sudden change in the strange elf. *Perhaps living so long with humans has warped his ability to act in a civilized manner,* Jess thought to himself, not liking the sudden odd kinship he felt with the other elf, who had made it clear he was a rival for Allie's affections.

"Because I was wrongly Outcast by the Guard and it is not in my heart now to expect any justice or fairness from anyone in that uniform," Bleidd said simply. Jessilaen shook his head slightly, unsure how such a thing could ever happen. Bleidd continued, "Know this though Commander; as soon as this danger is past I will offer my own court to her and we shall see who she really prefers. You may not like the outcome of that."

Jessilaen's head came up and his eyes narrowed, "Why tell me this now? Why ask for a truce and say that we should work together to protect her and then in the next breath give me reason to want you out of the way?"

"Perhaps I want to see you prove that the Guard are as honest and trustworthy as Allie believes you to be. Show me that you can seek real justice even when it would better suit your own purpose to see me framed for the crime," Bleidd said casually.

"And if I acted against you, how quickly would that turn her against me?" Jessilaen said.

"If you feel that way, then you acknowledge she cares more for me than you."

"If the situation were reversed maybe you would be the one who would not like the outcome," Jessilaen replied.

Then he took a deep breath and said "If we wish to cooperate to achieve anything we will have to stop arguing over this."

Bleidd shook his head ruefully. "Yes. It is obviously a subject we will have to avoid. That said, perhaps I can be of help to you in tracking down these Dark Court elves."

"How so?" Jessilaen said, not trying to hide his interest.

"Allie has made me promise not to seek revenge for her sake, but I made no oath not to seek them out. I know the city well and I have connections among the residents that you could never hope to reach. If they are here, in the city, I can find them."

Jessilaen nodded thoughtfully.

****

Allie emerged from the shower feeling slightly more able to take on the world and having had her cathartic cry, she felt far less emotionally on edge. She was vaguely worried that Jessilaen would be upset about finding her crying on Bleidd's shoulder, but he was just going to have to learn to accept that Bleidd was one of her closest friends, and she had no intention of losing that friendship now. Besides, whether Jess understood it or not, Bleidd needed her.

She dressed quickly in the same clothes she'd pulled on that morning, a t-shirt and sweatpants, before venturing out of the bathroom again. To her surprise she found the two elves she'd ducked in the shower to avoid dealing with standing there waiting for her. Her expression must have mirrored her feelings because Bleidd smiled and Jess looked rueful.

"Dinner's ready. Jason made spaghetti just for you." Bleidd said in a conciliatory tone.

Jess gave him an odd sideways look "I thought we were all eating?"

Allie couldn't hold back a giggle as Bleidd explained "It's an expression, Guard. It means he knows it's one of her favorite foods and cooked it special to please her."

Jess looked truly confused, "Is he a servant here? He always seems to be cooking for everyone else."

Allie was shaking her head, still giggling, but Bleidd looked annoyed "Of course not, he just enjoys cooking."

Jess clearly thought that was insane, but Allie's stomach chose that moment to growl loudly and the other two seemed to snap out of whatever strange mood they were in. If she didn't know better she'd swear they were acting like friends. It was a strange thought. "Come on guys you can argue the semantics of human idioms later. I'm actually hungry for the first time today and spaghetti sounds really good right about now."

She moved past them and down the stairs, feeling almost cheerful for the first time in over a week. The aroma of Jason's excellent spaghetti sauce filled the lower level and made her mouth water. In the kitchen she found Liz and Aeyliss sitting at the table while Jason shuttled plates and dishes from the counter to the various place settings and Syndra poured drinks into glasses. The Victorian's kitchen was spacious and the table was a long farm style set with a dozen chairs that could easily accommodate the residents and the two Elven Guard. Allie felt herself relaxing slightly at the domestic scene, strange as it was to see the red haired Elven woman, sword strapped to her side, sitting at the table. She moved to sit in her usual place on the hallway side of the long table and before she could pull her seat in she had Jess settling in on her right and

Bleidd sliding into the chair on her left. She looked from one side to the other, puzzled that with so many seating options they'd each choose to sit directly next to her, and caught Syndra across the room rolling her eyes. Liz, sitting at the far narrow end of the table frowned and then made a point of studying her silverware. Allie felt bad for her cousin, who she knew was a private person and was probably horrified by the intrusion into her home. Then again Allie realized her cousin hadn't seen her since she'd been injured. *Maybe she's upset at seeing my fabulous multi-colored face,* Allie thought, then, *I wonder why she never came and saw me in my room today?* It was an uncomfortable thought that she quickly pushed away.

Jason hustled over with a plate, smiling at her and ignoring the bruises. She smiled back.

"Awesome Jason, this looks great."

"I put extra cheese on yours," he said winking.

"Because I'm extra cheesy, right?" and they both laughed. It made things feel almost normal.

Syndra brought over the drinks: milk for Allie and the two Elven Guard, juice for Jason, water for Liz and beer for herself and Bleidd. Much to everyone's surprise Bleidd turned down the beer, getting a glass of milk instead. Syndra was speechless at this turn of events and kept giving Allie weird looks, which Allie returned with frowns and shrugs. She had a feeling that she'd get an earful from Syn later. Both the Guards were poking at their food uncertainly and she wondered if they had ever eaten spaghetti before. Instead of asking what it was or how one went about eating it they started surreptitiously watching the humans eat and mimicking them. Allie found herself smiling down at her plate as Syndra and Jason argued over the merits of the latest album from their favorite band.

"Are your meals always like this?" Jess asked her.

"On a good day."

"What a strange way to enjoy a meal." Aeyliss said when she finished eating. "Everyone talking–how can you enjoy your food?"

"We enjoy the food in between talking." Jason answered cheerfully. Despite his near phobia of elves he seemed to have gotten somewhat acclimated to the Guard's presence.

She gave him an appraising look that had Allie thinking the Elven woman was about to be disappointed. "Is it not better to focus all your attention on one thing at a time so that you can savor that experience to its fullest, rather than distracting the senses with many things at once?"

Jason shrugged, "I'm not that disciplined"

"Perhaps I could show you the advantages of such an approach," Aeyliss said with a look that made her meaning plain. Jason blushed but looked oddly flattered.

Syndra laughed, "Jason doesn't enjoy discipline–or women–so you're going to be out of luck on both counts."

Aeyliss looked a bit nonplussed, probably at the disavowal of women, "That's a shame. I'm certain I could convince him of the value of both."

"I don't doubt you could," Syndra said archly, earning raised eye brows from everyone but Allie. She was already aware of her friend's diverse interests and the two Guards who didn't know how unusual such an omnivorous attitude was. Aeyliss shifted her appraisal to Syndra and Allie repressed the urge to look at her friend to see whether Syn was returning the interest. There were some things she really didn't need to know.

Liz cleared her throat loudly, "So, Allie, you're feeling better?"

Allie wasn't sure if it was meant as a statement or a question but assumed the latter, "Yes, actually. Brynneth's a skilled healer and I spent most of today resting. Well that

116

and racking my brain trying to remember where I'd read about that ritual or something like it before."

"It's a shame," Liz said clearly making an effort at conversation, "that there isn't some master index for this sort of thing. Remember how Grandmother was always indexing her books? It always made referencing things so convenient."

Allie dropped her fork with a clang onto her plate, "Oh my Gods, Liz! That's it."

"What? What's it?" Liz looked alarmed by her reaction, and everyone else had fallen silent, looking at Allie.

"That's where I saw it. In Grandmother's grimoire." Allie couldn't repress a shudder at the memory.

"What are you talking about Allie. Grandmother didn't have a grimoire, she had a spell book," Liz said, looking uncomfortable.

"No. No. She had a grimoire from before. From a long time ago, before Dad and Aunt Mary where born. I found it once when I was in–Gods, like middle school I think. I was flipping through it reading and it was…"Allie stopped, looking at her cousin's skeptical expression. She took a deep breath. "It was dark stuff, Liz. Nothing like what she was doing when we were alive. I was reading through it and she found me and freaked out. I've never seen her so upset, before or since."

Jessilaen and Aeyliss both looked grim. Jess spoke carefully, "You are certain that is where you saw this?"

"I'm positive," Allie said confidently. "When she found me and took the book away, I was reading about what the grimoire called inverse fertility magic, the idea of using negative sex magic and prolonged death to create a desired effect. That's what was so familiar about the murders."

Liz blanched, and her other roommates looked stunned, but the Guard become suddenly animated. "To what purpose was this used?" Aeyliss asked

"I don't know, she took the book away before I finished reading that section. I only remember that much because she was so very upset about me finding the book."

"Do you have the book still? Is it in your store?" Jess asked.

Allie thought hard. "Not in the store, no. It should still be in the house."

"Here?" Aeyliss said sharply "This house?"

"Yes," Allie said, watching Liz pale and look around as if she expected the book to appear from thin air. "It was one of my grandmother's personal books. We kept them all after she died."

"She left them to you," Liz said quickly and then looked uncomfortable as everyone looked at her. "Well, I'm no witch. Or mage, or whatever," she mumbled.

"That's true, she did. I haven't really dealt with them though, since she died."

"Allie, that was 10 years ago. You're saying she left you all her magical books and you just–what–left them in a box?" Syndra said, sounding exasperated.

Allie made a face. "Kind of. Some of them are boxed up. Some are in the attic. Some are in my closet." She shrugged helplessly. "I just didn't want to deal with her personal stuff, so I sort of, you know, didn't."

"Fucking A, Al," Syn said, shaking her head.

"Well, it's still here somewhere. We just have to find it," Allie said defensively.

They all looked at each other for a moment. Jason shook his head slightly, "Sorry, I have to work tonight, I'm on 3rd shift today and tomorrow."

Liz also looked unhappy, already getting up from the table "I have to be at the theater. It's the second night of that new play and it was crazy busy last night. Actually if I don't get moving I'll be late."

Syndra nodded, taking charge, "Okay well you two get going and the rest of us can search. We may as well start in the attic. Just let me call Riordan and Walters and let them know we have some kind of lead," she looked at Jessilaen, "Maybe you should contact your Captain?"

Both of the Elven Guard shook their heads, "We have not found the book yet and Brynneth will be here at midnight to relieve Aeyliss."

"Yes, I will report to our Captain when I get back to the outpost; it may be that we can find the book before then."

Chapter 6 - Sunday

Just after midnight, the Guards switched and Brynneth arrived to relieve Aeyliss. The group was up in the attic, still searching for the book, and it took several minutes to explain to Brynneth what Allie had remembered and what they were looking for. He was not pleased to find Allie awake and exerting herself so hard, despite the reason, and when Aeyliss took her leave, he was still trying to convince her to go rest and leave the searching to everyone else.

Aeyliss walked through the darkness towards one of the cars assigned to their squad, thinking about what the girl had uncovered. *If she can find this book, we can learn the exact nature of the ritual. I can surely learn the flavor of the magic to track it back to its source,* Aeyliss thought, *and then this mystery will be quickly solved. Although if Jessilaen is right and the Outcast isn't guilty, there is no need for our involvement at all. Unless–it may be that this book is the same one that the Dark Court seeks.* That thought was unsettling. *I will have to share that idea with Zarethyn and see what he thinks of it.*

She crossed the expanse of lawn in front of the humans' home, her feet almost silent in the dry grass. Aeyliss did not understand this odd house, which seemed more like an Inn, taking on boarders, yet functioned like a family unit or small clan holding. Among her people no one lived this way; extended families lived together and when necessary, while traveling or for those serving in the Guard or military. Strangers might share living space but the boundaries demanded by society were very rigidly set. *These humans–and the Outcast and Aliaine–seemed oblivious to civilized social norms. I will never understand humans,* she thought ruefully.

There was a line of cars parked along the road with intermittent open spaces separating them. Each of the residents of the home had their own vehicle and those 5 cars usually parked directly in front of the house. Zarethyn had explained to all of them that the expanse was to be left for those vehicles, out of courtesy. She paused at the edge of the road, looking for the car that Brynneth had arrived in; she spotted it at the far end of the line of vehicles, parked just in sight where the road began to curve to the north and the woods dominated. Jessilaen's vehicle sat in front of it, where she suspected it would be staying for most of this assignment. Aeyliss shook her head to herself as she walked up the road to the other car. *I understand his attraction to the girl. She is comely and sweet natured, but this obsession with her is unnatural. I don't understand why Zarethyn is indulging him. Better to end it before it begins rather than to let it go on and end badly.* Aeyliss, like all elves, had been raised to eschew strong emotions as a dangerous diversion that led to tragedy one way or another. Either love would turn to hate over time or one partner would die and leave the other to grieve with the same intensity they had loved. She could not understand the appeal of such a thing; deep emotional bonds were best reserved for the surety of blood-kin.

Aeyliss was lost in her own thoughts as she reached the driver's side door of the vehicle, so the voice that spoke from behind the car startled her. She started to reach for her sword reflexively, a difficult proposition with the car keys in her hand, when the words registered and she relaxed slightly, recognizing Walters' voice. "Hate to break this to you, but it looks like you might have a flat tire."

Her eyes easily found his figure crouching down, examining the rear driver's side tire, and then belatedly she noticed the familiar car idling just down the road. *You fool, it is unforgivably careless to allow your own thoughts to distract you, especially now. Fortunate that it is an ally and not an enemy.* Aeyliss pushed aside her annoyance with herself and said "I am sure it is easily fixed."

121

"You should have a spare in the trunk. Have you ever changed a tire before?" he asked

She hesitated, "No, I have not, although I understand the theory of doing so."

"Well, lucky I came along then, I can help."

She nodded stiffly, embarrassed, and walked around to retrieve the spare. The key turned easily and she placed a hand on each side of the trunk and lifted, her eyes already searching the interior for the tire.

The pain was sudden and brutal, a burning that lanced through her back and kept burning, even after she felt the blade being pulled back out of her flesh. She opened her mouth trying to draw breath to scream and the pain came again on the other side; she felt as if her whole body was on fire now and she collapsed forward, falling writhing to the ground. Her back arched from the sheer agony and her head snapped back, hitting the pavement hard. Her mouth opened as she tried again to breathe and a rush of bright red blood poured out. Her hands clawed desperately at the asphalt and the spreading pool of blood, fighting to the last to live.

Walters stood over her, calmly, watching her die until the light left her eyes and she lay completely still. "Nothing personal. But I couldn't let you ruin everything I'm working so hard for here."

****

They searched for the book until Brynneth arrived, and ordered Allie to bed. She only agreed to go after carefully describing the exact book they needed to all of them four times and was finally forcibly escorted to her room by Jessilaen. She had thought she would be too wired to sleep but to her surprise as soon as she lay down she felt a wave of exhaustion overtake her. She dozed off quickly.

She wasn't sure how long she had been sleeping when a door slamming woke her up. Her eyes opened to the disorienting wash of red and blue lights alternating across her ceiling and wall; after a moment she realized it was the diffusing lights from a police cruiser. More than one cruiser actually based on the way the lights were dancing. She struggled up, still feeling groggy, and crossed to the far side of the room where her only front facing window was and where the light seemed most intense. The scene outside the window was so utterly surreal she closed her eyes, took a deep breath, and then opened them again, but the view remained the same. The road in front of the house was full of police cars–both human police and Elven Guard–all parked haphazardly with their emergency lights strobing. She felt the hair on her neck standing up, and her stomach clenched; whatever was going on it was clearly very bad. The air was thick with so much grief and anger that Allie could taste it, despite her shields and the wards on her room.

With a rising sense of panic she stumbled back across the room, struggling out of the clothes she'd been sleeping in and into the first pair of jeans and shirt she found, an old Henley she'd permanently borrowed from Jason. A quick glance at the clock told her it was just past 1 a.m., so she hadn't been asleep very long. She staggered out into the hallway and ran headlong into Bleidd who was coming up the hall.

"Allie, go back to bed," he said, sounding worried.

"Go back to bed? What the hell is going on–it looks like the entire police department is on our front lawn," her voice sounded hysterical even to her own ears but she didn't care.

"Come on Allie, "he said and physically moved her back into her room.

"Hey!" she was surprised that he was being so assertive.

"Go back to bed, you need to rest," he said as if this was any other night.

"Are you on drugs? What is going on out there?" she stared at him, wide eyed, almost more frightened by his strange behavior than the scene out the window.

"I think I picked the wrong day to stop drinking," he started, trying to sidetrack her again.

"Bleidd, for Gods' sakes, *what happened?*"

He hesitated for a long moment, and then with obvious reluctance said, "Aeyliss is dead."

"What!" she tried to push past him and he blocked her, grabbing her wrists and trying to hold her in the room. "Let me go! What the hell happened?"

"Allie calm down," he said gently, "running out there isn't going to help anyone." And then when it was clear she wasn't going to calm down, "Aeyliss was murdered near her car.'

Allie froze, her breath catching. She looked at him, mutely questioning. Reluctantly he went on, "The rear tire was flat–probably on purpose–it looks like she went to get the spare tire out and someone came up behind her and stabbed her in the back."

"Did she–did she fight back?" Allie asked, relaxing until he released her.

He winced. "It looks like it was an iron knife. The damage from the wounds was extensive–I doubt she lived long."

"Dear Gods," Allie breathed, horrified. Without warning she tried to dart around him, overcome with a desperate desire to get back in the attic and keep looking for the book that seemed to be at the center of all of this. He lunged after her, managing to catch her around the waist. She shrieked, fighting to free herself even as he tried to reason with her.

"Allie, Allie, calm down…"

"Unhand her." A voice said from the doorway. Bleidd looked up to see two Guards, Jessilaen and a stranger, standing there in full battle armor, the Guard equivalent of human SWAT gear. Unwillingly, he released his hold on Allie and she fell to her knees in the middle of the room. Under different circumstances he might have tried to argue with Jessilaen, but all of the Guard were radiating a cold fury over Aeyliss's death and Bleidd was not foolish enough to push any of them tonight. He locked eyes with the blond Guard, waiting for an unwarranted accusation of inappropriate behavior, but instead the Guard simply said "Captain Zarethyn wishes to speak with you, Outcast."

Bleidd bristled slightly at being denied even the use-name he had among the humans here, but before he could decide on a safe response Jessilaen gestured at the stranger with him. "Taishlin will escort you."

"She should not be left alone." Bleidd said shortly, nodding at Allie who was still kneeling, motionless, on the floor.

Jessilaen's eyes narrowed, "Nor will she be. She will have a Guard with her at all times from now on."

Bleidd eyed his rival as he walked out, accepting his escort to the Guard Captain with ill grace "How convenient for you."

Jessilaen closed the door almost in Bleidd's face and turned to Allie. She was kneeling with her head bowed down, her hair covering her face and he felt a twinge of worry at her unnatural stillness. "Allie?" he called gently.

She looked up and in the flickering lights that filled her room he could see that her face was streaked with tears. She wept silently and his heart broke to see her in such pain, even though he wasn't sure why she was crying. He took a moment and exerted the tiny bit of magic needed to dismiss his battle armor, and, clad again in tunic and pants, sat down next to her. She leaned into him resting her head on his shoulder. "It's just–it's just so much death. So much hopelessness. I feel like every time we make any progress it's all for nothing."

He stroked her hair, "No, not for nothing. We are closer to finding this killer than ever."

"Are we? I can't find the book, even though it's here somewhere. I don't remember much of anything useful from what I read 20 something years ago. And now Aeyliss is dead, either because the killer is afraid you were getting close or because the Dark Elves came here–for me..."she trailed off shuddering. "It all seems so futile."

"No, Allie, truly it isn't." He lifted her chin with his hand until her eyes met his. "It only becomes futile when we give up and let the darkness win."

"I don't know if I can keep fighting. It's just one thing after another. I don't have time to think and something else horrible has happened. Tonight at dinner things seemed so, so *good*, almost normal, and then I remembered about the book and it looked like we had a chance to solve this and now, now *this*," she looked at him, miserable. "I can't believe I'll never see her again and she died so terribly, Jess. It's all so much pain and loss and suffering."

"There's always hope, Allie. There's always something worth fighting for." He leaned in and kissed her, gently. She wrapped her arms around him, desperately, and kissed him back hard. She felt wild and out of control; the miasma of emotions in the atmosphere were overwhelming her self-control and her own emotions frightened her. He offered her something solid to hold on to, to anchor her in a reality that wasn't all death and suffering. She wondered if this was why elves were so quick to embrace sensual experiences, to use the physical joys to stave off the despair.

It was not in his nature or his inclination to refuse her. He met her passion with his own and kissed her more firmly, one hand finding her breast through the thin material of her shirt while the other wrapped around her waist. Without further urging she pulled her shirt off entirely and his breath caught, "Allie we don't have to rush this."

Some part of her knew that what she was doing was reckless and out of character for her, but she shoved that part aside. She silenced him with a kiss, not knowing how to explain the desperation she felt, the need to feel alive, to keep the dark emotions at bay. He moaned against her lips, his hands exploring her chest in ways that made her breath speed up and drove thoughts of tragedy out of her mind. She tugged at his shirt until he paused and pulled it off, and she seized the moment to slide out of her jeans. "Allie, we have as much time as we like," he tried again to get her to slow down, as she started unfastening his pants.

"I want you. Now," she said, wishing he could understand how she felt. How she didn't want to feel. She tried to show him with her body and his hesitation evaporated beneath her insistent hands and lips. He kissed her again, the naked skin of their bodies pressing together as he pushed her back onto the floor. She went willingly, grabbing his arms and pulling until he lost his balance and fell with her. They landed together next to the bed in a tangle of limbs.

He shifted his weight slightly, sliding himself between her thighs and she arched her hips up to meet him. Caught up in her frenzy he thrust forward; by the time he felt the slight resistance in her body, he had already pushed past it. He froze and she writhed beneath him, gasping, "Please, don't stop, please."

Slowly he resumed, giving in to her need despite himself. The feel of her body beneath his was too much to withstand when she kept urging him on, faster and harder.

Even after his own passion was spent she clung to him, holding him tightly so that he could not withdraw from her. They lay, twined together, their breath slowing. He lifted his head slightly after a while and tried to meet her eyes. "Allie," he said softly. "You should have told me you were a maiden still."

"If I had, would it have changed anything?" she asked. She was still holding him tightly, letting his emotions wash over her and counteract everything else. She felt a thousand times better now than she had before. He said nothing at first and she nodded slightly, "Then I'm glad I didn't."

"I could have been gentler with you; made it better for you."

"I didn't want gentle, and it was plenty good. Don't ruin it for me now. Besides, you're a guy. Aren't you supposed to be, I don't know, gloating or something?" She relaxed, feeling the texture of the carpet under her back and wondering what people usually talked about after sex.

"Gloating?" that seemed to amuse him. "Well, I suppose there is a certain satisfaction in knowing you belong completely to me."

She wasn't sure if he was joking or not, "Keep talking like that and next time you fall asleep around me I'll shave your eyebrows off."

He laughed lightly, "You told me to gloat. Or maybe you think I should be flattered?"

"Maybe you should be," she shot back, only half-joking herself.

Without warning his mood turned serious. "How old are you?" He sounded hesitant and she thought, *little late to ask that now, isn't it?*

"I'm 37. If I were human I'd be almost middle aged," she reached up to brush a stray lock of hair out of his eyes.

"And if you were Elven, you'd be a child." He sighed resting his forehead against hers.

"I'm neither. So where does that leave me?"

****

Bleidd was led down through the house by his escort and out into the yard. Standing near the road several hundred yards from where the body had been found was a cluster of a dozen Elven Guards–3 full squads–and he felt himself tensing even more at the memories that flooded back. Bracing for whatever unpleasantness awaited, he walked forward, knowing that at least they couldn't accuse him of Aeyliss's death as he'd been with the two other Guards the entire time.

As they arrived where the group was standing Captain Zarethyn looked up, giving Bleidd a measuring look, "Commander Jessilaen tells me that you believe you can find the Dark Elves that are in this place."

Bleidd relaxed slightly. "Yes, I believe I can find them, if they are still here to be found."

The Captain seemed to consider that and then, "He also says that you believe you were unfairly Outcast."

Bleidd tensed again, cursing himself for being too quick to let his guard down, even slightly, around this group. He nodded slightly.

"I find that very difficult to credit, but if it is true and if you aid us in this I may be able to assist you." Zarethyn said, his voice giving away nothing.

Bleidd repressed a grimace. *And what a lovely carrot you must think you have found to dangle for my cooperation*, he thought before saying "I find it equally hard to believe that you could assist me in any way,

Captain. But rest assured, if I can find these Dark Elves, I will, and it will be for you to deal with them."

The Captain's eye narrowed. "You understand why the humans were so quick to believe you were a suspect?"

"Oh yes, "he responded, bitterly, thinking, *and now the carrot is switched for the stick.* "I know."

"And yet you claim you are innocent of the crimes for which you were outcast?" Zarethyn's skepticism was reflected in the faces of the other Guards who watched the exchange.

"No," Bleidd said simply.

The answer obviously surprised everyone. "No?" the Captain repeated.

"No, I am not innocent, but yes I was unfairly punished," he gritted his teeth. "It was only a scant few decades after the end of the last war between my King and the humans. The local Guard didn't want to risk my– perceived actions–causing problems. So I was cast out with the belief that I would take my own life. Obviously I did not oblige."

Many of the gathered Guards were shaking their heads. Zarethyn pressed, "I do not understand how you can be guilty and innocent at the same time."

I have certainly chosen the wrong night to sober up, Bleidd thought. And then, seeing no way around it, he forced himself to speak, telling these strangers something he had not spoken of except in drunken fragments over the last 5 decades. "Believe it or not Captain, I was a member of the Guard once." He ignored the shocked looks, "I was assigned to protect a trade group; keep in mind the wars were still fresh in everyone's minds and all traders were under Guard. It was an easy assignment and much sought after because it was low risk and allowed time to experience human culture."

He paused slightly, frowning, "When we were with the traders as they did their business, one of the human merchant's daughters was flirting with me, and I foolishly saw no harm in returning her interest. I did not realize then that humans are as rigid about the age of consent of their offspring as we are and the girl was too young. It is so hard to judge with humans and I erred in assuming she was older than she was. Her father noticed her absence and questioned her afterwards and she broke down and told him that she had been with me–he was outraged and called the human police and reported me for what they call "statutory rape" and then he sought me out himself. I was arrogant and told him that the girl was no maiden, and in a fury he drew a small knife and attacked me. I killed him. When the police he had called arrived, they found him dead, clearly by my hand, and they did not believe that I had been defending myself. Rather, they believed that he had pulled his iron knife to ward me off. And then when they went to speak to the girl and she found out that her father had been killed, she told them that I had forced her. They would have seen me in their justice system and hanged for a rapist and murderer, except that the treaty gave the Guard jurisdiction. The Guard Captain–my Captain–knew my story was truth, but he would not risk starting new hostilities with the humans over one person. He spared my life and Outcast me to satisfy the humans' desire for vengeance. No one had survived being Outcast more than a few years and it seemed a solution to all their problems."

He stopped talking abruptly, and no one else broke the silence. Finally, Zarethyn spoke, "What was your name?"

Bleidd looked at him sharply, "It matters not. I am an outlaw now, so I take the name of wolf. It seems fitting."

"If, when this is all over, I can help you redeem your name, I will."

"I expect nothing from you."

Chapter 7 - Monday

Allie woke up alone in her bed with the morning sunlight falling on her face and looked up to see Jess standing at the far window, back in full armor. His face was unreadable, but she suspected he was thinking of Aeyliss. She bit her lip, unsure what to say, either about his Squad mate's death or about what had happened between the two of them the night before. She slid out of the bed and scooped up the first clothes she found on the floor, dressing quickly. Jess turned at the sound of her movement.

"Good morning, love."

At the word love, term of endearment or not, she felt herself flushing, and mumbled back a barely distinct "'morning." And then in a rush, "I need to hit the bathroom and get a quick shower."

For some reason that seemed to amuse him, and his lips twitched into a smile. "Of course, I will escort you."

She gave him a warning look and his smile widened, although his voice was serious, "I will wait out in the hall until you are done."

She rolled her eyes, stretched and realized that she felt considerably better today; the residual aches this morning where decidedly of her own making, and there was something oddly satisfying about that. For the first time since the Dark Court Elves had appeared in her store, she felt back in control of her own life. That thought got rid of any possible regrets she might have had for her out of character behavior the night before. She paused, eyeing the dull metal of his armor, "What's with the battle gear?"

He smile faded and he looked grim, "We do not know who killed Aeyliss, or how she was caught unawares, but Zarethyn does not want to risk another such death. We are all to work in pairs at all times and to stay in full armor. Had she been in armor, Aeyliss would have had a fighting chance, even against an iron knife in the back."

"Call me crazy, but aren't you working alone now?"
she asked

"Brynneth is here with me, and there are two
Guards from another squad here as well."

"Why?" she was genuinely puzzled by the extra
Guards.

"For whatever reason, my love, you seem to be at
the center of all of this. We must find the book and
understand what has been going on here and Zarethyn will
not risk you being killed or harmed," he said gently.

She had no idea how to feel about that and there
was that love word again. *I guess the store's staying closed
again today,* she thought, *that'll kill my bank account.*
Aloud she said, "I need to go to the bathroom," and ducked
out the door, almost colliding with Brynneth who was
coming out of Jason's room directly across the hall from
hers. Her first thought was to wonder how the Elven Guard
Captain would feel about both his on-duty Guards keeping
company during the night, although given the Elven love of
all things sensual and the presence of the two extra Guards
downstairs, maybe he wouldn't care after all. Then she
caught sight of Jason's chagrined face peering out of the
doorway of his room, and she thought, *Good for you Jason,
Carpe diem.* He looked like he was expecting criticism,
instead she said, as casually as she could, "Hey Jase, I'm
grabbing a quick shower. Any chance you might be able to
whip up some pancakes?"

Jason looked immensely relieved, "How about
chocolate chip pancakes?"

"You're spoiling me. And yes," she smiled at him
and dodged into the bathroom as he popped back into his
room. In an odd way she really was happy for Jason. He'd
always been nervous and uncomfortable around the elves,
at least the few who she'd seen him around. It had even
taken him months when he first moved in to get used to
Bleidd. Maybe this was a sign that he had gotten over

whatever weird issue he had about non-humans. *Or maybe he just decided Brynneth was really hot,* Allie though, smirking to herself as she turned on the shower.

A little while later, with her wet hair pulled into a rough braid, Allie followed her nose to the kitchen with Jess in tow. She had a feeling until all of this was solved she was going to have to get used to being followed around, even though it seemed unnatural to have someone walking behind her everywhere. *With any luck*, she thought, *this will all be over soon. And I can have my life back.*

Jason had cooked a heaping plate of pancakes, which sat like a mountain on the kitchen counter and Allie served herself with enthusiasm. Jess had walked over to stand with the other elves off to one side, talking quietly; she wasn't sure if they had already eaten or were abstaining from this particular meal. The two new elves were both male and dark haired, bearing enough of a resemblance to Brynneth that Allie wondered if they were from the same clan. Elven government was a monarchy, but within that structure it tended to be organized by clan groups, with each clan led by a clan head to whom the other members owed loyalty. In practice, each clan was an extended family who were all related by varying degrees.

Allie sat down with her food and began eating enthusiastically. Liz, who had refused the pancakes in favor of an English Muffin with marmalade, was, as usual, taking small lady-like bites, "Honestly Allie, I can't believe you're eating that. It's children's food."

"Relax and enjoy life, Liz," Allie said between mouthfuls. She was determined to hold onto her new attitude moving forward.

Liz gave her a long, disapproving look, "Sometimes you need to enjoy life a little bit less and be a bit more focused."

Syndra stopped chewing and glanced between the two cousins. "What's that supposed to mean?"

"I just think with everything going on around here some people should be a bit more professional." Liz sniffed.

Allie and Syn exchanged a puzzled look before Allie asked "And what does that mean?"

"I think you know what I mean, "Liz looked pointedly over to where Jess was standing talking with one of the new Guard.

Allie felt herself starting to get mad but tried not to let it show. She knew that Liz was under a lot of stress right now and also that she was used to lecturing Allie on exactly how Allie should live her life. Usually Allie took it without complaint. Liz had always watched out for her when they were growing up, and had often defended Allie against bullies when they were in school. Liz also knew how much Allie disliked confrontation and over the years the other woman had gotten used to Allie simply following where she was led. "I really don't know what you're trying to say Liz, so why don't you just spit it out?"

Liz frowned, "Well, quite frankly, if I didn't know better, having him in your room all night I might assume something inappropriate went on"

Syndra snorted loudly, "Inappropriate?"

Allie dropped her silverware onto her plate with a loud clang. Everyone fell silent and she found all eyes in the room–her roommates, Jess, Brynneth, the two new Guards–focusing on her. "Yes, I had sex with him. We had sex. I enjoyed it and I intend to do it again. I might die horribly tonight, tomorrow, the next day–and I am, by the Gods, going to make the most of whatever time I've got. If I want to have chocolate chip pancakes every meal, and sleep with someone I just met, and do whatever else I enjoy doing then, by the Gods, I will. I'm tired of being a victim. I'm tired of feeling out of control. And if you don't like that Liz, I'm sorry, but it's my life and I'm going to live it."

Her cousin's eyes had gone wide and round. Liz was used to Allie going along with what she wanted and had never expected resistance on this. She paled and then flushed, "Well I find it baffling that a few days ago you're assaulted–beat up, almost raped–and now you're jumping into bed with someone you barely know. What are you thinking?"

"I'm thinking that I was assaulted and almost *killed* and I don't want to die knowing I lived a great, moderate, boring life and never did anything I actually wanted to do for myself." Allie shot back, wishing she could make Liz understand. She resented her cousin, who had always had an active social life, boyfriends, and diverse interests, for acting like Allie trying to enjoy herself even a tiny bit as much as Liz did on a regular basis was out of line.

Liz stood up abruptly, shoving her chair back into the wall. "Well, when you realize what a huge mistake you're making being so irresponsible, I'll be here to help you fix everything, but don't expect me not to say I told you so."

Liz stormed out of the room, leaving stunned silence in her wake. The elves all looked thoroughly confused and Allie doubted they understood any of what had just happened, beyond that she and Liz had gotten into an argument. Bleidd was tight lipped, but Allie suspected that was probably over her loud declaration about sleeping with one of the Guard. Allie had expected Syndra to be the first to speak, but it was Jason who said, "Good for you Allie."

Syndra was nodding. "It's about time you told her to butt out. She acts like your mother half the time."

Allie shook her head, perversely feeling the need to defend her cousin, "She's always had to kind of look out for me when we were growing up. She just wants…"

"She's just flamingly jealous." Syndra talked over her. "And letting her push you around makes her feel like she's the boss, which she isn't. It's about time she start treating you like an adult and not her snot nosed little cousin."

"She's got nothing to be jealous of." Allie said, shaking her head. Syn gave her a long look. "Anyway, enough of that. I'll give her some time to cool off and then go talk to her. Meanwhile, after I eat I'll get back to hunting for that book. Once I can find that we'll be much closer to figuring this all out."

"I have to work later, but I'll help this morning." Syndra said.

Jason nodded, "I was out early last night–well, this morning. And I'm on 3rd tonight. I can help as long as you need me to this morning as long as I can catch a nap later this afternoon."

"Then we have a plan", Allie said, spearing another chunk of pancake.

"Pardon," one of the strange elves said, obviously hesitant to interrupt. *He probably thinks we're all entirely insane* Allie thought, caught somewhere between amusement and annoyance. "But if it's possible for you to restrain your dog after you eat, that would be helpful to us."

"Dog? What dog?" Jason asked

"We don't have a dog," Syndra confirmed. "We have a cat around here somewhere, whose probably hiding because of all the strange people, but no dog."

The elf looked genuinely puzzled. "We saw the dog when we came in. A large black dog at the edge of the woods."

Allie stood up quickly "In the woods! I bet he was in the woods last night too."

"What are you talking about, Al?" Syndra asked. Allie ignored her, heading towards the door that led from the back of the kitchen out to a small mud room and then the backyard. Alarmed the elves started to follow her but she stopped abruptly and turned, dodging past them and jogging down the hall. Syndra yelled after her, "Allie! What the fuck!"

Allie ran into the small sitting room off the right side of the main hallway which served as an unofficial library, her eyes scanning the shelves of books. Quickly she grabbed half dozen paperbacks off the nearest shelf, which she promptly dropped, unable to keep them all in her small hands. Casting her eyes around she noticed Liz's canvas sowing bag sitting near one of the Victorian style chairs and she upended it, scattering yarn, knitting needles, and half-finished afghan onto the hardwood floor. She shoved the books into the bag with an unusual disregard for them.

"Allie, what is wrong?" Jess asked, his voice cautious.

"He roams the woods at night," she said, distracted. "He might have seen who killed her. I mean maybe. Maybe not, but I can ask…"

The elves exchanged uneasy glances, "A witness to Aeyliss's death?"

"Yes! Maybe…" she replied, shouldering the bag and walking quickly back down the hall. Jess caught up with her and seized her arm, forcing her to stop.

"Allie, what are you talking about?" he said seriously.

She took a deep, steadying breath, "There's a kelpie who lives in the woods behind the house. He wanders sometimes at night in the form of a large dog–which is probably who you saw earlier–and he might have seen something. I didn't even think of it before, but we–I–can ask him."

"No" Jess said, shaking his head, "It's far too dangerous. Kelpies are difficult to deal with at best and the risk is too great to you."

It was her turn to shake her head," He's been my friend for over 20 years. He wouldn't hurt me. You, possibly. My other roommates, probably. But not me."

They stood staring each other down for several seconds as the elves waited for Jessilaen to make a decision. Finally, with obvious reluctance, he nodded and Allie took off towards the back door. All four of the elves followed in her wake, across the backyard and over the stone wall. As they entered the woods the elves fell back and fanned out, taking up defensive positions; Allie ignored them.

At the edge of the lake she reached out with her magic, hoping Ciaran would answer despite the elves. To her relief she saw the water ripple and moments later the kelpie emerged in his horse form. She opened the bag and carefully pulled out the books, trying to hold all of them without dropping them this time.

"Good morning Ciaran. I brought you some books."

The dripping, dark horse regarded her and the elves who were staying back well within the tree line. He spoke without changing his form, something that had unnerved her as a child.

"Good morning Aliaine. The books are greatly appreciated. I will take care that they are returned in the same condition they arrived in," and then, niceties observed. "You are keeping strange company these days."

Allie set the books down on a nearby tree stump. "Strange company, strange days. I was hoping I could ask you about last night."

The large horse head bobbed slightly in a nod, "I had heard you were injured Allie, I am pleased to see you are well enough now. Was the one who injured you the same one who killed the Elven Guard on the road?"

She could feel the tension behind her, "We don't know, but I don't think so. I was hoping that you might have seen something last night that might help them find whoever killed the Guard."

He thought about this, and she knew he wasn't trying to remember but deciding whether he would share whatever he'd seen. Finally he said, "I have no fondness for the Guard or desire to help them, but since you ask me, and it seems they are protecting your life, I will tell you. They may do what they will with the knowledge."

Allie felt an immense relief. "That would be appreciated."

"I was near the edge of the wood when a car drove on the road, and stopped, but its lights stayed on and its engine kept running. I only noticed it because cars either come or go, but don't usually idle like that. I did not linger though, but was roaming through the woods and had reached the far end when I smelled the blood and iron in the air. I ran with all speed back towards the road, but when I arrived at the edge of the woods the strange car was leaving and the Guard-woman was dead."

Allie was nodding when Jessilaen spoke. "And why would you rush to her aid?"

The kelpie turned and regarded the elf "Not to her aid, although perhaps my earlier arrival would have aided her, but to catch the one who killed her. There is no more delicious prey than a murderer, and this one had blood and death enough on his soul to make a feast for me. I had long ago promised Allie not to enter the yard of the house, and the road is the edge of my territory so I do not go past it, but the temptation of someone with fresh blood on his hands was great."

Something occurred to Allie as Ciaran spoke, "He was alone then? The killer?"

"Yes. Only one." Ciaran said, wushing air out in an equine sigh.

"That was very helpful Ciaran. We'll leave you alone now to enjoy the books. And let me know which ones you like best and I'll get more of that sort for you."

The kelpie nodded, "Of course."

He turned and disappeared back into the small lake and Allie shouldered the now empty bag and headed back to the house, her Elven escort in tow. As they reached the edge of the yard Brynneth finally broke the silence, "What was the point of that?"

"We learned that it was one person who killed her, and that he was waiting for her, in an idling car when she came out," Allie said bleakly.

"And that is significant in some way?" one of the strange elves asked. Allie realized that she had no idea what his name was and felt a twinge of guilt.

"Well, for certain it tells us that it wasn't someone she saw as a threat, since she had to know he was there," Allie said thinking, *and I strongly suspect that whoever it was knew when the Guard changed and was waiting for her specifically…* Instead she said, "Now to find the book."

****

As they walked back across the lawn she saw Jason waiting in the back door, looking unhappy. When they were close enough he yelled, "Hey Allie, there's two cops here. They want to talk to you."

"Okay, I'm coming in now." She called back, wondering why the police would want to talk to her. She hadn't seen anything last night and if she had it would be for the Guard to handle, since an Elven murder victim was their jurisdiction, unless the perpetrator turned out to be human.

Sitting in the kitchen, drinking coffee, were the two detectives from the joint task force. She was sure her face showed her surprise but Riordan gave his usual smile and stood up to greet her "Good morning, Ms. McCarthy. Your roommate let us in, I hope you don't mind."

"No, I don't mind," she said feeling inexplicably flustered, and then added, "Good morning detectives. Let me grab a cup and I'll join you."

She poured herself some coffee and sat at the table with the two town police. The Elven Guard had quietly melted into the background and Allie suspected that they wanted to remain unnoticed while listening. Walters sat and nursed his coffee, looking like he wanted to be anywhere else but there.

"How are you feeling?" Riordan asked "You look much better than I expected."

"Brynneth is a gifted healer, and I am feeling much better. I think the bruises will be gone by tomorrow."

Walters grunted slightly, "I always heard you should be careful accepting things from elves–but maybe you worked it out in trade?"

Riordan gave his partner a disbelieving look, but Allie wasn't offended, "It's never a good idea to be in debt to any being of Fairy, that's true, and I'm in his debt now, but honestly I haven't even had time to worry about it, between getting hurt and then Aeyliss being killed."

Riordan cleared his throat uncomfortably, "Yes, it was a shock to hear about that last night. It's not the sort of crime we expect to see in this neighborhood."

She looked at the Detective and tried to choose her words carefully. "It seems a bit much for coincidence that she was killed while we were looking for a book she could have used to track the killer."

Walters eyes narrowed. "There's no reason to see any connection between her death and the other murders."

Riordan looked less sure. "It's too early to know how or if her murder fits in to anything, but that's not really our bailiwick, that's for the Elven Guard to figure out. We're here to talk with you about what happened Friday."

Allie looked down, "I don't know what I can tell you about that."

Riordan leaned forward, "Ms. McCarthy, I understand why you might be scared. I saw the crime scene photos and the surveillance video. But we need to consider the possibility that whoever attacked you is connected to the murders. You said you wanted to help us and the best way to do that is to be honest with us now and maybe that'll give us a lead we can work with."

Allie bit her lip feeling truly torn. She couldn't tell the police why she was sure her attackers weren't their killers without compromising the elves refusal to acknowledge the Dark Court, which she agreed with.

"I do want to help you, and I will, but there's nothing I can tell you about this, except that I wasn't raped."

Walters gave her a long look and then seemed to decide to try a nicer approach.

"Listen, we know that this whole situation is tough for you. But from our point of view you need to understand we have to follow all the good leads. That's how investigations work. Whoever attacked you could be connected to our murders, could be our killer. We can't just ignore that."

"The people who attacked me were looking for a book, and when I couldn't help them they got violent about it." Allie reluctantly added, hoping that would be enough to convince them there wasn't any connection.

"You got beat up that bad over a book?" Riordan said skeptically.

"I think my attitude was more the problem, actually." She said wryly.

Riordan suddenly looked thoughtful.

"The Guard said you're looking for a book that might have info on the kind of ritual our killer's using and these guys come in looking for a book, but you don't see a connection?"

Allie swore to herself. "I don't know."

Both Detectives stared at her while she sipped her coffee, but when it was obvious she wasn't going to say anything else they stood reluctantly. Riordan sounded tired, "Well I'm glad you're feeling better. Thanks for the coffee and if you change your mind about pressing charges, give me a call."

"Or if you think of anything else about the murders," Walters added, eyeing the lurking Guard suspiciously "Keep us in the loop."

****

Riordan drove back to the station in silence, lost in thought, and Walters knew, even if he wouldn't admit it, that it bothered his overly politically correct partner to see the elves camping out in that house like that.

It should, Walters thought smugly, *I'd bet money they're shacking up with our 'expert' already, damn elves'll screw anything, anyway. Wouldn't put it past Lyons to be getting a piece of that either; rumor is she's pretty freaky. And I don't believe this rape story for a minute. I don't know what game she's playing at, but whatever happened was obviously part of something illegal she's involved in which is why she's trying to cover it up. Jim's just a big soft touch for a beat-up girl crying Rape! It's a damn shame whoever roughed her up didn't kill her–that would have solved my problem. But if someone else is looking for the book, that could be a huge complication.*

He turned to look out the side window so Riordan wouldn't see him frowning. *This world is too messed up, someone's gotta fix it. That's why it's so important to get this work done* he thought grimly. He hadn't expected the guilt he'd felt after he'd killed the Fairy cop. It hadn't felt right at all to kill any kind of cop, but he kept reminding himself that she was just an elf and it had to be done. When

Lyons had called and told them about her stupid roommate remembering the old woman's copy of the book, at first he'd been furious, but when she'd let slip the Guard schedule and when they changed shift, he'd seen a golden opportunity. And it had all worked perfectly, much easier than he'd feared. In fact it was almost disappointing how easy it had been to kill her.

Well, no more magical tracker means the magic can't be tracked he thought satisfied. Then he thought of the early morning phone conversation he'd had *Now I just have to trust and let the mixed blood bitch find the book for us, then take it…* He didn't like leaving anything in the bookshop owner's hands and he had a feeling that everything was spiraling out of control, but he had been forced to agree that it was the best course of action.

He hated sitting around waiting for something to happen.

****

"It's not this, is it?" Jason asked, holding up a leather bound book. Allie glanced at it quickly and shook her head. He added it to the pile of books they'd already checked and moved on to the next. The three friends, with two Guards hovering nearby, had been sorting through books in the attic for over an hour. Both the Guards were strangers to Allie; Jess had returned to the Outpost to offer a preliminary report–not that there was anything to report– and Brynneth was downstairs watching for Aeyliss's replacement who had been sent out to help cover the day shift.

Allie sat back on her heels for a moment, rolling her shoulders to work the knots out, and inhaling the musty but comforting smell of the old attic. The attic had always been one of her favorite places when she was a child, somewhere she came to hide when she was upset or to play on rainy days. The room stretched the length and breadth of the house and had long been used for storage of everything from holiday decorations to unused or unwanted items, including several old chairs and couches and countless boxes piled haphazardly around the space. Several years before her grandmother had died Allie and Liz had undertaken to line all the walls with short bookshelves which were filled with decade's worth of books, mostly once-read and discarded paperback novels. Interspersed in with those however were an array of others, including rare and expensive antique books and more recent but equally hard to find ones. Allie was having a hard time looking for her grandmother's grimoire because she kept getting sidetracked with other books that she knew she could sell in the store or that a customer had asked about at some point over the years. She had started a separate pile of books to smuggle out to the store as she went along and it was definitely slowing her down to divide her attention, but she couldn't help it. Jason and Syndra were searching with more speed, but they didn't know exactly what they were looking for so they had to keep stopping to double check with Allie when they came across something they weren't sure about. The end result was that after an hour the group hadn't gotten through even a tenth of the books on the shelves, and since their searches the night before hadn't gotten much further either they still had more then 2/3's of the books left to go through.

"Huh," Syndra mused out loud, more to break the monotony than anything else, "Wonder why your grandmother bothered to keep this ratty old dictionary? It's so outdated and messed up she might as well have thrown it away…"

Allie looked up just as Syndra was about to toss the book onto one of the teetering already-checked piles, and she lunged across the space between them, yelling, "No!" so loudly that she startled both the Guards into fully drawing their swords.

"What the fuck Allie!" Syndra yelled back "What are you doing?"

"That's it! That's the book! Can't you see it?" Allie felt elated as she picked up the grimoire for the first time in over 20 years. It was exactly as she remembered it: brown hand tooled leather smooth under her hands, cream colored parchment pages crisp despite its age, its weight somehow more solid than it should be for its size.

Syndra looked at her like she'd lost her mind. "Allie, it's just a battered old dictionary. Like super old. Pre-Sundering old."

She turned to Jason, holding up the book, and he nodded "It's an old dictionary. It looks like it's taken a bath, kinda wrinkly and moldy. Kinda gross." He wrinkled his nose.

Feeling a sudden foreboding she turned to the two elves, "What do you see."

The woman on the left hesitated a moment, "I am not sure, but it doesn't look like anything significant. An old worthless book as they say."

Wordlessly she held the book up to the other elf, feeling it tingle in her hands indicating active magic. He studied it for a long time, the seconds dragging out painfully as she felt her heart racing, "I–am not sure either. I cannot see it clearly."

Realization sunk in and Allie let slip a rare, "Oh fuck."

****

Allie was sitting down in the living room later waiting for the Guard Captain's arrival. He was summoned by the Guard assigned to her, who had been unable to understand her less than coherent explanations about the book. In the hours since the book had been found Jason and Syndra had both left and Allie had holed up on the living room couch, cradling the grimoire but unable to bring herself to open it. She wasn't sure why, exactly. Somehow she had thought that if she could find the book she'd be able to hand it over to the Elven Guard and her part in everything would be done–they could find what they needed from there without her. Like at her store, it should have been a simple matter of connecting the right person with the right book. But nothing was turning out to be that simple. Her last hope was Zarethyn; she knew that in order to achieve the rank of Captain in the Guard he had to be an adept mage and if even he couldn't see the book for what it was, she would have to accept that her grandmother's magic was too strong. It did occur to her to wonder if Liz could see the book, but her cousin had left earlier, while they were all up in the attic, and Allie didn't know when she'd be back. *And if she can see it, she might be in danger*, Allie thought frowning.

She was sitting on the oversized couch, staring at the room's wood paneling, the book in her lap, when Zarethyn arrived. He had Jessilaen, Brynneth, and the new squad member with him. The new elf was male, with black hair and a serious expression, Allie noted, feeling relieved he seemed nothing like Aeyliss. Unexpectedly they also had both human police in tow. Looking up to see the full task force gave her a strange feeling of déjà vu, despite the changed setting from their first visit, but it was broken quickly as Jess moved to sit next to her, resting his arm around her shoulders. She held the book up to the Captain, "What do you see?"

He frowned, contemplating the book. Walters spoke into the silence, "That piece of shit? It looks like something you hit with a weed whacker."

Riordan looked equally skeptical, and the other elves shook their heads slightly.

Finally Zarethyn spoke, "Are you certain this is the book you have been seeking Aliaine? It does not seem significant in anyway."

She had been expecting that response, but still felt her heart sink. "Are you sure? Absolutely sure?"

He looked displeased, and she knew she was bordering on rudeness to press him, but she wanted him to look again. He did, but shook his head, "I see an old human printed book, cheap, and of no special note."

She sighed, dropping the book back to her lap, "It seems that everyone sees something slightly different, but along the same lines–old, ruined, junky–not worth anything. This is it though. And it doesn't look like that at all. Like I told everyone when we started looking for it, its handmade, brown leather, obviously an antique but in good shape."

Zarethyn was staring hard at the book now, his brow furrowed, "It's enchanted."

"Looks that way," Allie said, and then winced at the unintentional pun. "If even you, Captain, can't see it for what it is then it must be a major enchantment. It must have taken my grandmother years to set it, although I have no idea why she'd invest that kind of energy in something like this."

"To hide it?" Riordan guessed, still not looking convinced but obviously willing to humor her and see where she was going with all of this.

"Yes, but why?" Allie said, "Why not just destroy it?"

Zarethyn shook his head "There is no way to know without knowing the full contents of the book."

"Yes, "Allie said, taking a deep breath and bracing herself, "And that brings us to the good news and the bad news."

"You can't read it?" Walters said suddenly, sounding uncertain. Allie was so used to his in-your-face attitude that his hesitation now caught her off guard.

"I can read it–although I have no idea at all why I can see and read the book and no one else can." She bit her lip, chewing thoughtfully.

"Perhaps because your grandmother intentionally set the enchantment that way" Jessilaen offered quietly. Allie winced.

"So, I'll bite, what's the good news?" Riordan asked.

"The good news is that if this is the book the–people–who attacked me in my store were looking for then they can't kill me, or seriously hurt me, because they'll need me to read the book for them."

"You call that good news?" Walters scoffed, "that still leaves room for a lot of shit."

"Yes, well, it's all about perspective. Assuming the, er, people who attacked me aren't connected to the murders, the bad news is if this book does contain information about the theory behind the ritual your killer is using–even the exact ritual itself–and I'm the only one who can read it, then as soon as the killer realizes that, it's going to be in his best interest to kill me as quickly as possible."

Jess's arm tightened around her shoulders and she resisted the urge to lean her head against him. Oddly she wasn't afraid for herself; she felt better having a few answers even if they weren't what she'd wanted.

Walters's voice was flat when he spoke, "You really think the guys who jumped you aren't connected to these murders?"

"I don't know why they'd want the grimoire if they already have the ritual," she said honestly and his eyes narrowed.

"It seems unlikely that this book has the ritual itself," Zarethyn said, reasonably, "More likely it contains the theory behind the ritual or other information that will lead us to understand why what is being done is being done."

Allie nodded, "I may have misspoken. Obviously though, there's something important in here and we need to know what it is."

"How would the killer find out you have this magic book no one else can read?" Riordan asked

Allie looked down at the book, and spoke quietly "How did he know to kill Aeyliss, the one person here who could have tracked him down magically once we found the book?"

Jess tensed next to her and she could feel his rage. The silence in the room was so complete she could hear people breathing. As the minutes stretched out she finally forced herself to look up; all the elves were radiating a cold fury that was more than a little frightening, even to her and she knew she wasn't its focus. The two humans were looking at each other, trying to communicate something silently.

"That's a pretty serious accusation," Riordan said grimly

Allie shook her head, "I'm not accusing anyone of anything. I'm stating the obvious–your killer has a way of finding things out. Maybe it's a leak. Maybe it's a spell. Maybe he wiretapped something–I have no idea–I just know that *he* knows. And if he has a way to find things out, whatever that way is, he will find this out too. It's inevitable."

Zarethyn's voice when he spoke was totally devoid of any emotion, "You believe this is why Aeyliss was killed?"

Why do you think she was killed? Allie wondered. "I think it's not a coincidence that he killed the one Guard that had the best chance of finding him. Her gift is rare– how quickly could you get another here with the same ability?"

Zarethyn locked eyes with her, searching, "It would be difficult. Months perhaps."

"Exactly," Allie refused to look away. "With her dead, finding him, even with the book, will be much harder."

Zarethyn nodded. "We will find him." His voice held unpleasant promises for the killer when that happened. Allie didn't feel sorry about that at all.

"I'm sure you will. But you, "her eyes swept the room, "need to make a decision, because the risk is too great of the investigation being further derailed if I'm killed. As I see it there are three options: I can read the book straight through as fast as possible and summarize it for you. The advantage of course is that you'd have some idea of what's going on pretty quickly, but the downside is you'd be relying on a summary and I might leave out important details unintentionally. I can read it out loud to someone else, sharing the info as it were, which will take longer. Or I can hand copy the entire book, which will take the longest of the three options but might be the best idea, overall. The risk of course is if I'm killed part way through."

Jess wrapped his arms around her. "You will not be killed."

"That's a happy thought, but it would be foolish not to have a backup plan. Or several," she said, refusing to look at him.

Walters was frowning, probably, Allie thought, at the idea that their whole investigation hinged on her.

Riordan looked thoughtful, "There's no way to break the spell on the book so other people can read it?"

Allie shook her head, "I don't think so, at least not quickly or easily. If it took years to set it could take months, at best, to remove."

"According to you," Walters said, "We only have your word that this even is the book. Maybe you're just looking for attention."

"You have no right to question her word," Jess cut in, clearly angry.

"You aren't exactly impartial, are you," the Detective sneered unpleasantly. "Standing up for your girlfriend."

"Walters," Riordan tried to interrupt, "remember the handbook."

"Detective, do not presume to insult any of my officers," Zarethyn said sharply.

"Screw the handbook, we're all trusting this case to someone that shouldn't even be involved, if you ask me." Walters was getting red faced, and Allie sensed that the tension and stress was about to erupt in a very dangerous way.

"Enough!" she said forcefully, and then with everyone still glaring at each other, "Enough. We can't start fighting now. Let's start here; I'm already under Guard. (She ignored Walters scoffing and prayed Jess would too.) Let me read what I can tonight and see what the book says. Maybe that will help give us some answers to start with. But think about how you want me to proceed from there, because it's too dangerous to keep things the way they are. One way or another, what's in the book has to be shared out somehow."

"Aliaine?" Brynneth said, speaking for the first time, "You had asked me to look for patterns with the timing of the deaths, do you remember?"

Everyone looked surprised, but Allie nodded, "Yeah, I remember. Did you find anything?"

"Yes, I did," Brynneth replied, "Although I do not know if it will mean anything to you. As far as I am able to tell all of the girls were killed on the night of the dark moon."

"Hmmmm," Allie frowned, thinking. "Well, that goes along with the idea of inverse fertility I guess. Fertility magic is done on waxing or full moons, so the dark moon would be the energetic opposite of that."

"That can't be right," Riordan said. "That would be four bodies over exactly three months but we started finding bodies 2 months ago and they aren't evenly spaced out."

"Looking at your reports, it would seem that the first victim found was the second one killed, and the second found the first killed; several of the bodies were not found immediately and so had begun to decay." Brynneth said calmly.

Riordan nodded thoughtfully, but Walters was shaking his head. "There's no way for you to look at those girls after they were found and know they were killed on whatever day of the moon."

"It's a tedious process," Brynneth said, sounding annoyed. "But it can be done with time and patience."

"Well, that gives me somewhere to start, anyway," Allie said, suddenly sick of all the arguing. "Between that and knowing the killer's targeting girls with mixed ancestry…"

"What do you mean–mixed ancestry?" Zarethyn queried; most of the others looked puzzled by her statement, but Walters looked really angry.

He probably thinks I'm saying that because I'm mixed, Allie suppressed a grimace, *and he thinks it's more attention seeking. Like being on some ritual murderer's ideal victim list makes me happy.* She tried to keep her voice even.

"All the victims had some degree of Fairy ancestry; I thought you knew that."

"Are you certain?" Jess asked quietly. She wasn't sure how they'd react to knowing it was Bleidd who had told her, but she trusted his perception. She nodded. The elves exchanged looks.

"If there's nothing else I need to get started on this. This book is over 500 pages of cramped handwritten everything. It's going to be a lot to go through and I don't know yet if it's coded."

"Coded?" Riordan sounded as tired as she felt. "What do you mean coded?"

"Most grimoires were written in code. Sometimes runic alphabets, where you have to know the runes to read it, sometimes substitution codes, where you need to know that one word or phrase means something else, sometimes key codes, where a key aspects of each spell or ritual is left out. It's all to ensure that the book can't be used by anyone but the proper owner," Allie said

"If it's coded, can you, um, break the code?" Riordan asked.

"I have to," Allie said grimly.

Zarethyn nodded abruptly, as if he had decided something, "Read the book and see what you can uncover; we will decide how else to handle it based on what you find. I believe you are correct in your evaluation of the gravity of your situation and the risk to our investigation should you be harmed. It would be best for you to come back with us to the Outpost, you can be protected there with less risk."

"No way," Walters said, as Riordan shook his head and added "I don't think that's a good idea."

The Elven Captain frowned, "It is the best course of action."

"How about we put her in human protective custody?" Walters said "She'd be safer with us, and then there'd be no conflict of interest."

"Conflict of interest?" Jess's voice was dangerous

"Hey, I call 'em like I see 'em," Walters said

"She would be safer at the Outpost." Zarethyn started before Riordan interrupted him.

"In human custody…"

"Stop! Just stop," Allie said, standing up and clutching the book. Jess stood up with her, his hand on her back. She couldn't help but draw comfort from the touch, a steadying presence as she spoke. "I can't just put my whole life on hold indefinitely until this is solved. I have a business to run if I'd like to keep paying my bills. I don't want to be horribly murdered but I can't run and hide either."

Since the police, Syndra notwithstanding, hadn't been protecting her so far anyway, she turned to the Elven Guard Captain, "I am deeply grateful for the offer, but if you cannot continue protecting me here then I will have to take my chances and get the book read and annotated as quickly as possible."

He shook his head, and Allie's mouth went dry. If he decided she qualified as a denizen of Fairy he could, theoretically, take her into his custody whether she wanted to go or not. But when he spoke it was with a grudging admiration, "From this point on, you will always have at least two Guards with you at all times, and another full squad assigned to patrol the area you are in, until this is resolved and the killer is captured."

She wanted to argue with him, because it felt like a ridiculous amount of resources being wasted on her, but she sensed it would be futile. The elves wanted vengeance for Aeyliss's death and they would do whatever it took, including babysitting her en masse, to find whoever that was. It offended her innate desire for personal freedom to think of having so many Guard with her all the time, and Gods knew how she'd explain it to Liz.

"That's a lot of effort for one person," Walters said, echoing Allie's thoughts.

"All things are part of a greater pattern; we cannot always see what the pattern forms. For whatever reason Aliaine is the key to what is going on here, on different levels. She will lead us to understanding the pattern and solving the crime." Zarethyn said calmly. Walters and Riordan both looked dubious, but the other elves, even the one who did not know Allie, were nodding. She had forgotten how much elves relied on synchronicity, the idea that things that appeared related, even if the relation was inexplicable, were in fact somehow linked on a deeper level. She wondered if his belief that her involvement was synchronous was why he was willing to let her make her own decisions about where to stay, and she wasn't sure if she should be grateful about it or worried about the added pressure for her to find the answers they needed.

****

When he finally finished his shift and got back to his apartment, Walters put his fist through a wall. He'd managed to keep it together in front of his partner, but inside he'd spent the rest of the day fuming. Bad enough that she'd found the book and immediately told the damn elves, but worse that she'd quickly put several pieces together about the ritual itself. He'd worked hard to make it look like there was no timing pattern and that dumb bitch turned right around and pointed it out to everyone. Up until now no one had realized the girls weren't entirely human– and damn if it wasn't a stone bitch to find each one of them–and there she went pointing it out.

How'd she even know? He thought, hitting the wall again. *How's she fitting it all together so quickly? Fuck! I should have killed her when I first realized she'd be trouble.* He was starting to wonder how he could do it, if it was worth risking shooting her, with the chance that ballistic evidence might trip him up where he'd always been so careful before, when his private phone rang.

He grabbed it convulsively, and the familiar voice was speaking as soon as he turned it on, "Don't panic. Everything's under control."

He took a deep breath, wanting to yell, but knowing better, "I can't see how. She has the book, she says no one else can read it and she holds onto it like it's stapled to her hand. And the Guards are always within touching distance, especially that one blond one."

"I have a plan. You may not like it, but we need to throw them a red herring." He had no idea how his contact could stay so calm.

"I could kill the mixed blood girl and steal the book," he suggested, trying not to get his hopes up.

"No. Absolutely not. You just said yourself she's never alone and it's too dangerous to try to orchestrate anything on your end."

"You don't think doing nothing's a bigger risk?" he said, wishing he'd get permission to kill her and knowing he wouldn't.

"No. Leave the girl alone. If she is the only one who can read the book then we need her alive." The voice was flat.

"I've done everything for the cause that needed to be done. No matter how unpleasant, I did it. I think you're letting your feelings get in the way now, and keeping us from doing what we need to do. We should take a vote," he pressed.

"We don't need a vote. I'm in charge on this and I'm handling it. And don't think I'm letting personal feelings get in the way. First chance you have you need to kill someone else, make it look like the ritual, but it won't be. It'll throw them off and make them question everything. And I know exactly who you need to kill."

The voice was resolved; he knew that tone and lowered his head, waiting to hear the plan. There'd be no arguing with it, and he chaffed, knowing that whatever it was he would be expected to do it without complaint.

He was getting really tired of handling all the dirty work and taking all the risk, but being expected to take orders without ever having his own opinion listened to.

****

She read until her eyes crossed and her neck cramped, but once she began she felt a desperate urgency to finish that pushed her to keep going. By mid-afternoon she was so tired she couldn't focus to remember what she was reading and a dull headache had started behind her eyes, but still she pushed on. Finally Bleidd appeared, ignoring the disapproving looks from the Guard–both strangers to Allie–and gently took the book out of her hands. She protested weakly, "Bleidd, I have to…"

"You need to eat and take a break before you collapse," he said, setting the book down carefully on the couch next to her. She sighed, resigned, and allowed him to pull her to her feet and guide her back to the kitchen, with the two Guard following like shadows. Liz was at the counter fixing tea, and without thinking Allie said, "Hey Liz, can I have some too?"

As soon as she spoke and saw her cousin's back stiffen she remembered their earlier fight. She stood awkwardly, feeling foolish, but Liz replied, "Sure Allie, hibiscus okay?"

"That'd be perfect, thanks," Allie relaxed slightly. Bleidd was grabbing crackers and peanut butter out of the cabinet so Allie went to the refrigerator and pulled out a block of cheddar and some leftover ham, meeting him at the table. "Are you hungry Liz?"

Liz waivered, then shrugged, "I have to be at the theater early so I should probably eat something now."

Allie pulled out a chair gesturing for Liz to sit as the other woman walked over with the tea. Bleidd had already poured himself a glass of milk and was slathering peanut butter on a cracker while pretending not to watch the two cousins. For a moment they all sat fixing little cracker sandwiches, eating, sipping drinks and not talking. Finally, feeling like she was doing an awful lot of apologizing and unsure if she should be, Allie said "I'm sorry we fought Liz, I don't want us fighting, especially not now."

"I just don't understand why you're so suddenly obsessed with this guy," Liz muttered sipping her tea, "You've only know him a few days. It's unnatural, like he put a spell on you or something."

"No spells, Liz, really, I'd know, but yeah it is weird. I can't explain it either." Allie shrugged, biting into a ham and cheese cracker. She chewed thoughtfully for a moment, "It's like he balances me somehow, like I–I don't know–like I'm drawing on him to ground myself in all of this chaos. He makes me feel sane."

Bleidd made a small noise and both women looked at him. His expression was distinctly unhappy. Allie felt uneasy, seeing it, "What? Why the weird look?"

He hesitated, and she pressed, "Come on Bleidd, you're freaking me out."

"It's probably nothing, "he said forcing himself to drink something from his glass. "Just for a moment there it almost sounded like what you were describing was what elves call "soul friends", it's a bond that can form between two people who are very close for a long time; the two join on a psychic level that allows for an exchange of emotions, wordless communication, that sort of thing."

Allie felt nonplussed, "I've only just met him, really, and we don't know each other well at all in practical terms."

Bleidd grimaced, "I know that. It's impossible anyway–it takes years to form such a bond and it's exceedingly rare. And no offense to you Allie, because you know your background doesn't matter to me, but I think such a bond is only possible between full elves."

"No offense taken," Allie said, still feeling unnerved.

Liz looked perplexed. "But couldn't that be why she's so head-over-common-sense for this guy?"

"I doubt it, it was just a random thought when she was describing how she felt with him," Bleidd shook his head. "Just forget I mentioned it."

"There are no random words, it's all synchronicity– isn't that what the elves believe?" she had meant it to be teasing, but he looked taken aback at her words.

"I do not understand how this could be important for you to know, "he said slowly. "It occurs only between full elves–not even between other Fey–and only very rarely. It takes years, sometimes decades to form. How could this be?"

Allie shook her head, "Don't look at me, this is the first I'm hearing of it, and I was just teasing about the synchronicity."

"Synchronicity moves in all things," one of the other Guards, a darker blond who looked strange standing in the kitchen in full armor, said solemnly, "It is the pattern behind all expressed reality."

Liz shifted slightly, "So this soul friend thing, is it always between couples or what?"

"No," Bleidd said. "The only ones I have ever known who had such a bond were sisters."

The Guard who had spoken before nodded slightly. "I knew two close friends who formed such a bond, and I had heard of a married couple as well, but I did not know them myself."

Allie shook her head, "I think we're all getting sidetracked looking for an explanation that isn't there. I love you Liz and I don't want to fight with you, but I didn't hook up with him because of some mystic whatever. Blame it on hormones, or pheromones, or wanting to feel alive after almost dying or whatever else, but it wasn't a magic spell or some sort of freaky soul bond making me do it."

Liz looked down at the table's worn surface, her fingers tracing the wood grain, "I guess I'm just not used to you acting like…"

"Syndra?" Allie suggested, and they both giggled. The tension was still there, beneath the surface and Allie knew that a lot of things were being left unsaid, but at least some effort to mend things was being made.

"So you found the book?" Liz asked as Allie went back to eating. She hadn't realized how hungry she was until Bleidd had dragged her in here, but now she was ravenous. She nodded, chewing as she made another cracker.

Liz kept tracing the table's surface, "I still can't believe that Grandmother even had that kind of book. She wouldn't ever talk about dark magic at all. The idea that this whole time she had an entire grimoire of it right here in the house is unnerving."

"Be glad you can't read it," Allie said, shaking her head, "It's macabre stuff, even early on."

Liz gave her a strange look, and started to say something, then stopped.

"Anything helpful so far?" Bleidd queried.

"Not directly relating to the case yet, but I'm getting a crash course in some hardcore witchcraft. I'd never suspected my grandmother of even knowing about this stuff, never mind doing it," Allie bit her lip, frowning at her tea. "But I'll push through if the answers we need are in there."

"Just don't push too hard, Allie. You have your limits," Bleidd said, softly. She met his eyes and the honest emotion there and looked away.

"I better hit the bathroom and then get back to reading" she said evasively, sliding out of her chair. "Thanks for the tea Liz–and making me stop and eat Bleidd. I needed that."

****

She retrieved the book from the couch and retreated to her room, sitting on the bed with the grimoire spread open on the blanket in front of her. She read with a renewed sense of purpose as the afternoon shadows lengthened and darkness fell. The Guard had stayed out in the hallway, giving her the illusion of privacy and she was grateful for it, because she was often unable to hide her reactions to what she was reading. At some point, as she sat reading in the dark room the door opened. She spoke without looking up,

"Jess, this stuff is horrific."

He sat next to her, reaching out to rub her shoulders, "You are pushing yourself too hard. You need to rest."

She shook her head, "No, I'm just getting to the part where she's talking about the ritual being developed."

"What ritual?" He sounded resigned.

"The ritual, the one the killer is basing his stuff on. Oh, right you don't know." She looked up "My grandmother was in the coven that created the actual ritual being used by the killer here, although he's modified some things. Is this more synchronicity then? My grandmother's book has the exact ritual in it?"

Jess was looking at her, open mouthed. She cocked her head to one side, "What?"

"This book has the exact ritual in it? Not just the general theories being used or similar ideas?"

"No, it looks like the base ritual being used is in here, although the part I'm at right now they–my grandmother's coven–is just beginning to frame the idea. I can see where it's going, though…What?"

"I must tell Zarethyn this immediately," Jess said, obviously agitated.

"Alright. You do that, I'll keep reading," She turned back to the book, yawning widely.

He hesitated or a moment, torn between telling her to rest and doing what he knew was his duty. Finally he stood up. "I will return as quickly as possible."

She nodded distractedly not looking up as he left the room.

He tried and failed to reach the Guard Captain on the phone and finally saw no choice but to drive to the Outpost. He traveled as swiftly as he could and returned within the hour with Zarethyn; they entered Allie's room to find her lying across the book sound asleep. Jessilaen took a deep breath, "I will wake her."

"No," the Elven Captain said, "Let her rest. If Brynneth is correct we have several weeks before the next girl will be killed, and with Aeyliss dead, Aliaine is the next logical target for the killer to eliminate to protect himself. It will serve no purpose to keep pushing her into exhausting herself."

"You still believe she is pivotal to finding this killer? Her role in this is not finished now that the book is found?" Jessilaen asked quietly.

"I may have thought so, but knowing that the exact ritual is in this book," he shook his head, contemplating the sleeping young woman. "No, her part in this is not ended yet."

"May I remain with her tonight?" Jessilaen asked.

Zarethyn turned his contemplation to his second in command. "Are you so certain already that your heart is lost to her?"

"It is what it is," Jess replied cryptically.

Zarethyn nodded, "Remain with her then, and see that she rests. I will stay here tonight as well. We will meet in the morning and see what she can tell us about what the book has revealed."

Chapter 8 - Tuesday

Allie woke up in the morning, in bed but fully dressed, with Jessilaen's sleeping form, also fully dressed, pressed against her back. For an instant she lay there trying to figure out why she was under the covers fully dressed, then she realized that she must have fallen asleep reading and Jess had put her to bed. It was an oddly comforting feeling, knowing that he was watching out for her. She sat up, trying not to wake him, but as soon as she moved he moved with her, making her wonder how long he'd been lying there awake.

She sat at the edge of the bed and felt her head dropping, as the strain of the past week hit her. He sat behind her, one leg to each side, and began rubbing her shoulders, "You're pushing yourself too hard."

"Why does everyone keep telling me that?" she sighed, relaxing as his fingers worked out the knots in her muscles.

"Probably because it's true," he answered gently.

"Hmmmm. Well, true or not I need to get dressed, get breakfast, and make my own report," she said, wishing she could just stay there and relax instead.

"Zarethyn is expecting everyone to meet at 9 this morning." Jess offered. She automatically glanced at the clock: 7:30 am. Plenty of time to eat.

"Okay, well, as much as I'd rather let you keep doing that for the next 90 minutes, better to get moving," she said. He leaned in and kissed her neck, making her breath catch. "That isn't helpful."

He laughed and pushed her up gently from behind, "Is that better?"

"More helpful yes, but I think I prefer the kissing." And they both laughed. Feeling more rested than she had in the past few days she took the time to find one of her better pairs of jeans and a nice charcoal grey sweater, not that she thought looking nice would make what she had to say later any easier. The approving look Jess gave her did satisfy her though. *Wow, Syndra would never believe I'm standing here caring what any guy thinks about how I look*, Allie thought ruefully.

After breakfast she gathered everyone, including all of her roommates and the four elves from what she had begun to think of as "her" squad into the living room. She had asked that the detectives be present too, but they were notably absent; the new squad member had said he was unable to get in contact with them, and Allie didn't doubt his word but was sure the human police wouldn't appreciate being left out. Jess had finally introduced her to the new member, Natarien, who Allie had to admit was both kind and friendly. Jason, Liz, Syndra, and Bleidd found places to sit around the room, while the elves all stood at near-attention in their armor. Allie went over to the room's fireplace and started a fire while everyone got settled. For early spring the morning had a decided chill to the air, and Allie wondered if it might even snow later.

Finally she couldn't stall any longer, and she turned to face the room.

"You have to keep a couple things in mind, okay? This was all about 80 years ago, within 20 years of the Sundering. Some of the wars were still going on and the body count was huge."

"This was before the Great Truce?" Syndra asked. The humans were frowning trying to put what Allie was saying in context. The elves had all lived through it and remembered it well enough without the refresher.

"Yeah, about five years before that. This was actually the worst part of the wars, I think, when the human lands were sending iron wielding armies into the Fairy Holdings and the fairies were responding with magical assaults that wiped out whole human cities."

Everyone nodded, and Allie continued. "My grandmother was born in the year after the Sundering. At some point in her late teens she joined a small coven led by a high priest who was very interested in dark magic. Even early in the book he was teaching her some hard core blood magic."

Liz interrupted, her voice tight "I just can't believe our grandmother was into dark magic."

"That's why we need the perspective," Allie said, and Liz gave her a long look. "No, really, Liz. It was in the middle of a massive war, two decades after the world basically fractured in a way that people thought was some sort of sign from the Gods, end of all things, omen. The way she writes about it in the book, dark magic, blood magic, was what a lot of people were turning to either for answers or to protect themselves."

Liz still looked unconvinced, but Syndra was nodding, "Yeah, I can see that."

"Right, well," Allie said going on. "A couple years into her training, when my grandmother was around 19 I think, the group's high priest went crazy, and I mean literally. Apparently he came from somewhere called "Texas" which almost entirely shifted to Fairy in the Sundering–it became the Great Southern Holding…"

"That is King Trassien's realm," Zarethyn said.

"Yes, that's the one. Well, after the Sundering his whole family, except for one son who was with him here at the time, were living in a Borderland town at the edge of that realm, and during the wars, in retaliation for a human raid, the elves destroyed the town and killed everyone in it. When he found out that his whole family had been killed he went nuts, locked himself in a room for weeks, and when he came back out he had come up with this idea for a way to repair the worlds."

"What?" Several people spoke at once, and Allie held her hands up.

"He was crazy. He came up with this series of rituals, based on the idea of using opposite energies; inverse fertility, death instead of life… all warped riffs on sex and death magic. He believed that a full series of these rituals, over the course of a year, would separate the worlds. But after the first three my grandmother lost her nerve. She couldn't bear seeing the girl's suffering and dying."

"I should fucking hope not!" Syndra burst out, while Liz looked down.

"Just keep in mind–and I'm not defending any of this–but it was the middle of a war. They convinced each other that a dozen deaths for the cause were better than the hundreds of thousands dying every day in the fighting over territory." Allie swallowed hard. "Anyway, my grandmother turned them in to the police–the human police of course, since there was no Truce there was no treaty and no Guard here, so I don't think the elves ever knew about any of this. The police tried to raid the high priest's home during a ritual and it ended really badly; the guy died as did several other coven members and he destroyed his own book rather than have it confiscated. The surviving coven members were never charged with anything, I think because they cooperated with police, and all the blame was placed on the ones who had died. From what my grandmother wrote in her grimoire all the books were destroyed and she told the authorities that hers was burned. I still don't know why she didn't, but that's why she hid it."

"Would it have worked?" Liz asked into the stunned silence.

"I don't think so. He was working on a flawed assumption about what had caused the Sundering that was popular at the time, but was disproven decades ago." Allie said, frowning.

"Are you sure?" Liz asked. Syndra gave her a disturbed look and Liz waved her off, "I want to know why my grandmother thought it would work, enough to do it in the first place."

"Well, honestly, I don't know but the theory isn't sound, so I can't see how it would have worked," Allie replied. "It would have done something, of course, all that energy has to go somewhere, but what it would do I have no idea."

"So, the killer is recreating these rituals?" Zarethyn asked, his voice flat.

"No, worse than that," she replied, rubbing her eyes.

"What can be worse?" Syndra asked sounding resigned.

"Whoever this killer is, he's taking the next logical steps. He's innovating and making changes to try to improve on the original. Most likely doing what the coven's high priest would have done when the first series failed, which they would have. The original victims were all human–this killer is targeting mixed bloods as symbols of the Sundering he's trying to undo. Basic sympathetic magic–using one thing to represent another related thing. In this case the girls are symbolic of the joining of the worlds and killing them symbolizes trying to separate the worlds again. The original used minor torture to create energy to power the spell but this one is using massive amounts of torture based on a separate theory the high priest talked about elsewhere in the book."

"What theory?" Zarethyn asked.

"I don't want to get into too much detail, because it's pretty awful stuff, but–he was onto something with that." Allie said shaking her head. "He found a way to use pain and suffering to create an echo–kind of the same theory that revenant ghosts are based on–a perpetual echo that acts like an energetic battery."

"Isn't that what blood magic does anyway?" Jason asked quietly.

"Oh no–usually blood magic is like any other kind of magic using a finite energy source. It's like if you have a cup of orange juice–once you drink the juice, it's all gone and you need to get more to refill the cup, right?"

Everyone, including the elves, nodded. She felt her skin crawling just talking about it.

"That's why blood magic is usually only used to create temporary effects or one time things and stronger sources–radiant Earth energy and ambient Fairy magic is used for bigger, long term things. The thing is the ambient stuff is innately weaker and you need more of it to do less. Blood magic is much stronger but the resulting energy raised is finite. This guy found a way to use pain, suffering, and torture to create an imprint of the pain that would act as a permanent energy source. He is using that to power his spell and each ritual strengthens it."

Zarethyn inhaled sharply. "That is impossible."

"It should be. But it isn't. He found a way to do it, trying to…" she winced and looked apologetically at the elves. "He was trying to find a way to use the energy he felt was being wasted when the Fairy prisoners of war where dying."

Everyone looked equally appalled. "But you see that was in an earlier section of the book before the ritual was developed; whoever this killer is, he's combining the two to create a much stronger effect. I still don't believe it can ultimately work, but it's impossible to say what it will do."

She walked over and picked the book up off a side table. "I know I offered to copy this out, but this book is far too dangerous to be kept. I don't know why my grandmother hid it, except that maybe some part of her felt guilty over her part in what happened, and she couldn't bring herself to let it go. Some of the things in here are worse than anything I've told you about so far. You have no idea how "dark" dark can be. I thought I knew but this is leagues beyond anything I could ever have imagined. If even half of what's in here got into the wrong hands the results could be devastating. I know you only have my word on that, but you're going to have to trust me that using the pain of someone being tortured as an energetic battery is actually not the worst thing in here. "

She walked over to the fireplace, pulling back the protective fireplace screen. She heard several people gasp as they realized what she was going to do, but she couldn't let her resolve waiver; in one swift motion she tossed the book into the flames, which flared blue and green as the magic invested in the grimoire fed the fire. She heard Syndra, mutter "Holy shit" behind her. She turned back to face the shocked faces of the group, "The book is gone now, but we still have to find this killer."

"How could you do that Allie?" Liz asked.

At the same time Syndra said, "That was our best clue."

"I read through the whole thing, I know everything that was in that book and if it's important I can tell you, but the things that were in there were too dangerous to risk getting out."

"That makes you a pretty big target Al," Syndra said unhappily.

"I know, but it's the only way," Allie took a deep breath, feeling relieved knowing the book was burning, and at the same time horrified that she' had just burned a book, "At this point it's better that I die and take what I know with me than that what was in that book get out."

"No," Jessilaen said sharply, "that is not acceptable."

"I didn't mean that I want to die," she said, wincing at the odd surge of panic she felt over his distress. "I meant that the book had to be destroyed and if I am killed, I had to know that the book was already taken care of."

Jess was tight lipped and still obviously upset, but Zarethyn was nodding, "How do we proceed from here?"

Having the Guard Captain ask her for direction was so unexpected that she found herself speechless. Everyone was looking at her, waiting expectantly so she licked her lips.

"Ummm. Well. Whoever this person, this killer, is he must be related to one of the original coven members. There's no other way he could know so much about the material in the book without knowing about the original group and its inner workings"

"Can you be sure there isn't another copy?" Brynneth asked.

"I can't be absolutely sure," Allie answered, "but I think it's almost impossibly unlikely. My grandmother's copy survived in part because she was the one who turned the group in so the police trusted her when she said she had destroyed her book. From what she had written the other books were collected and destroyed en masse. If you can track down the descendants of the original coven members, you can find your suspects."

"How do we do that without the book?" Syndra asked.

Allie pulled a piece of paper out of her pocket, "I wrote down the use-names that each member went by and all the identifying characteristics my grandmother mentioned. If you cross reference this with the police record from 80 years ago I think you can figure out who was who in the coven and what roles they played."

Syndra stood up, "I'll pass that on to Riordan and Walters when I go out to the gym later–they should be able to pull up the old records. But if its back that far it may take a while."

Zarethyn shook his head slightly, "One of us should bring the list in, and update the human Detectives, else they may think we are withholding information from them."

"Call them on the phone and update them that way, and you can tell them I'll be dropping the list off. Last I heard they were supposed to be out all day in mortal Earth getting hard copies of the coroner's reports for each victim and collecting the bagged evidence from the last girl to bring back to the station" Syndra said. Zarethyn hesitated but then nodded.

"Yes, we do not have the time to dally at the police station all day if they will not be there." He agreed. "If it does not inconvenience you Officer Lyons, I would be grateful for the assistance."

Syndra actually looked flattered, "No inconvenience. I usually hit the gym around 5 and they should just be getting back to the station by then. I can stop on my way."

Zarethyn nodded at her and turned to Natarien and Brynneth, "Head back to the Outpost and inform them of what has been learned so far."

The two elves bowed slightly and left. Liz, looking troubled, wandered out the door heading up to her room, with Jason following behind. They'd both worked late the night before, and Allie assumed they were heading to grab some sleep while they could. Syndra looked from her to the remaining elves and shrugged. "Well, I'm going to go run some errands. I'll be back around lunch time Al, if you need to talk."

Allie nodded as her friend headed out. Bleidd looked unhappily from her to Jess and turned and left without a word; she fought the urge to follow him. Before she could think of what to say, Zarethyn turned to Jess, "The patrolling Squad here needs to know what we have learned as well, especially that the book has been destroyed."

Jessilaen also bowed slightly, but on his way out he walked over to Allie and kissed her. She should have felt stupid about that but she didn't. She found an odd comfort in Jessilaen that she had already begun to depend on.

When they were alone in the room, with the last remnants of the book smoldering in the fireplace, she said. "I hope you understand why I had to destroy it."

"I do understand. I hope you are prepared for the danger you have placed yourself in," Zarethyn.

"Unfortunately, I don't think I had any choice. I couldn't allow the Dark Court to get that book and there are humans who would have used what was in it as well. I understand that it makes me a bigger target. I kind of wish I didn't," she said softly. "Then again I was already in danger, so I guess it's just a matter of degree."

"We will do what we can to ensure your safety."

She thought of Jessilaen. "He really loves me doesn't he."

"I'm not sure if that was a question, but yes, he does," the Captain said.

"As much as I hate to agree with Detective Walters, isn't it a conflict of interest?" Allie asked hesitantly.

Zarethyn shook his head slightly. "It is what it is. His feelings are unusual, but there is nothing that can be done about them now even if he wanted to change them. There is a greater risk of my brother being distracted if he were assigned elsewhere than of him failing in his duty with you."

Allie couldn't hide her reaction, "He's your brother?"

"Yes. We have the same mother," The Elven Captain said simply. Elves were matrilineal, so by their own view even if they had different fathers children of the same mother were full siblings. Allie suspected that by answering the question as he had Zarethyn was saying that he and Jess did have different fathers, which would explain why they didn't share more than a passing resemblance. The two being related was a strange thought and Allie wasn't sure how she felt about it. She knew, of course, that elves had no concept of nepotism and that it wasn't uncommon, with the way the social structure was set up, for clan groups to live and work together. She just hadn't stopped and thought about how that would impact the Guard; she had grown up in a large Fairy Holding with more than a dozen clans, but she realized that she actually knew very little about how the local Queen's Holding functioned.

"I'm not sure if this is polite to ask or not, so I apologize if it seems out of line, but is Brynneth also related to you?" she couldn't resist asking.

Zarethyn smiled. "His father is our mother's great uncle, but he belongs to a different clan. We, Jessilaen and I, are part of clan Firinne, while Brynneth is clan Leighis."

Allie decided to push her luck a little since Zarethyn seemed willing to answer her questions. "Clan Firinne, that's the ruling clan here, isn't it?"

He nodded, "Queen Naesseryia is also clan Firinne, but we have no direct relation to her."

Allie's relief must have been obvious, because he actually laughed, a light sound that made her want to smile too.

"You are not disappointed?" he asked "Many would hope for a closer connection to the throne."

She shook her head vehemently. "Absolutely not. That's the last thing I need in my life, believe me." She was silent for a moment, thinking. "Honestly all I want is a nice quite life, a couple good friends, comfortable home, business turning enough of a profit to keep me going. I have no interest in politics, or thrones, or lines of succession."

He gave her a long look and she wondered if she'd said too much, but he didn't question her about her own background. "And where does Jessilaen fit into these plans?"

She blushed, "I'm not sure yet. But like you said, it is what it is; there's nothing to do to change it. So we'll just have to wait and see where it goes."

****

Later in the day Brynneth returned for his shift and Zarethyn took his leave of Aliaine. He was growing fond of the girl, who he judged to be both clever and brave, and he had had to admit that he was not entirely displeased that his brother was so taken by her. Others in the clan had been far less accepting, and Jessilaen was already being pressured to put aside the mixed blood girl, but Zarethyn knew his brother too well. Once Jess had chosen a course, he would see it through to the end.

The Elven Captain moved quickly through the humans' house seeking the Outcast elf. He needed to speak to him before leaving but he had little time to spare; he already spent too much of his attention on this one case when he had other squads he was also responsible for. And yet, he was certain that this case was special and that his attention was needed to see it resolved. As he moved into the kitchen he found Bleidd leaning against a counter, eating an apple.

"Have you had any success?" Zarethyn asked bluntly.

The Outcast, chewed for a moment, his expression not entirely friendly, "I have not found their exact location, but I am certain they remain in town. I tracked them to one hotel, but arrived after they had left, and then to a type of tavern humans have with girls who dance. They were kicked out after starting a fight over one of the girls, and she disappeared shortly afterwards."

"You believe they killed her?" Zarethyn asked, cocking his head to the side.

"I believe they did her harm. I do not know with certainty if she lives or died." Bleidd said flatly. "I am following their trail from there. If they are still here, and I believe they are, then I will find them."

The Elven Captain nodded. "Continue searching then, until you find them."

****

She woke slowly, a foul taste in her mouth, like metal and blood and cotton. She tried to swallow and realized she'd been gagged, and her heart started to race. She was cold and she felt the roughness of stone beneath her; her arms and feet were bound tightly, holding her body down in an uncomfortable spread eagled position. She forced her eyes open and squinted in the candle light that illuminated a small forest clearing. Standing next to her was a cloaked figure, as if he had been waiting for her to wake up. She struggled uselessly against the ropes that held her down.

"I'm sorry about this." A chillingly familiar voice said. She felt a wave of sheer fury that almost eclipsed the fear. "I've never killed a human before, and I didn't ever want to. But you have to understand that your death is necessary. They're getting too close. I'd rather it be that damn mixed blooded bitch tied there–she deserves it and you don't–but there's never a moment when she's alone. And something has to be done to throw them off, to make them think everything they know is wrong. Your death will do that."

He dropped the cloak to the earth and she looked away not wanting to see the naked flesh that had been concealed underneath. She tried not to lose herself to panic as he started speaking again in that same matter-of-fact voice.

"This won't be the real ritual, of course. It's the wrong time for that, you know that much already, and you aren't the right sort, but they have to think it's real, so I have to go through all the motions at least. Nothing personal. It's all for the greater good in the end and even though it isn't part of the ritual, your death will help the ultimate success of the cause."

She felt hot tears burning behind her eyes and ground her teeth down on the gag furiously.

****

He stood over the body for a long time after she died, feeling frustrated. This wasn't how it was supposed to be. He'd done exactly what he'd been told to do–done it even after he found out the book was gone forever and they knew almost everything now–but it didn't feel right. None of it felt right anymore, and it was all that damn half-blood bitch's fault. If only he could get her out of the way, he was sure it would all be good again…

Finally he shook his head. There was a lot to do yet before his work would be done and he couldn't afford to be distracted now.

Walters untied the body and lifted the corpse carefully, stepping out of the circle's protective wards. It would be a short walk to the waiting metal tub, which was already full of bleach, and he was thinking ahead of the perfect place to leave this one, when two shadows stepped out of the trees.

"Beautifully done," the first elf spoke as the other nodded.

He felt a burning rage and wondered, if he dropped the body could he reach his gun before they reached him? Sensing the direction of his thoughts the talkative elf raised a hand placatingly.

"Peace. We have the same ultimate goal, I think. We came here seeking the book you use for your ritual only to find that someone is already enacting material from the book to good effect."

"How do you know about the book?" he asked, grudgingly curious and willing to play for time.

"We knew about it 80 years ago, but thought all the copies had been destroyed then. Only recently did we learn that a copy might still exist, and that information led us here."

"Well you're too late," he said shifting the corpse slightly, "All the copies have been destroyed. I pieced what I know together from family lore and bits of material that were handed down from my grandfather. That dumb half-Elven bitch had the only copy left and she destroyed it."

"Did she?" the elf sounded disbelieving.

"Yeah, burned it before I had a chance to steal it–or before you could." He couldn't hide his anger over the wanton destruction of something that should have been his. Was supposed to have been his.

"Did she read it first?" the elf asked casually.

"It doesn't matter to me if she did or not. I needed that book. It should have been mine. My great-grandfather was the high priest of that coven and those were his teachings, his ideas. It was supposed to be mine." He fumed.

"Indeed." The elf said sounding bored, "We can do nothing to replace what has been destroyed but since we seek the same goal perhaps we can aid each other in different ways."

"And how can you help me?" he asked not trying to hide his scorn.

"We can aid you in completing these rituals. We may be able to lead those who seek you onto a false trail," the elf said smiling unpleasantly.

For the first time he stopped and considered what the strange elf was saying. He certainly wasn't getting any help from the others, just hard orders and expectations. "And what do you get out of this?"

The elf shrugged, his companion a silent shadow at his back, "If you succeed where your ancestor failed then we get the world back as it was before when we were allowed to do as we willed, without being controlled by weak Bright Court sycophants. If you fail we may still learn something of your methods which would be of use to us, since the book is lost. Of course we need a place here to operate out of; someplace we'd be safe from prying eyes."

He nodded, slowly. The idea of working with these elves was galling, but the help they offered might mean success instead of failure, and at this juncture he was feeling desperate to salvage all the effort he'd put in so far. He shifted the body again, feeling the dead weight pulling at his arms. "Nothing else? That's all you want?"

The elf smiled wolfishly, "If you could deliver the mixed blood girl to me, I would consider our agreement officially sealed."

His eyes narrowed, "That's almost impossible. She's always surrounded by Guards."

"With everything you have accomplished so far, I am certain you can find a way." The elf said, still smiling. "And you would achieve several goals with one stroke: the girl would be removed as an obstacle from your path, you would have your revenge on her, knowing what she would suffer with me, and it would distract and mislead those who track you."

The killer nodded thoughtfully. They wouldn't like it—he'd been told repeatedly to leave the girl alone, and none of them would ever agree to allying with elves for any reason. But he wouldn't technically be hurting the mixed blood himself, and he wanted the bitch to pay for destroying the book. And it was past time he had some help in getting things done. "Yeah, "Walters said slowly, "Maybe we can work out a deal."

Chapter 9 - Thursday

Allie woke up screaming and thrashing, the dream so real that at first her familiar bedroom and Jessilaen's warm body against hers as he tried to restrain her, seemed dreamlike. She screamed hysterically, wordlessly, totally disoriented by the sudden shift to full consciousness. Only Jess calling her name over and over, his concern palpable to her empathy, finally got through to her. Like a switch being flipped without warning her body suddenly relaxed as the last of the dream's echo left.

She realized that she was in a tangle of blankets at the end of her bed, Jessilaen lying mostly on top of her having tried to keep her from hurting herself as she flailed in her sleep. Her door was wide open, and all four of the extra Guard on patrol had rushed in, swords drawn, as well as Brynneth and Bleidd, crowding her tiny room uncomfortably. Under normal circumstances she would have been mortified to have everyone currently in the house standing in her room while she was in such an awkward position and without a stitch of clothes on, but at the moment she didn't care. She lay there, her heart racing, body shaking, trying to sort out actual reality from the dream.

Jess sensed her body relaxing and eased off of her slightly, "Allie?"

She looked at him, her eyes wide and still panicked, "Was that a dream or is this a dream?"

Brynneth moved quickly across the small space from the door, sheathing his sword as he moved, kneeling down next to her and resting his hand on her neck. She felt his gentle healing energy flowing into her, mitigating the effects of the huge amount of adrenaline and cortisone flooding her system. She took a deeper, slower breath as he nodded, "Good, slow breaths. You are safe now."

"What was that?" she asked still feeling disoriented.

The elves exchanged glances. "Have you ever had a vision before? Does the gift of Seeing run in your line?"

Allie shook her head, "No, and never. It was like a dream but not exactly. I mean it was more real than a dream but..." she trailed off. "I felt like someone was trying to pull me or call me to them."

She hadn't gotten the words out of her mouth when all the other elves moved, except Jess and Brynneth, taking up defensive positions throughout the room. Even Bleidd raised the house wards to their full extent, the magic surging up from the building's foundation to encase the old Victorian in the strongest possible shields. Her breath caught slightly as the rush of magic in the room pressed against her, "No, not like someone trying to force me somewhere. I'm explaining this badly."

She struggled up out of the tangle of blankets, heedless of her nakedness, and sat at the edge of the bed, feeling dizzy. Brynneth steadied her and she felt Jess's hand resting on her back.

"It was like–like someone I knew, someone familiar, reaching out and I wanted to go to them, they needed help, they were scared."

She felt her breath speeding up and Brynneth looked up alarmed. "But I couldn't reach them. But I saw... it was a ritual circle. That's why I couldn't get through, it was holding me back. And there was a person, tied down, and they were being hurt."

She turned and looked at Jess, who was looking at Brynneth. "I think I saw one of the murders," she said slowly, "How is that possible?"

All the elves looked uneasy; no one lowered any of the wards or relaxed their defensive stances. Jess answered her uncertainly, "I do not know. It sounds like a vision of some kind, but I have never seen anyone in a vision react so violently. You were sleeping peacefully and then, without warning, you convulsed and began screaming. I could not wake you."

She shook her head, still shivering from the after effects of whatever had just happened. "I don't understand this. There is no human magic I know of that works this way."

"I have seen many things in my years in the Borderlands, but nothing like this," Bleidd said quietly from near the door.

"It is not like any Elven magic I know of either," Brynneth said. "But there is someone at the outpost who knows more of such things than any of us here. Perhaps he can tell us what this is and whether it is a threat to you."

Allie felt her mouth go dry and turned to look at Jessilaen. "Do we have to go now?"

"No," he said shaking his head. "It will have to be arranged and only Zarethyn can do so. We will contact him and let him know of what has transpired here. You should rest."

She started to stand reflexively and he reached out for her looking concerned. Brynneth grabbed her before she could get to her feet, and she pulled back from him as well, his armor cold against her flesh. "No. No sleep." She shook her head emphatically. She was certain she would not be able to sleep or get any rest again. Possibly ever.

"Allie, you must rest." Jess insisted, and she looked at him miserably.

"Aliaine," Brynneth said gently, "I can help you. I can use a minor charm to ensure that you sleep without dreaming. And if the wards are kept up that should prevent any outside influences from effecting you."

She looked from Brynneth, to Bleidd, and finally at Jessilaen, before capitulating. With obvious reluctance she laid back down in the bed, pulling the covers up with the depressing certainty that she would never feel warm or safe again. Brynneth touched her forehead gently and she felt her entire body relaxing; her last conscious thought was to wonder how her roommates would get back in the house with the full wards up.

****

She slept the rest of the night dreamlessly, and despite her concerns the night before, when Jess woke her just after dawn she did feel better. The dream from the night before was still frighteningly real, more like a memory of an actual event than a dream and that worried her. But the elves seemed convinced that they could find answers about what had happened.

Part of her was worried about how deeply involved she was getting with the Guard–not just Jessilaen but the Elven Guard in general. She worried about how in debt she was to Brynneth for the times he had healed her and to the others for protecting her. It was a really bad idea to be in debt to any being of Fairy, whether that debt was intentional or not; she wasn't sure though if they were counting everything as part of their duty as Guards. She made a mental note as she dressed to ask Jess later. As if that wasn't enough to worry about, she was also concerned that whatever was going on with her was distracting everyone from focusing on catching the killer before he found his next victim.

At some point in the night Brynneth had left and Natarien had returned, so she found herself being escorted out to the Guards' cars by him and Jessilaen with the other squad remaining at the house to continue patrolling the property.

As she was led up to the dark green Guard vehicle she suddenly realized that she had never been inside one of the Guard cars before. The outside of the car was fairly non-descript in that way that unmarked police cruisers had, where they tried so hard not to stand out that anyone looking at it could guess it was a cop car. It was built for speed, and without any iron components it was much lighter than it looked, giving it an edge against other cars its size in acceleration. Allie had heard rumors that the Guard cars were a bitch to drive in windy weather or on ice because of the lack of weight and had always wondered if that was true; she suspected looking at the layers and layers of set spells coating the car that they probably used magic to compensate, making it a moot point.

Jess opened the rear door for her and she slid in, curious about the interior; he and Natarien sat in the front, separated from her by a thick Plexiglas wall. Allie was familiar enough with that from riding in one of the town's squad cars with Syndra that she didn't even think about it. The rear seat was soft—she ran her hands over it and decided it probably was real suede. A big step up from the Ashwood police cruisers' vinyl seats, but then, the human police didn't have magic to waste cleaning up the inevitable messes that happened in the back of squad cars. *Only elves*, Allie thought as the car drove east towards the Outpost, *could make police cars luxurious*.

The 20 minute drive passed in silence and Allie found herself growing more and more nervous with each passing mile. She had never been to the Elven Outpost before, nor did she entirely understand who she was going to see. What she did know was that this person must be very important indeed if it took the Guard Captain to arrange this meeting, and part of her couldn't believe that she was in the middle of all of this. Her stomach was in knots by the time the road broke free of the trees and the Outpost came into view. *This is what a medieval castle must have looked like* Allie thought, overawed despite herself. The sight also brought back unpleasant memories from her childhood, things that she'd nearly forgotten in the intervening years.

Crannuaine Outpost–known ubiquitously even among the local elves simply as the Outpost–was a huge stone building that rose 5 stories, rivaling many of the trees around it in height, and stretching nearly a thousand feet, the length of the clearing. The road curved to the right and divided; the main branch passed through a heavily armed gate, which she knew was the passage into the Fairy realm; beyond that gate was a parking lot for the tourists, although she'd never seen it, because cars were not allowed into the Fairy realm proper. People walked or rode fairy horses in the Elven lands, for the most part, because even the modified technology that allowed cars to work in the Borderlands tended to be difficult and hard to maintain in the fully magical atmosphere beyond the border. The other branch of the road ran parallel to the front of the building from right to left before disappearing into a tunnel in the stone edifice. The entire effect was grand and ancient, although the power lines running to the building and prominent satellite dish and antennae visible on one section of the roof did remind Allie that this was still at least partially mortal Earth. As far as she knew, true Fairy lacked all of the technology and other modern perks associated with Earth, although with the availability and strength of magical energy so much could be compensated for that one might never even realize it.

The car pulled up to the main entrance, a short staircase that led up to a large double door which reminded Allie strongly of the entrance to Ashwood's cathedral. A Guard in full armor, including helm, was standing at attention on either side of the doorway and Allie felt herself swallowing hard. Her nerves were a mess and feeling like she was about to walk into a situation that was way over her head wasn't helping. She wanted to close her eyes and be back to her regular life, heading to work in her regular book store, hanging out with her regular friends. When the car stopped Jessilaen got out and stepped back to open her door, *Well, maybe not back to my regular life entirely* she thought watching him.

Taking a deep breath she climbed out of the car and let him lead her up the stairs. Natarien drove the car on and she watched it disappear into the tunnel in the side of the building. Walking up the stairs she realized that while the stone steps were rough for traction, the rest of the stone, granite by the look, was polished smooth. It gave the walls of the building an oddly reflective look in the light. The door was massive, wooden, and with brass metal work that shone despite the exposure to the weather. As soon as she and Jess reached the landing at the top of the stairs the doors swung open and before she could second guess the wisdom of what she was doing she stepped in to Ashwood's Elven Outpost for the first time.

Allie had expected something fittingly archaic, but she was disappointed. Beyond the door there was a wide reception area with the sort of comfortable seating you'd expect at a doctor's office. At the back of the room was a long counter with three windows and three waiting receptionists; behind them along the back wall she could see a cork board plastered with notices, desks with computers, and a door. In the waiting area there were several people, human tourists by the look of them, sitting in the chairs, probably waiting for passports to be cleared, and a few others that were obviously Fey waiting for various appointments. As they walked in a phone rang and one of the receptionists answered it cheerfully. *This is surreal,* Allie thought, *it's just like the DMV on mortal Earth.*

Jess led her to the left through a door that required a magic passcode to enter; she tried to ignore the strange looks and whispers from some of the people in the waiting room. *They probably think I've been arrested,* she thought, finding he idea oddly amusing. *I think my life would be simpler if that was the case actually.* The hallway stretched back as far as she could see, with doors intermittently along the right hand side. She decided that the wall on the left was probably the outer wall of the structure. They passed a dozen doors and then finally came to one that Jess opened. Allie realized that she would be hopelessly lost in this place very soon and that thought did not help her relax. The new door opened to another large room, this one sectioned off by groups of desks in clusters, each with computers, phones and large white boards. After a moment she realized it reminded her strongly of her visit with Syndra to Ashwood's police department; this must be the Elven Guard equivalent of a squad room then.

In one corner a Brownie was cheerfully sweeping the hardwood floor. He didn't look up as they entered, but Allie couldn't help staring briefly since she'd never actually seen a Brownie before. He was a walnut brown color all over, skin, hair, and clothes, and he had a small stub nose, which she knew meant he was a Highland Brownie and would be missing his fingers and toes from the first knuckle up. There was no one else in the room.

Jess led her back to another door, and she repressed a slightly hysterical giggle. She had no idea where they were going, but there either wasn't a direct way to get there or he was looking for someone else first. The next room proved to be Zarethyn's office, a cheerfully decorated, brightly lit place that was nothing at all like what she'd expected. The Guard Captain himself was sitting behind his desk filling out paperwork. He looked up as they entered and smiled.

"Good morning, Aliaine. Is this your first visit to the Outpost?"

Damn, of course we're speaking Elvish, she thought, smiling pleasantly.

"Yes, it's an amazing place."

"Indeed it is. When there's more time you will have to take the full tour," he said and she wondered if there was an actual tour, with a tour guide, or if he was just trying to use a human colloquialism. She fought the urge to giggle again as he went on.

"Unfortunately we have a tight schedule this morning and we're expected in the reception hall. As you can imagine, it was very difficult to arrange this and we must adhere to the time table. I'm sure you understand."

Oh my Gods, do they have a gift shop? Trying not to let any of her thoughts show she said, "Of course I understand."

Jess wrapped his arm around her shoulder, a strong comforting presence and guided her out of the room and through another maze of halls and doors. At this point Allie wasn't even paying attention to where they were going. It wasn't like she could run for it anyway.

The reception hall turned out to be a long rectangular room with a crystal chandelier and tapestries on all the walls depicting significant events from Queen Naesseryia's life. The floor was hardwood, polished until it glowed and there were no electric lights here, everything was lit by ambient magic. It was so much more like what she'd expected from the outside that Allie actually found herself relaxing a little.

Zarethyn led her forward to where a strange elf was standing at the far end of the room, beneath a tapestry showing the Queen's coronation. The Queen's images showed her to be willowy, with long pale blonde hair held back by a delicate crown. The strange elf was also tall and blonde, probably from the same clan, Allie guessed, and he was dressed well in dark green silk. Allie guessed that this elf and the Queen were likely related, probably more closely than the loose ties Zarethyn and Jessilaen had to her. Zarethyn introduced her simply and Allie curtsied, an elaborate high Court move that she was surprised she even remembered how to do properly. She shoved aside the thought that it was ridiculous to be doing high Court anything in jeans and a sweater and faced the other elf. He was old, far older than any elf she had ever seen. His age didn't show the way human age would; he looked like any other elf at first glance but he radiated Power in a palpable way that was more than a little bit frightening to someone like Allie, who had been raised to reflexively fear and mistrust powerful people.

Despite her best efforts not to show her feelings, or perhaps because he was very skilled at reading people, the old elf, who had been introduced as Tharien, seemed to sense her fear and he spoke gently, "Peace to you child, you are safe here."

Allie bowed her head, overwhelmed and speechless. He reached out and rested one hand on her hair, as if it had been planned that way, and she could feel his energy swirling around and through her. It was a bizarre feeling and she wasn't entirely sure she liked it. After what seemed to her like a very long time he finally lifted his hand again, and a moment later she looked up. He was staring above her head, thoughtfully. When he finally spoke he still sounded meditative.

"You asked me to come and see this child Captain, to find out if she has any gift for Seeing that might explain her unusual dream. She has no such gift, of that I am certain, but I am glad you called me here and glad I came, for I rarely see such a gift as this."

Allie turned her head slightly to give Jess an uncertain look, although she didn't dare speak or move further than that. It was enough for him to come up behind her and embrace her anyway, and to her surprise Zarethyn also stepped up and placed a reassuring hand on her shoulder.

"Do not fear, child," Tharien said, smiling slightly. Allie did not feel reassured.

"I am sorry if I am frightening you," the old elf said gently to Allie, who was feeling very much like a particularly interesting bug under a microscope "You know that some people are gifted with certain abilities, beyond simply being able to use magic?" Allie nodded and he continued.

"You are an empath, which means you have the ability to read the emotions of people around you and of places. In time you may learn to harness this ability to use emotional energy to fuel your magic."

Allie was thinking furiously. There were no empaths in the Dark Court because they usually burned out or self-destructed very early, so her knowledge of empathy as a magical ability among elves was very limited. Her grandmother had not wanted to train Allie's ability since Allie had been so uncomfortable with it, so she had never learned to do more than shield out the emotions of others. The idea of using emotions as a magical power source was strange, but she was familiar with the idea of emotional energy as a type of food; many Dark Court beings lived on negative emotions, consuming the emotional energy of fear, anger, or pain the way humans ate a hamburger. It wasn't a particularly happy train of thought. As she was thinking Zarethyn had asked if her ancestry was a factor and the old elf was answering no. Allie tried to carefully frame her own question, "Pardon, may I ask something?"

Tharien smiled, "Of course."

"I'm... unsure exactly what this means. I can feel what other people are feeling, that part I understand, because empathy is a common gift among humans, but I don't understand the other part or how that relates to– whatever that thing last night was," she tried to choose her words carefully.

He seemed genuinely surprised, "Empathy is common among humans? Truly?"

It was Allie's turn to be surprised, "Well, yes. Many humans have some degree of empathy. I've dealt with it since I was small but I mostly only know how to block other people's feelings. I've never heard of anyone using empathy for anything except to read other people's emotional states."

Tharien, nodded thoughtfully." Fascinating. Your gift then must come from the human side of your ancestry. It is a very uncommon gift among elves, and noteworthy because it allows one to see the true feelings behind the polite surface. It is unwise though not to learn how to control your power; you may be more open to the influence of those around you than you realize. With practice you could learn, I believe, to track emotions like a scent on the wind. More than that though, you will be able to use the energy you sense, as if it were any other magical energy. The other that I knew with this ability, once he had mastered it, was something to be seen. As to your dream, it likely was not a dream but either an emotional echo of the event, if you have a strong enough connection to the place it occurred in, or someone you are connected to emotionally is involved. Your gift allows you to form strong bonds with those you care about and such a connection would allow for communication, particularly of emotions, although since you are entirely untrained it is impossible to know who you may have connected to or for you to control it. It would be wise to seek training to avoid being unduly influenced by others."

Allie felt her mind reeling. It was unnerving to look back at your life and wonder how much of it had been influenced by other people. Was that why she had been so upset after Aeyliss died? That night when she awoke she had been overwhelmed by despair and grief; was that her own feeling or was that the massed feelings of the Guard who had been all over the property investigating their comrade's death? She felt her skin crawling at the thought that she was so open to outside forces and Jess tightened his hold on her. That sent her mind in another direction that was just as depressing. And yet she couldn't help but feel better, more grounded, stronger as he supported her. It was unsettling to suddenly be aware of how much she'd come to depend on his presence in such an extremely short time. She spoke again, just as carefully as before, "Sometimes I have felt like I am drawing strength from… people I care about. As if their emotions are… keeping me going when I don't think I can go further."

He nodded thoughtfully, "This I have not seen before. It could be a human aspect of the gift, but I believe it more likely that it is an aspect of using emotions as magical energy. It is possible that you can use emotions also as personal energy."

Allie swore to herself. Repeatedly. That sort of thing was dangerous territory indeed, and she was going to have to learn how to better shield herself as quickly as possible, to prevent herself from accidently doing it. So far there was no indication that her use of Jess's energy, minor and unintentional as it had been, affected him in any way, but she wasn't willing to take that chance. Struggling to keep her face impassive, she said "I have a lot to think about"

"You have much to do, I think, and there is still great danger around you. If ever you wish to further discuss this I will gladly tell you all I can," the old elf smiled again and Allie nodded trying to smile back.

Jessilaen and Zarethyn had stepped back as well and both bowed deeply; taking the cue, Allie curtseyed again, praying this meant an end to the meeting. She felt like her head was going to burst and she couldn't think straight. The high ranking elf nodded slightly, and Jess guided Allie back and out of the room. As soon as they reached the hallway and the door closed she leaned against the nearest wall and covered her face with both hands.

The Elven Captain, touched her shoulder lightly, "Why are you distraught Aliaine? That went very well."

"Yes," Jess agreed, "It may be a challenge to master such an unusual ability but it will be a powerful skill."

He stopped as she dropped her hands and gave him a long look. "I don't like the idea of using other people's emotions like some sort of personal battery," she said gritting her teeth.

He looked exasperated, "You have no reason to see it that way. Does breathing the air in this room take anything substantial away from anyone? You have a gift to use what others are not even aware of to your own advantage. You hurt no one in doing so, and it increases your own power. It is an advantage that should be made the most of."

"And what if it does take something away from others? What if hurts them?" she said, unable to not say what she was thinking.

"You do me no harm when you draw on my emotions for your strength," he said gently. "I am absolutely certain of this." She shook her head trying to look away, but he held her chin and met her eyes with his. "Allie, I am over 700 years old. I know my own energy and my own self. Trust me when I say this—you have never taken anything from me that I noticed or missed. If my feelings for you help in any way, then you are more than welcome to them."

"And what if," she said flatly, "what you feel for me is because I created some sort of connection with you?"

"If anyone needs to worry about that Allie, it should be I," he replied, equally grave. "Tharien said nothing about you being able to influence or control what others were feeling, only that you are sensitive to the emotions of those around you—perhaps what you feel for me is entirely based on the projection of my own feelings about you."

She bit her lip, "That doesn't sound right."

"Try to project what you are feeling now, if not to me then to Zarethyn," Jess said. His brother nodded encouragingly, obviously curious. She took a deep breath and focused on sending out what she was feeling, which was mostly fear. After a moment both elves shook their heads slightly. She frowned and without thinking, tried to open up to them, and since she wasn't sure what she was doing, she simply lowered all of her personal shields. The next thing she knew she was flat on her back on the floor with their worried faces filling her field of vision. Jess was saying, "Fetch a healer."

"No," she mumbled still dizzy, "No, I just did something stupid. Give me a minute."

She struggled to sit, both elves kneeling to support her; she could feel worry radiating from them. She heard someone walking at the other end of the hall and sighed, feeling a surge of concern and interest from the stranger. She brought her personal shields up as fully as she could and the outside emotions disappeared.

"What happened?" Zarethyn asked, when it was clear she had recovered a bit.

"I'm an idiot," Allie said ruefully. "I couldn't project to either of you so I thought I'd try reading you, but I wasn't thinking of where we were or to extend my shields out, or anything else remotely intelligent. So I just dropped all my shielding which I probably haven't done since I was taught to shield in the first place. I hadn't realized–I must have subconsciously been blocking all the external emotions to a point where I wasn't letting myself acknowledge any of it at all. Sometimes things leak through, if a person is close to me or touching me, and I guess I just started to think of that as the limit of my range, which it really isn't. So then I just dropped all my personal shields and it was like–it was like–total sensory overload."

The two elves looked at each other, and then Zarethyn asked, "What is the limit of your range when you are unshielded?"

"I don't know, but for a second there I think I felt the whole Outpost." She shuddered slightly at the thought. Zarethyn's eyes went wide.

Jess reached out and stroked her hair, "Are you sure you are well enough now?"

"Less dizzy, yeah. This is going to take a long time to get the hang of, I think," she said, climbing to her feet with their help. As soon as she touched Jess's hand she felt his emotions flooding back in.

Crap. she thought, worried. *That's not right, with my shields fully up at most it should be a vague feeling. What the hell did I just do to myself?*

"Don't push yourself," Jess said, concerned. Allie decided that she shouldn't tell them about her problems shielding now. They were freaking out enough and it was obvious that empathy was something they had no real understanding of, so it wasn't like they could offer any help anyway.

"I have to. We have to find this killer and I can't be a distraction to you-"she stopped, her breath catching. "Come on, we need to get back to the house, now."

"What is it?" Zarethyn said alarmed by her sudden urgency.

"I got totally sidetracked feeling guilty about..." she glanced at Jessilaen. "And then zapping myself. Anyway, I wasn't thinking–he said the dream wasn't a dream. I was picking up on something, the emotion from the victim. It can't be the place, because I've never seen that pace before or I would have recognized it. I felt like the person was calling me, pulling me to them, so it must be the person. Someone I have an emotional connection to, like he said."

Zarethyn looked grim, "Someone else has been killed."

Allie shuddered slightly. "I'm afraid so. But I have no idea who. I couldn't see them clearly–I couldn't even tell you if it was a man or a woman. It was a clearing in the woods, boulder shaped, sort of like an altar–the person was tied to it, and there was someone else there, hurting them– and candles around the perimeter, marking the boundary of a ritual circle. The circle was blocking me I think…I don't know. I couldn't reach them, and they kept pulling at me."

"Stop, Allie. Enough," Jess said forcefully. "Don't put yourself back there again. We will go as swiftly as we may back to your home and start by checking to see that all your housemates are safe. Then we can work out from there, until we find whoever this may have been."

She took a deep breath, feeling her heart racing. Zarethyn looked thoughtful, "It may not even be someone you knew personally. You have devoted yourself entirely to reading the grimoire and memorizing its contents over the last few days. Perhaps that created an emotional connection to the ritual itself."

"Is that possible?" she asked, finding the idea comforting and unnerving at the same time.

"I do not know, but it seems no more or less likely than anything else at this point," he replied.

"Come on my love; let us go" Jess said, urging her down the hall, "The sooner we know what is going on the sooner you will have some answers."

"I just hope my answers help your investigation," Allie said, realizing that for the first time being called "my love" didn't make her stomach twist.

****

Zarethyn accompanied them back to the house, as did Brynneth, meaning that Allie was crammed in the back seat with two of the Guard. She hadn't looked forward to dealing with the physical proximity of anyone else. Since dropping all her shields and knocking herself silly she kept getting ghostly impressions from anyone within a few feet of herself, no matter how much energy she put into her shields. However sitting between Jessilaen and Brynneth, with both of them radiating concern, was actually comforting. She tried hard to block them out at first but eventually gave up when it became clear that it was futile.

Once she stopped fighting it she found their emotions were indeed helping her feel more refreshed, and while she couldn't stop finding that disturbingly similar to the Dark Court beings that fed on emotions, she also couldn't deny that she was obviously not doing them any harm or even noticeably effecting them in any way. Unlike the beings she knew of from her childhood who fed off of emotional energy and drained their victims in the process she seemed to be absorbing their emotions like a plant taking in sunlight, taking what was there without diminishing it.

As they came around the curve in the road she immediately knew bad news was waiting. A marked police car was parked in front of the house along with the unmarked car that she'd gotten used to Riordan and Walters driving. She looked away, resting her head on Jess's shoulder, trying to grasp the last moment before she had to deal with whatever this was, but all the Guard were assuming the worst and the emotional tone from both Brynneth and Jess had turned tense and grim. She fought to get her shields back up as fully as possible, and found it easier now that her energy level was better. After a moment she managed to block both of them almost entirely.

I am really going to have to think about how much I'm being influenced by other people's emotions, she thought, trying to distract herself. *Up until now I was operating blind, just letting myself go with the flow, but now that I know I can't keep letting myself act because someone else feels a certain way.*

The car stopped at the end of the line of cars and Allie had no choice but to get out when the Guard did. She felt a growing sense of dread as she crossed the lawn towards the house, following the Guard who were walking in formation. She was certain the official approach was to prepare for whatever they were about to learn. They walked up the steps to the front door and she felt a rising sense of panic. The last time she'd felt this way was the day she'd returned from work to find the police and ambulance here after her grandmother had collapsed. That thought only increased the feeling of foreboding.

They walked in the door and Allie could hear Bleidd yelling, his voice furious.

"I had nothing to do with any of these murders and certainly not…" he cut off abruptly as soon as he saw the Guard.

When they walked into the living room she saw the two Detectives standing near the windows, Liz sitting on the couch clutching a tissue, Bleidd in front of the fireplace, and Jason sitting on the loveseat, his eyes red-rimmed. She knew then, and the moment she knew her reconstructed shields collapsed and she felt all the outside grief rushing through her. She felt her breath catch, her head dropped, and for an instant everything went gray; she thought she might pass out. And then nothing. Emotional flat line.

She looked back up to see Jess looking at her with real concern. He and Brynneth both broke ranks and came over to stand on either side of her; Jess pulled her in to his chest as if he were shielding her from a blow, but she felt numb. She stood stiffly in his arms, her mind blank. Brynneth reached out, his hand gentle against her neck, and she noted the healing energy in a detached way.

"Is she going to pass out?" Liz asked, sniffling.

"I'm sorry, Ms. McCarthy." Detective Riordan sounded like he meant it. "I hate this part of the job. Officer Lyons–Syndra–was found dead this morning. It looks like our killer."

She felt herself nodding. The Detective frowned, slightly "I know how upsetting this must be for you. All of you, of course, but you were close friends with her."

Allie nodded again, her eyes focusing on the line of cars out the window. Walters spoke suddenly. "You should know they found her body in the parking lot of your store. I'm sorry. She was a good Officer"

Of course they did, the killer wanted to make sure I knew it was supposed to be me, and he only took her because he had to, Allie thought numbly.

Riordan shifted uncomfortably. "It looks like we need to rethink the direction we were going in with this. We have a witness that saw two people dumping the body, early this morning–Rick and I got the call and got there within 20 minutes. She hadn't been dead for very long-less than 12 hours."

Liz got up abruptly, and walked over to Jason, grabbing his hand and pulling him up with her. "We don't need to hear this. And I don't want to know. She shouldn't hear it either. It's bad enough we just lost our friend, we don't need the gory details."

"She's been helping on the case," Walters said, trying to sound reasonable, "I'm sure it's hard to hear but if we're going the wrong way with what we've been thinking we need to get on a new track really quick now. This guy's killed 2 cops, counting that Elven Guard, not to mention 4 girls, and if we still need her help she's going to have to tough it out."

Liz looked furious, but when Allie didn't move, she gave up and dragged Jason out of the room. Allie heard their footsteps going up the stairs and a door slamming. *Is this still the dream? Maybe I'm still sleeping,* she thought. Jess spoke into her hair, "Can you listen to this? Or do you need a moment to grieve your friend?"

His voice washed over her like water, and she did not respond. He looked sharply at Brynneth who was frowning. Walters spoke again "We don't have time for grief right now."

"You are being cruel Detective," Jessilaen said.

"And you're thinking with your…"

"Rick!" Riordan cut him off quickly, before turning back to the elves placatingly. "We're all upset right now and emotions are running high. But we need to get this figured out before this gets any more out of control. If this is a group instead of an individual, that makes a big difference for this investigation."

"You are certain her death was caused by the same killer?" Zarethyn asked. "The time is wrong and Officer Lyons doesn't fit the victim profile."

"Maybe you were all wrong–or she was–about the timing and the victims being not human. They all looked pretty damn human to us." Walters said, regaining some of his normal belligerence.

"Same M.O." Riordan said wincing slightly before anyone could respond to Walters. "She was raped and cut up, her throat slit, then…"

Allie realized she was going to throw up and moved with a speed that only those desperate to reach a bathroom can have, dodging out of Jess's loose hold and away from Brynneth's hand. She shot down the hall, ignoring the shouts behind her, and skidded into the dark bathroom, managing to slide across the tile on her knees and reach the toilet just as her stomach reversed itself. She knelt there, retching long after there was nothing left to throw up.

Jess came in and crouched behind her, holding her hair and rubbing her back, and in desperation she extended her shields out around him, letting his emotions fill her space. It helped, enough that she could stop throwing up and catch her breath as the toilet flushed.

Vaguely she heard raised voices arguing somewhere else, but she didn't care. She felt broken and lost, and she could feel her grief like a physical thing, threatening to consume her. She clenched her jaw tightly, feeling a keening wail rising up in her throat and afraid if she started she'd never stop. Jess's voice finally penetrated her overwhelming reaction, riding on the current of his love and worry.

"I am so sorry, my love, my heart, what can I do to help you? Tell me, talk to me…"

She turned, swallowing hard, "Water. Please."

He did not move and she was surprised when a hand offered a small paper cup of water. She looked at it for a moment, not comprehending and then recognized the cup as one of the disposable ones that were kept stacked on the bathroom counter, and a moment later that the hand belonged to Brynneth. She took the cup with shaking hands and drank, ignoring the burning in her throat. As soon as she was finished she collapsed back against Jess again, feeling the keening in her chest.

Jessilaen looked helplessly at Brynneth, "I do not understand this."

"I saw her…being tortured…"Allie forced the words out, swallowing hard, "she was trying…to reach me…I couldn't…but I saw…in the dream…I *saw* it…"

Jess stroked her hair, "Breath Allie, just breath."

"I feel like…I'm going…to start…screaming…and never stop," she gasped.

Brynneth also reached out then, so that she was pressed between the two Guards, and she could feel his concern along with Jess's. She latched onto the emotion as another source to help ground her, and was able to calm down slightly.

"That's better. I feel a little less like I'm coming apart at the seams now."

"You're picking up on our emotions?" Jess guessed.

Allie nodded then admitted, "I can't shield for crap. Whatever I did at the Outpost, when I dropped my shields and fried myself, I really screwed something up. I can't keep my shields up and I keep getting all kinds of outside stuff filtering in."

She swallowed hard, not sure if the water was going to stay down, "I knew on some level it was her, I think, but I didn't want it to be. When we came in and I realized, and it was like in that moment, I lost all my shields again and then everyone else's grief went right through me and everything went numb. And then Riordan was talking about what happened and I suddenly realized that was what I saw and I just snapped." She swallowed hard again "And then I couldn't get my shielding back up anywhere near enough to block things and it was all just a swirling mass of horrible feelings. You both being here, touching me, I can feel your emotions and it's soothing. I feel much more grounded."

"Jessilaen you said something similar to this happened before, after Aeyliss's body was found." Brynneth said.

"Yes," Jess said, resting his cheek on the top of her head, "she was upset to the point of despair then, but nothing nearly as extreme as this."

Brynneth contemplated the idea for a moment. "I do not know what you did to yourself by dropping all your shielding at the Outpost; it may be that you temporarily burnt out your own defenses or weakened your ability to protect yourself. Or you may have been blocking your own ability on an unconscious level until now and being forced to acknowledge it called it to the fore."

He spoke directly to Jessilaen. "It seems that she may be very open to outside emotional influences when she is sleeping and also when she is in an open emotional state.

When she is conscious and in control she seems to keep her shields up at a higher level that blocks out both the good and the bad. The last time you said she reached out to you and afterwards she was able to block the emotions of the other Guard and separate herself from the despair that had seized her?"

"Yes," Jess agreed.

"And Tharien said she can use emotional energy… interesting." Brynneth nodded to himself. "It may be then that she uses the positive emotional energy to rebalance from or recharge from extreme emotional distress."

"Great, except that it looks like negative emotional energy knocks me flat on my butt. That's a pretty huge problem, isn't it?" Allie asked looking at Brynneth.

"Only as long as you are fighting against the energy of those emotions, or allowing them to overwhelm you." He said gently.

"You think I can change how I react to it?" Allie found it easier to focus on discussing her struggle with negative emotions than to remember why the negative emotions were there at all.

"I believe you find comfort in emotions that are more pleasant and you reject or fight against those that you consider frightening," he said.

She nodded, "You may be right, but it's not something I think about. It's like a reflex."

"Even reflexes can be changed, with effort."

She took several deep breathes, focusing on grounding and centering. It was a children's exercise, something her mother had drilled into her as far back as she could remember, but one of those things that it was easy to get lazy with. Eventually she felt more balanced and carefully brought her shields back up; they still felt different than they had been before she'd dropped them at the Outpost, but they did feel more solid. Even with both elves in physical contact with her she was able to block them out, and that was progress of a sort. "Okay, we need to get back out there, before Detective Walters decides we're in here having a ménage à trois."

Both elves looked blank at the unfamiliar term, which seemed ironic to her, and Allie rolled her eyes.

"Never mind, we just need to get back out there."

"You should rest," Jess said, as she struggled awkwardly to her feet. "There is nothing to accomplish if you push yourself to collapse."

"Honestly I don't even know how I can help with anything at this point. They don't think what I've been saying so far is right and I burned the only evidence we had to support what I'm saying-"

"Why would they question your word?" Jess said, genuinely puzzled.

"Human law isn't like Elven law. Human's lie, outright, and the court system is... really complicated. Sometimes guilty people are freed because the evidence isn't strong enough, or because the jury believes the lie instead of the truth." She tried to explain.

"That is madness. How can any system function in such a way?" Brynneth scoffed.

"In Fairy no one lies, so the truth is a matter of finding the right people and asking the right questions. On Earth it's about finding evidence that can't be easily disputed. Magical evidence is a really difficult thing and some courts still don't accept it. The cops don't want to rely on me and have it go to court–if it's a human–and see their whole case get thrown out. They want concrete evidence. The book would have been that." She winced, "I imagine that they are pretty pissed with me for destroying it."

"Then why go back in there?" Jess asked

"Because Syndra was my best friend," she said, feeling tears burning behind her eyes, "and I am going to help catch this guy if I can."

Both elves nodded, and to her surprise Brynneth rested a hand on her shoulder, squeezing briefly, "I believe that you will, and anything I can do to aid you I shall. Do not hesitate to ask. I will not allow my niece's killer to escape."

Allie felt her eyes getting wide, "I'm sorry, I didn't realize Aeyliss was your niece."

"Indeed. My youngest sister's daughter. I would do much to see her killer brought to justice."

"I will do everything I can." Allie said seriously.

The group reemerged into the living room to find the two human police and the two Elven Guard squared off, arguing over how to proceed. Bleidd was nowhere to be seen, and Allie assumed, like Liz and Jason, he'd had enough of the details and left.

"That's not how investigations work," Walters was saying, his face red.

"What he means," Riordan added, clearly trying to play diplomat, "is that we can't just go on intuition and guesses when we have evidence that points the other way. We have witnesses who described two people dumping the body, who look a lot like the two who attacked Ms. McCarthy-"

"How is that possible?" Allie blurted out, without thinking. Everyone turned and looked at her with expressions ranging from concern to disdain.

"I mean, I couldn't give you a description of them, and I thought the video wasn't clear, how could you know the suspects are the same?"

"Same general height, same cloaks–and that reminds me, if you could get us the video from your store for last night we can probably see them on the parking lot camera," Riordan said.

Walters, with an effort to speak calmly, continued, "We need to accept that we were going in the wrong direction with this. This guy, or group, isn't going to be caught with mumbo-jumbo magic. We'll solve this case with old fashioned police work."

Now that Allie was back, the elves were watching to see how this would play out and trusting her and synchronicity to carry the argument. Allie was shaking her head, certain to her core that they had been close to the killer already. "This isn't right. It's misdirection. Why kill Syn at all when he could have picked any victim?"

"Maybe your involvement is pissing the killer off," Walters said coldly, "Maybe it was the two who beat you up in your store and they found out you burned the book they wanted and so they killed your best friend in retaliation."

Allie felt like she'd been punched in the gut, and she struggled not to start crying, knowing that tears would be a sign of surrender. "Maybe you're right about her dying because of me," she forced each word out. "Maybe it's my fault she's dead, because it should have been me. But that just proves *I'm* right. I wouldn't be a threat to the killer if I wasn't."

Walters gave her a look of grudging admiration, but he wouldn't give in, "Or maybe it was a message to me and Jim to try to push us off the case or warn us. She was your friend, but this isn't all about you, no matter what the elves think. Maybe killing a cop was a message to us."

Allie decided to press her luck, "Did you have any success with the list she gave you?"

Riordan looked at Walters, who shook his head. "So far it's a dead end. But we'll keep working on it."

Allie had a sudden inspiration. "What if I could find the crime scene? Would that give you something for a traditional investigation?"

"That's impossible," Walters dismissed the idea immediately.

All the elves looked at her intently. Riordan hesitated before asking "How?"

"I think I saw the place in a, kind of like a dream. I think, maybe, I have enough of a connection to it from that to find it," she said, trying to sound more confident than she felt. Actually she was hoping that she could use her connection to Syn and the experience of her friend's death to follow the emotion back like Tharien had said. She just had to figure out how to do it now instead of years from now.

"Can you do this?" Zarethyn asked.

"I'm not positive I can. But I can try," she answered honestly.

Walters was shaking his head, "We're relying too much on you already. You shouldn't even be part of this– you aren't a cop and your expert advice hasn't gotten us anywhere."

"Detective, Aliaine has been essential to our progress to this point." Zarethyn said flatly.

"Oh I'm sure she's been essential to you," Walters sneered, giving Allie a pointed look. "But I don't see you getting anything substantial done except hanging around here."

"Don't insult us Detective," the Elven Captain said, his tone dangerous.

"I just don't see her doing anything but being a complication and distraction. And making herself seem important when she shouldn't be. Now she's obviously doing a lot more for you than for us…"

"Rick, that's enough" Riordan said, trying unsuccessfully to shut the other man up.

"…and maybe she's a great lay, but you're not focused."

Walters tried to keep going but he'd pushed the elves too far. Not, Allie thought, by insulting her or even implying they were getting side benefits, but by implying they were derelict in their duty. Elves might be very sensual by nature and have different priorities than humans, but they took duty and obligation very seriously in their own way. Walters was yelling, all the elves had stepped towards him, also speaking; an intimidating site in their armor. Riordan was trying to stay between them, hands up. She couldn't hear what he was saying but she was sure it was an attempt to calm things down. Finally he grabbed his partner's arm and more or less pushed him out the door. Luckily for both of them the elves stood their ground.

She didn't need empathy to feel the tension in the air, and she realized that the task force falling apart like this could only benefit the killer–and maybe that, ultimately was the point of killing Syndra in particular. She spoke into the wake left by the human police, "This is bad."

The elves turned and looked at her, and she shook her head. Zarethyn was clearly still piqued, "We will not tolerate being spoken to that way. That detective oversteps himself."

"That detective is a bigot," Allie said, feeling tired, "but divisions now aren't going to help us."

"We do not need them." Natarien said curtly before turning to his Captain. "I will go and observe the uniformed officers."

Allie disagreed, but instead of arguing said, "What officers?"

"There are uniformed officers in Officer Lyons' room, checking for any evidence that might relate to her death." Zarethyn said, more kindly. Allie felt herself automatically flinch at the idea of strangers going through Syndra's things, and Jess came over to stand with her, pulling her against his chest as he had when they'd first heard the news. This time though she allowed herself to be embraced, wrapping her own arms around him and resting her head against his chest. The sound of his heartbeat, even through the armor, was reassuring on a visceral level and she was suddenly glad that the Elven Guard were there and that they were what they were. It was a disturbing feeling though, for someone who had always been wary of what the Guard represented and who was determined not to get pulled into Elven culture. She realized that in the last week her life had changed so radically that she almost didn't recognize it.

"If I can find the site of the murders, I need to. That will help give the police the evidence they want, and it'll give you a place to start hunting for the killer." Allie said.

"I'm afraid we don't need to look for him," Jess said gravely. "I believe he is stalking you. If we protect you he will come to us."

"Or he'll just keep killing everyone I care about, until I wish I was dead," she said. Jess tensed, and she swallowed hard, fighting tears. "No, I need to start fighting back, and this is the only way I know how."

Zarethyn nodded. "How can we help?"

****

They had been driving around for hours already, down all the main roads and side roads of the town, working their way out into the old farm lands at the outskirts. Allie sat in the back seat of one of the Guard vehicles, with her eyes closed trying to focus on the energy of the dream-vision and Syndra, without getting overwhelmed by her own emotions. It was a tedious process, but they were making progress.

They had tried starting at the store, which had also given her time to grab the surveillance video the police wanted and stick up a rough sign on the door apologizing to her customers for the shutdown. After getting that done she'd been unable to get any kind of emotional feel from the area, which seemed very odd to her. Frustrated she had suggested they drop off the video at the police station and afterwards Jess had come up with the idea of driving around letting her act like an antennae trying to tune in on the energy. At first it had seemed equally futile but to her surprise as they drove she realized that by focusing on where she felt uncomfortable she could slowly feel her way towards what they were looking for. It was a slow method, but the closer they eventually got to the site the stronger the discomfort grew, until she was sure she could actually feel a tingle of the pain and fear she remembered from the dream.

When she told them to take a left onto one of the old farm roads she knew they were nearly there. Her stomach knotted and she felt her fists clenching, "Slow down, we're almost there."

The car slowed and she felt the energy surge, along with something else, something she couldn't quite describe.

"Stop."

"Here?" Natarien asked, uncertainly, "There is nothing but empty fields."

"I know, pull the car over and park." Allie said, then added, "Please."

As soon as the car rolled to a stop she was jumping out, leaving the two Elven Guard to catch up. She stood for a moment getting her bearings; there was nothing in sight but old wooden fencing running along the road, and long stretches of empty fields. She hopped the fence and landed easily in the grass on the other side.

This field was being reclaimed by the woods now, but looked like it had still been in use within the last few decades. The grass was high and heavy bushes were everywhere but the largest trees were young birch, with a few saplings of oak and maple mixed in.

She began making her way into the brush at a slight angle to the road only to have Jess grab her wrist and force her to stop. She was going to complain until she realized both of the armored Guard had their swords drawn. When he spoke, Jess's voice was low, "We can feel something here as well, Allie. You have done enough in leading us this far; let us call for reinforcements now and fall back until they arrive."

She wanted desperately to argue– she could feel the emotional trail she had been following pulling her forward into the tree line across the field–but one look at the odd, disturbed look on both the elves' faces convinced her not to argue. "Okay. If that's what you think is best."

Jess looked relieved and she realized he had expected her to argue. *You have no idea how much I want to argue,* she thought, *but one or the other of you would probably just pick me up and carry me back to the car anyway. So I'll behave.*

Feeling like she was failing somehow, she turned and went back to the road. All three retreated to the car, where Jess used his Guard-issued cell phone to call the Outpost, and then at Allie's urging the human detectives as well. *I really should get a cell phone,* she thought idly as they waited for everyone else to arrive, *but I'd probably lose it in the first day. Or break it.*

The Elven contingent showed up first, and to her extreme annoyance Jessilaen made her sit in the car, while he got out to talk with Zarethyn and the others. She counted 5 cars, which meant that at least they were taking her seriously. Now if only the human police could be as accommodating.

Will you listen to yourself, Allie, she thought suddenly embarrassed. *What has gotten into me? Before all this started I didn't think there was anything special or important about me at all, and now I'm sitting here feeling resentful that I'm not right in the middle of the action. I get one boyfriend and someone calls me an expert in something and all of a sudden I have delusions of grandeur.* It was a humbling thought and she settled down into her seat trying to get some perspective.

This should be it. I found their crime scene; my part in this is done now. What else can I do, really? I gave them the ritual, the information from the book, now this. Maybe I can get back to my real life now. Gods know if I don't get the store re-opened soon I'm screwed financially.

She was starting to nod off with Natarien sitting still as statue in the front seat when the car door opened. She shook herself out of her doze and looked over to see Riordan crouching next to the car. "Hi Detective."

"Well, I don't know how you did it, but you said you would and you did," he said, sounding mystified.

"You found it then? The crime scene?" she couldn't keep the eagerness form her voice.

"Yeah, we found it. It took a while to get at it, I guess there was all kinds of wards and spells and things. Strange magic, the elves said," he gave her a long look, "they're pretty upset about everything actually. I guess they can't quite figure out some of what's going on out there–its stuff they've never seen before. I can't say that makes me feel very comfortable."

She nodded in sympathy, then dared to ask, "Where's your partner?"

He gestured with his chin up the road, "He's interviewing people that live around here to see if they saw or heard anything strange lately. He's pretty shaken up–you wouldn't know this but Rick actually grew up around here. Finding a major crime scene practically in his backyard has him freaked out."

"I can imagine," Allie said feeling an unexpected sympathy for the unlikeable detective.

"I wanted to thank you for pushing this after we told you to back off. The crime scene is our biggest clue so far and it's our best chance at some solid physical evidence." Riordan said.

"You're–you're sure it's definitely your crime scene then?" she asked hesitantly.

"We found four more bodies, buried out near the site. Well, the elves did. Older ones, but not badly decomposed because of the cold. It looks like after the ground froze he switched to dumping them in parking lots rather than risk leaving them lying out in the woods where someone might have stumbled across one. Whoever this guy–or group, I guess–is he's clever. With the weather warming up, if we hadn't found this site now he probably would have switched back to it and stopped dumping the bodies and we'd have thought he moved or stopped."

The detective sounded tired, "We've got a crime scene unit on the way out and the elves are processing the magical stuff. It'll take days, maybe weeks to sift through everything."

"Do you still think Syndra's murder was part of this ritual, or..." Allie started to ask, but the detective held up his hand.

"I appreciate all your help. We'd never have gotten here today without you, that's for sure. But we still have to be careful not to jump to conclusions. Until we prove otherwise, her death looks like one of our murders, and I don't see why our killer would go to all that trouble if it wasn't part of his plan." The detective's voice was firm, so Allie nodded. Riordan stood up and thanked her again before heading back towards a cluster of police cruisers she hadn't noticed down the road. He passed Zarethyn who was walking towards her.

The Elven Captain stood next to the car for a moment, gathering his thoughts, before speaking, "You have done us an invaluable service, Aliaine."

"Please, call me Allie." She said, sure it was probably a breach of etiquette but sick of hearing her full name all the time. She had a sinking feeling when he mentioned service, since the last thing she wanted was for the Guard to start seeing her as potentially useful in other cases.

He looked startled at being given the nickname, but nodded, "Certainly, Allie, if you prefer."

Eh, it sounds weird when you say it she thought *I guess I'll get used to it.* "The strange energy here–it's from the ritual, isn't it?"

He nodded, looking unnerved, which worried her. Seeing an adept mage who, she guessed, was probably over a thousand years old disconcerted by anything magical was disturbing.

"Yes. I must admit something to you–I did not doubt that what you told us was in your book, but I did not believe such a thing could in truth be done. Even seeing it now, with my own eyes, I almost still cannot believe it. It is just as you said though–standing within the ground that marks the killer's ritual space, it as if the ritual is happening right now. It is a most disturbing feeling indeed, and the energy swirls like a whirlpool. We fear that it has significantly weakened the fabric of the Worlds here."

"What would that do?" Allie asked, wide eyed.

"Not separate the worlds again, but perhaps tear a hole through to a third world. It is hard to say with certainty."

"So in trying to split the two worlds he was actually making the Sundering worse?" Allie found the idea appalling.

"It seems so. We have sent for a High Adept to see what can be done, if anything, to repair the damage. It may take a long time, perhaps more than a year for her to arrive, but the phenomena seems stable as it is," Zarethyn said

"What if the killer finishes the cycle? They said they found more bodies, which makes the total, what? 8? That we know of for sure. What if he kills the last 5 that he needs to complete a full year?"

"We will not allow him to continue. It is clear that he presents a great danger to both worlds and must be stopped," Zarethyn was trying to be reassuring but Allie did not share his optimism. "As it stands though, your part here is done. Natarien will take you back to the house now and we will try to join you later when we may."

"I'm still under Guard then? You don't think with the book gone and this place found that maybe my part in all of this is, you know, finished?" Allie said, trying not to sound hopeful.

Zarethyn gave her a sympathetic look and crouched down to pat her leg reassuringly. "I believe that this killer will continue to see you as a threat because of what you have done so far, and as well he may seek vengeance for your interference. I believe you are correct that he killed Aeyliss, and that he did so to prevent her from tracking him, and–I am sorry–that he killed Officer Lyons not only to distract us all and throw us off his scent but also to upset you personally. The fact that it did not work, and led you to push to find this place, will only enrage him further. I would be remiss in my duty to have allowed you to get us so far in this case at such risk to yourself only to abandon you to danger now. And we do not know if the Dark Court agents still seek you, something else that I must resolve."

It occurred to Allie suddenly that the Guard might be using her for bait in both cases and she found the idea very troubling. *Bleidd warned you not to trust them and you did anyway,* she thought. *And maybe they were thinking the whole time that even if you couldn't actually help them with leads you could help them by being a tasty bit of cheese in the trap...*

She bit her lip, looking down, "You know I am kind of tired, maybe I should go home."

The Elven Captain misinterpreted her reaction, "Do not worry Aliaine–Allie–we will not let harm come to you." He squeezed her leg reassuringly, before standing and closing the door. Before stepping away he nodded to Natarien who nodded back and started the car, "I will get you back to your home Aliaine" Natarien said kindly, "and the others will follow as soon as they are able."

She swallowed her paranoid thoughts, and tried to speak evenly, "I appreciate that, Natarien. When we get back, I'll fix something to eat. As a guest in my home, you're welcome to have some, if you're hungry."

He smiled, "I would not refuse a good meal."

****

They sat in the kitchen eating the quick chicken stir-fry that Allie had thrown together after they returned to the house. It was late afternoon, but since she hadn't had lunch she decided that an early dinner was in order and Natarien, who had never had stir-fry before, was too curious to refuse the new food. Allie was fairly certain that he was young, for an elf, because he was willing to engage in small talk and proved eager to ask questions about human society–usually the older elves were more reserved and unwilling to admit to their ignorance about human culture unless they had to. To her surprise she found herself enjoying spending time with him, even if most of it was giving him a crash course in human culture.

She was in the middle of trying to explain about human names, a subject that consistently baffled the elves, when Bleidd came in, "No the first name is a personal name and the second name is kind of like the clan name, sort of, but most people in formal settings are called by the second name–Hi Bleidd, there's stir-fry on the stove, if you're hungry–and using a first name denotes a level of intimacy."

"That seems very confusing. If everyone is addressed by clan name then how are individuals identified?" Natarien frowned, "And how do shortened names fit in?"

"Nicknames? Well they would also denote intimacy, sometimes, but sometimes it's just if the person doesn't like their name. Like I don't like mine, so I ask people who use my first name to call me Allie," she said between mouthfuls of food.

Bleidd stood for a moment watching this exchange with a bemused look on his face, and then went over to get a bowl out of the cabinet. She watched out of the corner of her eye as he grabbed a drink form the fridge and was disproportionately relieved to see him take a soda. She had feared Syndra's death would push him back to drinking and she had been enjoying sober-Bleidd.

Natarien nodded thoughtfully. "So it would be more appropriate to call you Allie?"

"Well, I prefer it, yes. But of course, among elves it denotes a close bond, so..." she shrugged. He chewed and considered. Bleidd sat down at the table with his plate and drink as Natarien was finishing; Allie had talked so much she still had half her meal left. With a polite nod to both of them the Elven Guard stood up. "If it is alright with you I would like to speak with the squad that is patrolling the grounds."

She wasn't sure why he needed her permission. "Sure. I'm not going anywhere."

He nodded again, almost a short bow, and headed out the back door. She watched him go, and then looked at Bleidd. "So, how are you holding up? I meant to talk with you earlier..."

"It's been a difficult day," he said shortly.

"They found the ritual site. Where the altar is and all that," she said awkwardly.

"They found it, or you found it for them?" he asked pointedly.

"I found it," she said. They both fell silent, eating. Finally she said, "Bleidd, I want you to know. I need you to know. She probably died because of me."

"No," he said shaking his head and looking up at Allie.

"Yes. And I don't want you to get hurt too, because of this. You and Liz and Jason are my family. I think you should all be extra careful."

"Allie, I love you," he said. She looked at him like he'd grown a second head, feeling the unexpected emotion from him as he spoke. Flustered he kept talking, "I know this isn't the best time to tell you. I know you're with that Guard right now. But Syndra dying made me realize that I need to say this to you because we don't any of us know what is going to happen. And I can't bear the idea of anything happening to you and you not knowing how I feel about you."

"You–what?" she sputtered. "You love me? You're telling me this now?"

"I should have told you sooner, but…"

"You should have told me this a lot sooner! Gods' damn you Bleidd!" she put her head in her hands. "Why? Why all those years ago when I was reaching out to you, flirting, hinting–I mean I know I was subtle, but you knew I was interested! You gave me that whole "let's just be friends, platonic love" talk. And I spent the last *10 years* resigned to just being friends. I accepted things as they are. And now–now! You're going to tell me that you love me! I want to punch you in the crotch, you moron!"

He winced, "I deserve that. I thought…I knew how young you were…too young, I thought. I didn't want to take advantage, and I thought I could wait for you until you were old enough…"

"You thought, you thought. , Oh my Gods! And you couldn't involve me in any of this thinking?" She looked at up him, wondering if she did hit him if he'd hit her back. It was surprisingly tempting to try. "What do you want me to say to this?"

He stood up and walked around the table and she stood as he approached, tensing, "Allie, please. Please. I know I'm doing this badly. But I do love you. I've loved you for a long time now, and I just want you to know that. I want you to know how I feel."

"Great, now I know," she said, still furious, *My best friend just died, my boyfriend might actually be using me as bait to catch a killer and now my other best friend is confessing his love. This day is unbelievable,* she thought. "What do you want me to do with this knowledge?"

"I don't want you to do anything, Allie, I just, I want...," it was strange to see Bleidd floundering and searching for words, "...I want you to consider my court too."

She looked at him in utter disbelief. He grabbed her hands, "Don't say no, Allie, please, think about it. Don't you love me too?"

"Of course I do." she said without thinking, and then winced, "Bleidd, that doesn't change anything."

He kissed her, leaning forward and covering her mouth with his. She was so shocked she stood there and let him, her mind reeling. She had fantasized many times over the years about something like this and a small part of her wanted to give in to it. But the rest of her was too angry with him; after a second she pulled back and shoved him away. He staggered slightly, his expression hurt, and she punched him in the chest. "What is wrong with you? I can't freaking handle this right now, okay? I practically had a nervous breakdown this morning, I'm trying to figure out how to be an empath as quickly as possible. Everything is falling apart, and I–can't–handle–this!"

She was near tears, and she watched him struggle with his own emotions. She was learning first hand that Elven emotions were dangerous things, volatile and strong, and through her ragged shields she could feel his love warring with rage. She fought to calm herself down and get her shields back up, "I'm not rejecting your, your court, okay? Okay? But I can't deal with this right now. And if you really care about me you'll stop pushing this, okay?"

He took a deep breath, "I'm sorry Allie that was out of line."

"Don't apologize," she muttered, sitting back down to eat, not because she was hungry but to get away from him without being obvious about it.

After a moment he sat back down as well and resumed his meal. Then, as if her words were just registering, "You're an empath?"

"Always have been. And I seem to have blown a fuse through sheer stupidity and flipped my empath switch permanently to on," she said not wanting to have to get back into that whole story.

He sighed, "That will make the funeral difficult for you, if you do not have your ability under control."

"Yeah, I guess, but I have to go," she replied, determined not to miss saying goodbye.

Chapter 10–Sunday

"We should have all the pieces," Allie said frustrated. "I don't understand this. We know what the ritual is and why it's being done. We know where it's being done and that the number of victims is higher than we thought. We know it has to be a descendant of one of the original coven members. We know he probably killed Aeyliss because she could have tracked him down, and Syndra to throw us off the track. I feel like it should be obvious who the killer is and we just aren't seeing it," Allie said rubbing her eyes.

It was the morning of Syndra's funeral and the four Guards were with her as she prepared to go to the service. The entire Ashwood department and representatives from many other local human police forces were going to be there, and the elves had sent a couple squads as well, out of respect, which Allie appreciated.

"This killer is canny and manages to stay one step ahead," Zarethyn said. "We will catch him, but it will not be easy."

"It hasn't been so far," Allie agreed, pulling at the hem of her black dress. She hated wearing dresses. "I just feel like we already have the answer and we aren't seeing it."

The days since finding the stone altar had been almost anti-climactic in their normalcy. Jess had stayed by her side nearly continuously as she and Liz planned the funeral, and she got her store cleaned up and re-opened. Although working with several Guard hanging out in the store was both strange and not conducive to business, at least she felt slightly more normal, and Jess had been with her through it all, no matter how tedious.

But in the back of her head she had started to question whether he was staying with her to be supportive or because the elves thought the killer would make his move soon. Thanks to the empathy which she still could not block out, especially when physical contact was involved, she knew he did love her, but she doubted that would stop him from using her to catch the killer if it seemed expedient. It made her question their future once his duty wasn't so conveniently aligned with her life, which was depressing but easier to think about than never seeing Syndra again.

The rest of the roommates were each struggling in their own ways to deal with Syndra's absence. Liz had taken it upon herself to handle packing up Syndra's things, working so quickly to clear her room that Allie had resorted to sneaking in during the night and filling a box with things she wanted to keep for herself. Since Syn didn't have a will or any next of kin, Liz had decided to donate all of her possessions, including her car. Liz's boyfriend Fred was helping her push the paperwork through the probate court in town hall where he worked.

Jason was picking up extra shifts at work and only coming home to sleep; Allie wasn't sure if he was planning to come to the funeral or not. And she had been trying to avoid Bleidd, still not ready to deal with his declaration of love.

"Are you ready?" Jess asked her as the rest of the Guard all headed out the door.

No, Allie thought, swallowing a sudden surge of tears, but she nodded and followed him anyway, pulling on her old leather jacket. It looked strange with the formal funeral dress but she thought Syn would appreciate it and it was too cold not to wear a coat. She had no idea how the elves stayed warm in their metal armor, unless they used magic.

The ride to the town's only funeral home was tense and silent. Allie was riding in the back of the Guard car again, this time with Jess and Natarien. She had realized

earlier that the elves were a bit baffled by the complex
funerary rites human's had; in Elven culture the body was
cremated privately and close kin would hold a memorial
service later to honor the person's life. She'd never stopped
and thought of how strange the human customs must seem
to them, but last night at the wake, when she'd had to
explain that it wasn't the funeral, and then try to explain
what would happen the next day, it had become clear that
the entire concept was bizarre to them.

The car Allie was riding in was driving between
several other official Guard vehicles in a small procession.
Zarethyn had chosen to send three squads, including his
own, to Syndra's funeral as a sign of solidarity with the
local human police community. Even though Allie knew it
was basically a public relations move and possibly also a
precaution in case the killer tried anything, unlikely as that
seemed, she still appreciated the gesture.

When they pulled up outside Sweeney's Funeral
Home there were police cars, marked and unmarked, as far
as the eye could see. Allie was assaulted by a wave of grief,
anger, and unhappiness, that made her catch her breath.
Worried, Jess pulled her against his shoulder, stroking her
hair, "You do not need to do this. If it is too much for you
we will return to your house."

"No," she said, gritting her teeth and putting as
much energy as she could into her battered shields. "No.
She was my best friend. I need to do this. But if I pass out,
you can say I told you so later."

He looked alarmed at that but Brynneth was
opening the door and she was pushing him out, giving him
little choice except to get out of the car or make it obvious
they were disagreeing. He pulled her along with him,
keeping her tucked against his side as they walked up to the
little door that led in to the building. He had quickly
learned that physical contact had the strongest effect when
she needed help with outside emotions; her growing

dependence on him made her feel needy and comforted by turns.

As they walked into the funeral home Allie was once again assaulted by bitter memories of her grandmother's death–the same nondescript hallway leading to the same blank room, the same heavy scent of flowers, the same underlying smell of death.

Unlike her grandmother's tiny family service though, Syndra's ceremony was packed with people, including friends, lovers, and rows of uniformed police. The Elven Guard squads stood in a row along the back wall, their armor gleaming under the electric lights. Allie looked to the front where the heavy oak coffin sat with a large framed picture on top of Syndra in her uniform smiling out at the room, and her feet would go no further. She saw Liz and Bleidd sitting in the front row with several empty seats, she assumed for herself and Jason, but she could not make herself join them.

She whispered up to Jess, "Can we stay back here with the rest of the Guard?"

He looked confused, but nodded, guiding her to an open space along the wall, "If you prefer, we may stand with the Guard. But are you certain you would not rather sit?"

"I'm certain," she mumbled. And so she stood against the wall, weeping quietly, throughout the entire service, which was lovely. Several people got up and said nice things about Syndra, including Liz, who spotted Allie while she was talking and kept trying to catch her eye. Allie avoided her though, focusing on making it through to the cemetery. She could not let herself totally break down until it was all over, so she held on to her self-control by a thread.

The car ride to the cemetery provided some respite, and when they all gathered again at the grave side–Syndra's picture now resting on an easel next to the coffin–

Allie was starting to feel less ragged. Folding chairs had been set up in long rows to accommodate the crowd and this time Allie sat with her friends, Jess still by her side. Bleidd, on her other side reached out partway through the lowering of the coffin and took her hand, and she could feel Jess's irritation radiating out on the other side. It provided a good distraction so that Allie wasn't thinking quite as much about her friend's body going into the cold ground.

It was a small explosion but somehow all the more dramatic for that. The flames leaped and consumed Syndra's picture as the gathered mourners jumped to their feet in alarm. Someone pointed to the northern end of the cemetery and Allie spotted the two slim forms there; she had no doubt it was the two Dark Court elves, although she had no idea why they would show up to publically disrupt the funeral. It made no sense and there was something deeply counterintuitive to the action. Everyone was yelling and several of the armed police officers had drawn their guns. A moment later the Elven Guard who were present ran towards the woods, flying over the ground like deer. Jessilaen hesitated, his hand clenching on her shoulder, and without thinking she said, "Go! Don't let them get away."

He started to step away and stopped, and to her surprise Walters, who was standing nearby, said "Go–she's surrounded by cops. Go catch those bastards. We'll get her back to her house."

Jess nodded and ran off at a right angle from the others, Bleidd running with him, trying to guess where the Dark Court elves would have been heading. Allie watched them run, praying they'd both stay safe and hoping that Bleidd would remember his promise to her not to seek revenge. Walters reached out awkwardly and put a hand on her shoulder. "Come on. I think that pretty much ended the service. We'd better get you back to the house where the other Guard are before anything else happens or your boyfriend'll filet me."

Allie couldn't help smiling slightly, despite the circumstances. She felt a wave of anxiety from the brawny detective. *Maybe Walters isn't so bad*, she thought wiping away the last few tears. *He's an ass, but I guess he has a good heart underneath it all.* She spared a final look at the coffin being lowered into the earth. *Goodbye Syn. I'll never stop missing you.* "Yeah, I guess we better get going."

Liz shook her head, her nose red from crying, "I can't leave yet, I have to finalize a few details with the cemetery manager. You go on though. I drove myself; I can't leave my car here anyway."

Allie reached out spontaneously and hugged her cousin. After a moment of stiff surprise Liz hugged her back. They were still not on the best of terms, in fact besides discussing Syndra's arraignments they'd barely spoken, but Allie hoped her cousin knew how bad she felt about everything.

She and Detective Walters walked through the milling crowd, everyone still agitated from the disruption, towards the parking lot. Walters had parked in the far corner and by the time they reached his car she was tired and ready to go home. She was surprised to see he was driving an older heavy car, the kind that was common on Earth but not usually seen in the Borderland areas because it had a lot of iron in it and was hard to keep running. She turned and was walking towards the passenger side door, thinking that he must pay a fortune to someone to keep the car running, when she felt a sharp pain in her head and everything went black.

****

Walters lifted the unconscious girl out of the trunk in the dark and carried her to the shed behind his house. It was amazing how well the plan had worked–his new allies had created a distraction as promised and all of the Elven Guard had chased after them like cats after a mouse, leaving the girl unguarded. It had almost been too easy then, despite all the human police milling around, to grab her, and no one suspected him. He'd hit her from behind, drugged her, and stuffed her in his trunk while everyone was still chasing rogue elves. His private phone rang several times but he ignored it. This was the best plan and he knew success was in his grasp; the others would realize he was right.

When the altar had been found he'd been sure everything was lost, but suddenly it was all turning back in his favor. The troublesome mixed blood bitch was out of the way; he'd managed to do it without technically going against what the rest of the group wanted, something he knew he could make them understand, and when he handed her over to the two elves he'd seal their bargain. Although he'd rather see her bleed out in his ritual to pay for her interference, the idea of what she'd suffer made him happy. He hoped it took her a long time to die.

He dropped her unceremoniously onto the shed's concrete floor, rolling her over with his foot, and he pulled off the jacket she was wearing and tossed it in a corner. Grabbing an old strip of towel he kept as a rag off of a shelf he tied her wrists behind her back. Then just to be sure he pulled out the rag he used to drug all the girls with, soaked in a potent anesthetic, and held it against her face for a few more seconds. There was a risk that he'd overdose her and kill her, but he didn't care too much–after all, he'd promised the damn elves the girl, but he'd never promised she'd be alive, and if she died, he'd blame her death on them. When she was totally limp he dropped her head back to the concrete. He quickly pulled off her shoes, throwing them onto her jacket; he'd take both and burn them now since she wouldn't need them and it was too risky to keep any of her things. Now he had only to wait for his new friends to return and he could hand the girl over before heading back out to work.

****

Allie woke up in the dark, and her first thought was that she was cold. Her head hurt, and there was a strange metallic taste in her mouth. She tried to roll over and slowly realized that her hands were tied behind her back. Nothing made sense, but it was hard to think with the pounding in her head.

Somehow she managed to get to her knees, and then her feet, staggering as everything seemed to spin. She almost fell and her shoulder hit something; after a moment she realized it was the wall of an aluminum shed, the kind gardeners used to store tools and small equipment. She tried to walk and fell again and without warning found the surface she hit moving as the door to the shed opened. She hit the cold earth and lay there for a moment, still not sure what was going on. It was so hard to think and her mouth tasted bad. She struggled up again and took a few more steps when she heard someone swearing–before she could turn towards the voice, she was tackled and driven to the ground with so much force she heard her ankle snap. The surge of pain cleared her head a little, but she couldn't get her eyes to focus.

"You stupid bitch!" Someone was growling and then a fist hit her, hard in the back. She grunted and the person hit her again and again, until she started to cry. "Stupid bitch! You're ruining everything!"

She felt helpless and frightened as her mind tried to make sense of what was going on. The person pinning her down stopped hitting her and for a moment she could hear his ragged breathing above her. Not the Dark Court elves then, this sounded distinctly human, and despite herself she could feel waves of savage anger and fanatical determination from him.

Is he the killer? Did he kill Detective Walters and kidnap me? But why? Why not just kill me too? I don't understand this.

A moment later the person's weight lifted and then she felt him grabbing the back of her dress. He dragged her the few feet back into the shed as she writhed and tried to kick, tossing her down onto the concrete floor. Before she could recover he had picked up something from a set of standing shelves against one wall and rolled her onto her stomach. He knelt on her back, and she heard the distinctive sound of duct tape being measured out, then he quickly untied her hands, dragging her right wrist up to her left elbow behind her back. She felt the tape being wrapped around her arms. He re-tied her hands that way on both sides leaving her no room to move. It pulled her shoulders painfully tight and made it hard to get a full breath. She heard herself whimpering and he got up kicking her hard in the ribs. She curled up reflexively, as much as she could, as he moved to the back of the shed. She heard a heavy metallic dragging sound as he moved something over in front of the little door; she could feel the iron even from there and repressed another whimper.

I have to open my eyes, she thought fighting the dizziness and after effects of whatever she'd been drugged with. *I have to see who this is.*

Before she could manage more than to weakly thrash her head from side to side, he was back and had grabbed her hair again. He gagged her with the rag he'd had her hands tied with before, and she took advantage of the moment and managed to crack her eyes open. The face that came into focus was such a shock that she froze and he shoved a wet cloth under her nose. She tried to struggle and he ground the cloth into her face; she smelled the same sharply metallic scent that had filled her mouth and everything went grey....

****

"I am certain she is not dead," Jessilaen repeated, his voice ragged but unwavering. "I would know if she were."

Unexpectedly the Outcast spoke up as well, "I agree, Guard. She is not dead, at least not yet. If we hope to keep her that way we must find her with all speed."

The group of Elven Guard - Zarethyn, Jessilaen, Brynneth, and Natarien - as well as Bleidd and Detective Riordan had gathered at Allie's house. The remaining Guard squads and police were searching the cemetery and surrounding area, so far without success. Zarethyn had ordered Allie's cousin and other roommate placed under Guard until she was found as a precaution, something that her cousin had resented greatly. He had not relented though, fearing that they should repeat their error in losing Allie by allowing harm to come to any of her remaining friends or family.

Zarethyn looked from one to the other after the two elves spoke. He knew both blamed themselves for Allie being taken during the funeral, after they had left her unguarded, a burden he shared. When the Dark elves had appeared so blatantly they had all reacted without enough thought, and assumed that the half-elf would be safe surrounded as she was by so many human police. It had been a real shock to return after a fruitless pursuit to find that Detective Walters had been attacked and Allie was gone. "How is Detective Walters?"

"He's fine," Riordan said, sounding like a man who was nearly at the end of his own strength. Zarethyn looked at him sharply, wondering if the human had the fortitude to see this through to the end. "They sent him home to recover but he's insisting on working his next shift. Wouldn't even go in the ambulance. Looks like someone came up behind him and shoved some kind of drugged rag under his nose. He said he got a strong dose of it before he even realized what was going on, and next thing he knew he was on the ground, which is where the other guys found him. I know it doesn't count for much, but he feels awful about the whole thing."

Brynneth was spreading maps out onto a folding card table that Bleidd had set up in the living room. "The question is why did he not kill the detective?"

"You say that like it's a bad thing." Riordan said angrily.

"Not at all, but it is illogical. It would have been easier and safer for the killer to eliminate the detective instead of leaving him alive and a potential risk."

"Maybe. But maybe it was a time issue. He was surrounded by cops–maybe he saw an opportunity to grab Ms. McCarthy when he saw her with just one cop walking out to the car and decided to seize the moment, but was trying to be fast before anyone else noticed. He comes up behind them–not hard with so many people, they wouldn't have noticed someone in a parking lot–and he knocks out Walters and then grabs the girl. He gets her in his car and takes off in the confusion before anyone even notices." Riordan said

Brynneth didn't look convinced, but didn't press the point. Jess tried to get them re-focused "We must find her. She was saying this morning that we have all the pieces of the puzzle, but we are failing to put them together. We must see what we are missing before it's too late."

Zarethyn nodded. "What is the common thread, besides Aliaine?"

No one spoke.

****

As the hours went by she tried to rest and gather her strength, ignoring the pain. The concrete was cold under her cheek, her ankle throbbed in an insistent way that made her think it was probably broken, and she was desperately tired, but she found that she could draw strength by focusing on Jessilaen. At first she thought it was only her imagination, but as time dragged on she was certain that the more she focused on him the stronger the connection to him became. Bleidd had told her that in a few cases elves could psychically bond to each other on a deep level that allowed for an unspoken exchange of emotions and thoughts. Of course he had also said this was an extremely rare occurrence which took years to form and was almost certainly impossible for her due to her father's mortal blood.

As an empath, she could also form emotional connections to people, like the one she appeared to have had with Syndra, although she hadn't ever been aware of them before. And yet she was increasingly certain she could feel Jess's presence in her mind, his fear for her, desperation, and rage were distinctly not her own. Either he really was there, in her head in some way, or she was finally losing her mind from the stress. She wondered if this was an Elven thing or an aspect of the empathy like the connection she had had to Syndra, or some strange hybrid of the two. She felt a burning rage and terror thinking of Syn, but struggled to push it aside.

Maybe–maybe, somehow I do have that soul bond with him, and because of my gift with empathy, amplifying the emotions and solidifying things, that's why it's stronger and it formed faster than anyone thought it should. Maybe somehow that's what's allowing me to reach out and connect to him at this distance. That's an awful lot of maybes... It seemed impossible and she didn't think it was supposed to work this way.

So far she hadn't been able to read anyone who wasn't either in physical contact with her or very close by unless she dropped all her shields completely, which she'd already proven was a bad idea. She was fairly sure Syndra had reached her only because of the agony the other woman had been suffering at the time, resonating through their connection and touching Allie's sleeping mind. Still it seemed too much for coincidence that she was the key to the elves solving these murders, which had led her to meet and love Jessilaen, and now her own life depended on the Elven Guard finding her and this tenuous connection to Jess might be the only way for her to be saved and for the killer to be caught.

I could almost believe in Elven synchronicity after this, Allie thought, *if I'm still alive after this, that is. I wonder though, if this is all part of a greater pattern–if I met him and we love each other because it's supposed to save me now, or at least catch the killer–how? How does it work?* She closed her eyes trying to think past the throbbing in her head. *I can feel what he's feeling, so he can probably feel what I'm feeling too? Maybe, maybe not. I couldn't project anything to him when I tried at the Outpost. Bleidd did say that people who have this connection can use it though, can communicate with it, but how? My own empathy has always been receptive only. But Syndra pulled me to her...*

She tried to roll over, to relieve some of the cramping in her shoulders from the way her arms had been tied and hit her foot against the iron railing he'd put across the inside of the door to keep her from escaping. The metal seared the exposed flesh of her ankle, and she writhed away reflexively, tears streaming from her eyes as every single injury added its pain to this new agony.

At the same time though she was vaguely aware that the feeling of Jess-ness surged stronger and more clearly; she even had a momentary, disorienting glimpse of maps laid out on an unfamiliar table. *I think I just saw through his eyes,* she thought, gasping, and trying not to vomit behind the gag. The physical pain was almost overwhelming and it was easier to focus on this new revelation than on what her body was going through.

Stop and think Allie, she told herself, *there's something about this–it was in the grimoire,* she realized, *it's the same idea behind cutting up the girls–using pain to fuel magic with a set spell to create an amplifying effect. Pain as an energetic battery to create a long term effect rather than creating a one-time power surge. That's what the book said. Tharien said my own gift allows me to use emotions to power my magic... but my own emotions? My own pain... instead of other peoples... If I can channel my own pain into this energy-echo spell to amplify my natural ability I should be able to use it to reach to him, to get him to hear me.*

She felt a momentary uncertainty about the wisdom of this; there was no way to know if it would work at all or what long term effects it would have on her or Jessilaen and she could very easily create something permanent that she'd regret later. *Yeah well, at least I'll be alive later to regret it,* she thought grimly.

She took a deep breath and allowed herself to feel the pain of every bruise, scrape, and blow. She sensed the energy building and struggled to divide her attention, so that she was still feeling the pain while also setting the spell to gather the energy and set up the energetic echo that would create the permanent power effect. She wrestled with it and then without warning the spell fell into place with an almost physical snap. She took the channeled energy and used it, reaching out to Jess; she could feel what he was feeling now as if he were next to her and when she closed her eyes, she could see through his, but still she could not get him to hear her. She ground her teeth down on the gag in frustration. The spell had worked, had amplified her natural ability, but not in a helpful way.

Then it occurred to her to use the emotional energy as well, since the set spell was in place and needed no more effort from her. If she doubled the energy–doubled the effect–maybe that would give her the extra reach to communicate with him. She took a deep breath and repeated the process, this time intentionally bringing up all of her emotional pain; all the feelings of grief and guilt about Syndra, the fear for herself, the anger and betrayal that this was all at the hands of someone she–and Syndra–had trusted. The emotions rose like a wave and she wasn't sure she could control it. It was much harder to get the spell set this time and she was sweating and panting on the cold floor when it finally worked. The spell fell into place, resonated, and melded with the first one. Unexpectedly it did not double the effect; it increased it by orders of magnitude. Allie felt a moment of panic as the combined energy surged and overwhelmed her. The tingle of magical energy became a painful burning, like grabbing an electric fence, and she felt her whole body convulsing slightly as the energy went into the only outlet she'd given it–herself. It was over in an instant, the spells still holding and radiating energy. She lay limp and stunned on the floor, feeling very much like a blown fuse.

She had no idea what she had just done to herself, and there was no chance to worry about it. She could only hope it was enough to reach Jess and get a message through, and she would have to worry about the consequences later. This time when she reached out to Jessilaen, with the combined energy of the two echo-spells powering her it was noticeably easier. She could see clearly through his eyes, and she felt his sudden disorientation as he subconsciously acknowledged her. With rising excitement she tried again to speak to him.

"Jess, can you hear me?"

****

Jessilaen was standing looking down at the maps spread out on the cheap table, trying to see what possible pattern they could be missing, while the others went over everything they knew for the third time, when he felt suddenly dizzy. He staggered slightly and grabbed the edge of the table. He heard his brother asking, "Jessilaen, what is it?"

And then Allie's voice was in his head.

"Jess, can you hear me?

He fell to the floor, caught completely off guard by the uncanniness of it.

"Allie?" He thought back automatically.

"Yes! You can hear me! Finally!"

He imagined he could feel an excitement, almost exhilaration, that wasn't his own, and it was quite unnerving. He wondered if this was how it always was for her, and if so, how she could stand it without going mad. Zarethyn and Brynneth had rushed to his side and were trying to understand what was wrong; he looked up, disbelieving, "It's Allie, she is speaking to me."

"Speaking to you?" Riordan said, shocked, "Speaking to you how?"

"Telepathically," Zarethyn guessed correctly, "Although that skill should be well beyond her."

"Allie has a way of working around her own limitations," Bleidd said briskly. "Ask her where she is."

"I can hear them through you," Allie replied in his mind, before he could pass the question on. *"I don't know where I am exactly. In a shed, probably a backyard. But it's important, you have to know–Walters is the killer."*

As soon as the words reached him he surged back to his feet, enraged. Riordan flattened himself against the wall, obviously afraid that the elf had lost his mind. The other Guards were trying to restrain him, as his brother pled with him.

"Jessilaen what is it? Tell us. You must share what she is saying, we cannot hear her."

"Walters." He growled, "Detective Walters is the killer."

"No," Riordan said, his face going pale. "That's impossible. Not Rick. No way."

Jess turned to glare at the human and the man shrunk away from the burning rage in his eyes. "Allie says it is him and she has no reason to lie."

"It makes sense, Detective, distasteful as it may be for you. He had inside knowledge of the case from the beginning. Aeyliss would have trusted him enough to give him her back near her car, and Officer Lyons would have trusted him as well. Indeed all the victims would have trusted him, if only because he was a police officer," Zarethyn said grimly.

Riordan grimaced. "I know he doesn't like elves, but I can't believe he feels so strongly he's willing to kill people to push the worlds back apart with some crazy ritual. He isn't even a mage or witch."

"That you know of," Bleidd said, "He could have been hiding that part of his life from others."

Riordan winced, "I still don't want to believe it. But the ritual site was on an empty lot near his parent's house. Didn't seem suspicious at the time."

"And he was the one who was supposed to check the list of descendants from the original coven, and said it came up empty," Zarethyn said. "Who would waste time double checking? And I wager we shall find his name on the list of descendants."

"Where is she?" Bleidd interrupted.

"She does not know. In a shed somewhere, she says," Jess answered quickly. Then he held up a hand to get them all to quiet down.

"Are you alright? Have you been harmed?" He was trying to focus on Allie but unsure how this communication worked.

"I've had better days," she answered evasively. *"I'm tied up and... I think my ankle is broken, so I can't walk, at least not far. Don't worry about me now though, you need to catch him! He doesn't know you know it's him. This is your chance to get him, before he gets wind you're on to him and escapes. You can get me after you get him."*

Jess was shaking his head, and Bleidd grabbed him before Zarethyn pried the two apart, "What is it? What is she saying?"

"She will not tell me how badly she is hurt, beyond a broken ankle. She's bound and cannot escape, I don't think. She wants us to apprehend Detective Walters before he knows we have learned his identity and escapes," Jess said, feeling frustrated.

"Is he still there with you?"

"I don't know. He hasn't killed me yet, so he's got to be waiting for something, but besides calling me a bitch, we haven't exactly had a conversation." Allie replied.

Jess looked back up at the others, "She doesn't know where he is right now, but she thinks he might be waiting for something, and that is why he has not killed her yet."

"Perhaps he plans to use her in his ritual?" Natarien suggested, frowning.

"No," Zarethyn said, thinking quickly. "It is well after dark now, if he planned to use her in that way he would already have begun, and he cannot hope to hold her alive until the next dark moon." He glanced at Riordan and then switched to Elvish. "No, the Dark elves attacked at the funeral, an uncommon, blatant tactic for them, and it provided the prefect distraction to allow for her to be taken."

"You believe they have allied with each other? To what purpose?" Brynneth asked in the same language.

"What are you saying?" Riordan asked, confused. The elves waved him off.

"They attacked her before for the book. Perhaps he found them before we could and told them she had destroyed it after reading it. He could have offered her in exchange for their assistance. Or they may even have approached him first, asking for the same thing," Zarethyn said thoughtfully, still in his own language.

"So you believe he is holding her captive intending to trade her to the agents of the Dark Court?" Bleidd asked.

"What's going on?" Riordan asked again, starting to recover from the earlier shock enough to be annoyed.

"It doesn't matter Detective, except that the ones who disrupted the funeral were elves who came here to cause trouble, and it was they who attacked Aliaine in her store. They were seeking her grandmother's book, and now that she's destroyed it they may be seeking her in its place."

"Allie?" Jess asked.

"Okay, now I'm really scared. But, still…you still need to catch Walters" Allie replied.

"Listen, I need a warrant to arrest Rick," Riordan flinched as he said it, "And we don't have nearly enough to get that. We have to find Ms. McCarthy first, alive, so that she can testify against him."

"For once Detective, we are entirely in agreement," Zarethyn said. "Aliaine must be found alive as soon as possible." He looked at Jessilaen. "Can she help guide us to her?"

"*I think so. I can feel you and see through you–I think if you start searching like we did for the ritual site, I can tell you when you are getting closer or further away*," Allie answered immediately, and he relayed her words.

Zarethyn looked startled, "She can see through your eyes and hear us right now? She is not relying on you to tell her what we are saying?"

"Yes, she is present with me. It is difficult to describe. It does not work both ways though, I can hear her speak, here, but I cannot project myself to her, "he replied, unhappily.

Zarethyn looked impressed. "I do not know what magic that is then. It is not true telepathy if she is not relying on you to relay information."

"Wait," Riordan said, "let's be logical here. If we just start driving around it could take hours to find her."

"What do you suggest, Detective?" the Elven Captain asked.

"Let me think. He must have faked being knocked out at the cemetery, so he couldn't have–he must have had her in the trunk of his car," Riordan said, pacing as talked, "Yeah. He knocks her out and gets her in the trunk, then pretends to be knocked out himself. No one's going to check the trunk of his car. He refuses the ambulance, gets sent home, and drives off with her in the car while we're all still searching the grounds."

"That is ingenious," Bleidd said, "And no one would have any reason to suspect him."

"*Allie? Is that what happened?*" Jess asked.

She replied slowly, "*I don't know. I turned to get in his car and everything went black, then I woke up here.*"

Aloud Jess said, "She doesn't remember if that is what happened, she said she was knocked out as she turned to get into the car."

"He won't be at his own place; it's an apartment in the middle of the downtown residential district. He isn't at the ritual site–no sheds out there." Riordan said. "Ask her if she can hear anything–cars, kids yelling–anything."

"*No, it's silent. I hear an owl.*" Allie answered immediately again

"She says she hears an owl, but nothing else," Jess relayed.

Riordan shook his head, then stopped suddenly snapping his fingers. "His parents' house! He must be out at his parents. It's been on the market since they died, but he hasn't had any luck selling it. It's about a half mile from the ritual site, quiet area, no neighbors for miles."

Everyone was already moving for the door, and Jess thought to her, "*Be strong my love, we are coming.*"

****

Allie pulled herself back from Jessilaen's mind, only to find that she could still sense him to some degree and hear what was going on around him as a background murmur, as if it were occurring in another room.

Well crap, she thought, hoping he couldn't still hear her, *I knew this was a risk, but if this is permanent it's going to get super annoying really quick…if this is permanent this might be more than annoying. I might have fused myself into his head forever which is going to make for some really awkward moments. If this relationship doesn't work out–even if it does–I could find myself a little too aware of exactly what he's thinking about someone else's butt or...oh this could get really bad. I do not want to get a guy's perspective on a lot of different things. And I'm sure I don't want to know what he's feeling all the time, or what people around him are saying all the time. Well, there's nothing I can do about it now except hope it fades.*

She rested her cheek against the concrete floor, trying to think. *Okay. They are coming for me. Great. But if Zarethyn is right, then the Dark Court elves are also on their way and I'm supposed to be some kind of pay-off. That isn't going to end well for me. So what can I do?* She tried, carefully to shift her weight again.

Her shoulders were a burning agony at this point and she cursed Walters casual cruelty in binding her that way. *Damn the stupid duct tape anyway! If it was rope I might be able to get my hands free—wait a minute. Tape. It's tape. And I have a charm to remove adhesive—that should work!*

She thanked the hours of frustration dealing with cleaning up secondhand books at the store that had motivated her to create the simple charm to remove adhesive residue, and quickly got the little charm in place. Within moments the tape on her arms loosened and fell away and her arms rolled forward. The sudden freedom increased the cramping exponentially, and the flood of blood returning to her numb lower arms burned. She wept unabashedly until she heard Jess's worried voice calling her.

"Allie what is it?"

She fought to control herself and respond. *"It's nothing. I managed to free my arms, but the circulation had been restricted so it hurts. I'm fine."*

She could practically taste his worry. *"We are nearly there now."*

And then the door to the shed opened, a bare bulb overhead flickering on, and in a panic Allie did the only thing she could think to do; she pretended to be unconscious. She heard the iron railing being dragged aside and heavy footsteps, and her heart raced. Walters swore and kicked her hard, but she managed to stay limp. He was leaning over pulling the loose strands of tape away when the second voice spoke, a voice she had only heard once before but would not soon forget, "What is wrong?" The Dark Elf asked, sounding annoyed.

"Nothing," Walters growled back, "She got her arms untied, but looks like she's still out of it."

"I doubt it. Likely our arrival was fortuitous and she was about to escape your crude prison," The elf said condescendingly.

"Hey I'm the one who got her here remember? And she isn't going anywhere, her ankle's broken," Walters shot back.

"Really?" The elf's voice was closer now and Allie felt rising panic. "Which one?"

"Left. Snapped it when I tackled her," Walters sounded curious now.

"Well, then let us see how unconscious she truly is." Without any further warning he lifted his foot and struck full force at her broken ankle. The pain was immediate and savage; Allie writhed on the floor screaming behind the gag, her cramping arms grabbing weakly at her leg. The elf laughed lightly, "She seems to be awake now."

"You want me to re-tie her arms?" Walters asked, as if having a woman screaming on his floor was a perfectly normal occurrence. Then again, she thought, maybe for him it was. He must have been getting ready to go back on duty; he was wearing the suit she thought of as standard issue detective wear, with his gun in its shoulder holster. The Dark Court elf, without his cloak, stood over her. He was fair haired and wore a non-descript dark tunic and trousers with a knife and sword at his waist. In the doorway of the little shed stood the second elf, looking like a mirror image of the first.

"No need. She can't do us any harm and she's far more fun this way," The closer elf responded. He reached down pulling the gag off, taking some of her hair, which was caught in the material's loose knot, with it. She hardly noticed the pain, but when he reached down and picked her off the floor by her hair she cried out again, her hands clutching his wrist. She could not put any weight on her bad ankle now, and tried desperately to balance on her right foot. His emotions swirled around her, a disgustingly familiar blend of lust and satisfaction, and she couldn't seem to block him out. He grabbed her face with his free hand. "How does it feel, little mixed blood girl, knowing that you are here now because of fools and stupidity? That your own lover left you to chase after us and let you fall right into my hands?"

He leaned forward breathing deeply along her throat and in her hair, "I can still smell him on you. But I promise you, very soon, that will change." And he laughed again, delighted.

"Stop playing with her Ferinyth, you have plenty of time for that later," the second elf spoke from the doorway, brisk and business like.

"But I've been looking forward to this," the Dark Elf said, his free hand tracing the line along the top of her dress, just below her collarbone. She shivered. "Are you frightened?"

"Yes," she whispered, because it was true.

"Good," he said smiling, and then slapped her hard across the face. She staggered, losing her one-footed balance, his hand in her hair momentarily taking all her weight. Before she could recover he released her hair, grabbing her right arm with both hands as she started to fall and breaking her wrist as easily as if it were kindling. She fell to the floor screaming. In her mind she heard Jessilaen's voice again, but she dared not try to answer him.

"Ferinyth, let us conclude our deal with the officer first," the second elf said again sounding bored. "The girl can wait–and do not forget I need to question her yet about what she may know of the book. She has used some of its magic, I can feel the energy here…"

"You spoil all of my sport, Daeriun," the elf Ferinyth, complained. Allie lay on the floor, panting in pain and thinking furiously; there was very little she could do magically in this situation. Her own abilities were more about leverage and influencing small things than any direct magics. She could shield herself and protect herself from any magic they tried to use on her, because she was rather good at protective magic, but little else. And despite her success in reaching out to Jess she dared not try to use the echo-energy to power anything else she could think of from the book because she was afraid now, despite her desperate situation, of the consequences that she might create.

"You can have your sport later, "Daeriun replied firmly, "After our business is concluded."

"It's alright," Walters said, his emotions making Allie feel sick. "You wanted the girl, you got her. He can do whatever he wants with her now."

"You're welcome to watch," Ferinyth said. Allie's eyes fixed on Walters' gun and she had an inspiration; when she was young her Grandmother had taught her a little charm to keep the poachers who sometimes stalked the woods near the house from killing anything by hexing their guns. Seizing the moment, Allie used the distraction of the elves to quietly set her spell on the renegade cop's gun, thankful that the weapon was almost all plastic. It was a little thing but it made her feel slightly better.

"You cede her to us then? You agree our alliance is made?" Daeriun pressed. He clearly wanted Walters to verbally acknowledge what he was saying. If the cop had more experience with elves, Allie thought, he'd be a lot more careful about what he said to them and how he said it.

"Sure, yeah," Walters said. "You get her and the use of this house, and I get your help when I need it to keep the investigation off my back."

The Dark Court elf nodded, "Then it is done." Allie felt a ripple of energy as the spell the elf had framed set up; probably a basic geis to prevent Walters form breaking his word, even if he changed his mind later. The human killer seemed oblivious as he watched Allie try to roll over on the floor. The first elf, Ferinyth, knelt down, smiling wolfishly. and grabbed the top of her dress in both hands ripping it down the front, "Now, my turn."

****

Jessilaen was despairing as the car flew down the dark road towards the house that Detective Riordan had identified. He had tried repeatedly to get Allie to speak to him again, but after one brief response he could hear nothing more from her, although he was certain that he could feel something disturbing, something he suspected was pain. The first time he had felt it, like a ghostly aching, he had reached out to her and she had answered, telling him she had freed her arms and they hurt. The second time the shadow pain was worse and she would not answer him at all. He grew more and more afraid for her with each passing minute.

His squad's car was following Detective Riordan, with the other squad of Elven Guard who had been at Allie's home behind as well. Zarethyn had summoned further aid from the Outpost but they had far to travel and it was unlikely they would arrive in time to be of any help. Jess feared that they would all be too late and the thought was more frightening than anything else he could imagine. It was hard for him to believe that someone he had not even known existed a few weeks ago had become so essential to his life, but the thought of her death now was unacceptable to him.

As soon as Riordan's car stopped in front of the house Jessilaen leaped out of the door of his own vehicle, hitting the ground running. He could hear the others shouting at him to wait but Allie's screams echoed in the chill night air and the sound of her suffering was unbearable. He ran towards the source of the noise even as it suddenly stopped, around the dark bulk of the house, across the backyard. As soon as he saw the small building at the edge of the yard, he knew it must be the shed Allie had described and he shot towards it like an arrow, drawing his sword. A figure in the doorway turned and Jessilaen barely managed to dodge aside as the Elven mage threw a fireball at him; it coruscated as it hurtled past his head. He never slowed. The strange mage ran into the yard preparing another spell, but before he could cast it Zarethyn was there and the two mages engaged each other. Jess had crossed most of the yard by then, trusting his brother to handle the Dark Court mage and knowing he had to get to Allie.

When he was still a dozen feet from the door the murderer, Detective Walters, bolted, running towards the woods. For an instant Jessilaen hesitated, and in the next breathe the second Dark Court elf appeared, his sword reflecting electric light off its blade as it swung towards Jessilaen's face. He brought his own blade up, deflecting the blow.

"You can fight me, Bright Knight, or you can save her, but you do not have time to do both." The Dark Elf taunted him showing the small knife he held in his other hand, bloody to its hilt. Then he retreated, daring Jessilaen to choose whether to follow his enemy or save his love. Out of the corner of his eye he saw the flashes of color as

Zarethyn continued to battle the Dark mage; the rest of the Guard could not be far behind. He lunged forward and darted into the shed without turning his back on his enemy. A moment later Natarien ran past, giving chase, with several elves from the other squad close behind.

****

Zarethyn ran behind his brother into the back yard and watched as Jessilaen was nearly hit by a sorcerous fireball. He moved up as quickly as he could to engage the Dark Court mage in the center of the open space as Jess ran heedlessly towards Aliaine. The other mage was powerful and he found his own spells ineffective in breaking through the Dark Elf's defenses, while the other's attacks were hitting him with enough force to stagger him back. He did not think he had the ability to defeat this foe and the other members of the Guard had all run past; he began to sweat in the chill air unsure how he would win. His opponent threw an energy whip at him that caught him and knocked him off balance and he found himself flat on the ground, gasping. The strange mage walked over casually, drawing the energy for the final spell that would destroy his enemy. "You Bright Court are all the same, all weak and ruled by your concern for others," he sneered.

Bleidd appeared from the other side of the house, hitting the mage from behind before the spell could be finished or the other elf could realize he was there. The energy of the spell backfired into the mage and the Outcast elf, knocking both to the ground and Zarethyn watched the Dark Court mage convulse with Bleidd's dagger buried to the hilt in his back. Before either elf could get up they could hear Walters yelling, "Put the gun down Jim, don't make me shoot you."

Looking up they saw the two police detectives facing off across the yard, guns drawn. Riordan shook his head. "Don't do it Rick. It's over."

"No, it's not. It won't ever be over, no matter what happens to me. I'm only one person trying to make things right. If I fail others will continue the work," the killer said, furious, pulling the trigger on his gun with an audible click. He looked baffled when the gun misfired and even more surprised when Riordan's bullet slammed into his chest a moment later. He fell without a sound, and his former partner was running towards him before he hit the ground.

****

Jess found Allie in a spreading pool of blood on the concrete floor. He fell to his knees next to her, calling her name, and her eyes opened.

"*I can't breath,*" she thought to him sounding more dazed than frightened.

"*Hang on my love,*" he thought back, quickly assessing her injuries. He had started to turn to call Brynneth when the healer appeared, kneeling down in the blood.

"Her lungs are punctured." Jess said, terrified, as her eyes fluttered shut again.

Brynneth nodded, moving quickly to place his hands over the stab wounds in her sides. The healing energy flowed like water as Brynneth worked a major enchantment to heal the critical injuries. Staring at her pale face, Jess watched for any sign of success and nearly wept when she suddenly drew a full breath.

"*My love?*" he thought tentatively.

"*It's better. He's healing the worst of the worst parts.*" Allie replied, sounding a bit sleepy but more like herself. "*They panicked when they heard the cars, and the car doors. The mage wanted to take me with them but the other one–the other one didn't think they could get away with me so he...*"

"*You are safe now*," Jessilaen answered, reaching out to hold her hand as Brynneth finished his work. She turned her head towards him and he was certain he could feel her emotions now, mostly relief; it was still a strange thing and he had no idea why he was feeling what she felt but he clung to the sensations.

"*Jess, I have to tell you something, something I did and I think it might have been a bad idea now, but at the time there didn't seem to be any other way*," she looked at him, and her pale, bruised face made him weep. "*Please don't cry!*" she said, alarmed.

"I can't help it. I almost lost you and I can't stand the thought of it, or knowing that you suffered as you did because we failed you," he said aloud. Brynneth glanced up but stayed focused on the healing.

"*Don't blame yourself. We all trusted him–oh! Did you catch him? Did he get away?*"

"Don't worry about that right now. Try to be still and let Brynneth help you," Jess looked anxiously at the medic who was still framing major spells over her battered body.

"*Jess–this talking in your head thing. I did that. With a spell. I kept trying to reach you, to use the connection we have, but it wasn't enough. I mean I could reach you, but you couldn't hear me or feel me. I didn't know what else to do so I–I used a spell from the grimoire. The spell to create permanent energy sources*," Allie felt his surprise and rushed on, trying to get it all out. "*I used my own pain and my own emotions and I focused all the energy on strengthening our connection through my empathy so that I could communicate with you. And it worked but I don't know exactly what I did or how I did it, and, um, I kind of think it might be permanent too and I don't know how to fix it."*

She had expected him to pull away or be angry, but he simply tilted his head to one side thoughtfully. "Interesting. So your spell amplified what was already there into something stronger, strong enough to allow you to—what? Project yourself into my mind somehow?"

Brynneth gave Jess a strange look from the corner of his eye, but the Guard commander ignored him.

"Do you know what the extent of this is yet?"

"Extent? You mean what can it do? Well not entirely, but I can feel what you are feeling, kind of all the time now. And if I push I can reach out to you and hear you in my head, and see what you are seeing, and what you are hearing—and of course you know you can hear me if I speak to you." Allie was glad for the distraction of talking with Jess, instead of thinking about how much her body hurt. Brynneth was having a hard time getting her ankle to heal; she could feel the spell he was trying to set on it slipping a little each time he tried to use it. When she closed her eyes she kept reliving those last instants when she had been stabbed in the sides and found herself unable to draw a breath, and the memory left her terrified and shaking, even knowing she was safe now. She'd rather talk about her spell mistake than ever think about it again.

"Interesting," Jess said again, thoughtfully, "although perhaps these effects will fade with time."

Allie wasn't so sure about that, knowing the nature of the echo-power spell, but she didn't want to argue with him. Brynneth finally straightened up, looking unhappy.

"Aliaine, I have done as much as I can. Your life, at least, is in no further danger, but the damage to your ankle is partially beyond my skill to heal. I have done what I can for it."

Jessilaen frowned, "How bad is it still?"

"She should not walk on it, not now and not for a few days at least."

He hesitated and then spoke directly to Allie, "I fear that even with time you may have a permanent limp and it may always give you some pain." Brynneth sounded frustrated as he spoke, but what Allie felt from him was regret.

"That's okay, really. You've done more for me anyway than I can ever repay, and at least I'm alive to have a limp," Allie said trying really hard not to think about the feel of the hard boot sole impacting her broken ankle. It seemed that every little thing was bringing back memories of the events that had caused each injury, and she swallowed hard, trying not to cry.

"You owe me nothing Aliaine, truly," Brynneth said. "There is no debt between us."

"How can there not be?" Allie asked, feeling tired and confused.

Brynneth sighed, "Alright, then I release you from any debt you owe me. You have done more to help us find the one who killed my niece than we could ever have done on our own, and it would be ill grace of me, after what you have suffered for helping us, to ask any repayment."

"And any debt you owed I would pay anyway," Jess said briskly. "So do not fret about it."

She shook her head, feeling worse, since they had needed to come rescue her and had to heal her, it seemed wrong somehow to have that all wiped away. Jess reached down, gathering her up into his arms, and she tucked her head against his chest, suddenly wanting desperately to be anywhere else except this horrible place.

"Please get me out of here."

He stood easily with her in his arms, and for the first time since Syndra's funeral, she felt safe.

****

Zarethyn stood and extended his hand to the other elf, helping Bleidd to his feet. The Outcast hesitated a moment and then accepted the hand up wordlessly. The backyard was oddly silent now, without even the normal night sounds of the forest to fill the air. Zarethyn quickly assessed the rest of his squad, hoping that the others might have managed to capture the second Dark Court elf.

Jessilaen was emerging from the shed carrying Aliaine, who was pale and bloody, but seemed alert; Brynneth stood next to them his hand on her shoulder. His brother looked ragged, although there was no indication he had suffered any injury. Zarethyn felt a momentary twinge of worry and found himself wondering, not quite idly, what would have happened if they had arrived too late to save the girl; he felt a grim certainty that for good or ill his brother's life was irrevocably intertwined with Aliaine's now. What that would mean for his future Zarethyn could not guess.

Natarien stood at the back of the open space holding pressure on a bleeding gash in his side, his eyes searching the tree line where the other squad had disappeared chasing the remaining Dark Court elf. The Guard Captain had little choice but to accept that at least one agent of the Dark Court had escaped them, although he could be satisfied in knowing the more dangerous of the two was going nowhere. The fallen mage lay still in the grass, Bleidd's knife still embedded in his back. Zarethyn worried about the elf who had escaped, but that was a worry for another day; nothing could be done about it now. The squads he had called for backup should be arriving soon and they could be sent out to see if any trail could be found, and as well the human police would be swarming. He could already hear the sirens wailing in the distance.

Detective Riordan crouched over Walters' body, talking quickly into his radio, but Zarethyn doubted the injured killer would survive. He felt a sense of satisfaction, despite the apparent escape of one of the Dark elves, and a nagging concern that Walters may not have acted alone. His people had all survived, they had arrived in time to save Allie, and Aeyliss's killer was dead or dying.

When it had become clear that her killer was human the Guard Captain had faced a moral quandary: to let the human justice system handle the killer, and risk the man being set free, or to seek his own justice and risk the fragile peace that held the two communities together. This outcome, he felt, was ideal.

Looking up, his eyes met the Outcast elf's and he came to a decision. Pitching his voice loudly enough that everyone still in the yard could hear him, he said "You named yourself wolf once, after being Outcast by the Elven Guard, but I say now that you have acted with honor and are an honorable person. I declare you Outcast no more, Morighent of Clan Soileireacht."

The former Outcast's eyes went wide at the sound of a name he had not heard spoken in over 50 years. He stood still for a moment, unsure what to say. Such a thing had never been done before; being Outcast had always been a death sentence for those who suffered it and no one had ever had it repealed. As a Guard Captain though Zarethyn had the authority to speak judgments of law that could not be overruled, except by the Queen herself, and while it hadn't been done before he was within his rights to do it. Finally Bleidd–Morighent–nodded slightly and then walked over and pulled his blade out of the fallen mage's back. Zarethyn smiled slightly to himself, wondering what the strange elf would choose to do with his life now.

****

Jess carried Allie into the house, wrapped in his cloak since her dress was ruined. He had argued that she should stay at the Outpost but she refused, wanting to see her cousin and Jason, and be in her own room. As soon as they entered the house they found Liz waiting in the entry way, looking exhausted.

"Oh my God, Allie. Are you okay?"

Her cousin hugged her, almost pulling her out of Jess's arms, and she felt a surge of fear, anxiety, concern, and anger. She caught the sideways glance Liz threw at Jessilaen and tried not to sigh.

"I'm alive, Liz, which is more than I can say for Detective Walters."

"Oh my–what? What happened?" Liz looked truly stunned, leaning back against the wall as if she needed the extra support.

"I'm sorry I thought you knew–Jess can you put me down on the couch?" Allie asked, distracted.

"Absolutely not. You should not be walking on that ankle," he said in a tone that brooked no arguments.

"Fine, carry me to my room, and Liz you come with us and I'll catch you up," Allie said, exasperated.

"What happened to your ankle?" Liz asked weakly.

"It was pretty badly broken," Allie winced as she tried to talk to Liz over Jess's shoulder while he carried her up the stairs. "Walters kidnapped me at the cemetery."

"What?" Liz shook her head, disbelieving. "No. That's not possible. He's a cop."

"It's true Liz. He knocked me out and took me to his parents' house and locked me in this shed. He was the killer, the one killing all the girls, and he was going to hand me over to the, um, the other people looking for grandmother's book, the ones who hurt me at my store last week. He had some kind of deal with them to trade me for their help."

"I don't believe it," Liz said shaking her head.

Allie felt Jess stiffen, thinking her cousin was questioning her word.

"I know it seems crazy but it's true," she said quickly, as he carried her into her room and set her gently on the bed. "But the Guard and Detective Riordan got there before the bad guys–I mean Detective Walters and the other two–could get out so they tried to kill me."

Liz made a small noise in her throat and Allie stopped.

"I'm sorry Liz. I'm okay, but Walters was shot and he died before the ambulance got there."

Liz went and stood in front of Allie's window, looking out over the garden. "But it's all over now, right?"

Allie looked at Jess, who sat down next to her and took her injured ankle into his lap.

Jess spoke quietly. "Walters said it would never be over. I fear that he knew something we didn't, even at the end, and that it may not be finished yet."

"You're just saying that because you don't want to leave," Liz said.

"Liz, don't say that…"Allie started, but her cousin interrupted.

"We've had the Guard here all night. I had to call out of work tonight because how could I go in followed by two armed guards? And we had Syndra's funeral this afternoon and then you disappear. I've been sick with worry all night. I just want this all to be over with. Allie. I want our lives back," Liz said plaintively.

"I know Liz. I'm sorry. I think, maybe, it is over now," Allie said, flinching away from her cousin's distress.

Liz gave her an inscrutable look, threw one last hostile look at Jess and then left. Allie looked down, and Jess shifted, easing her ankle off his thigh so that he could sit next to her. She leaned against his shoulder, something she felt she'd been doing far too much of lately. "Do you really think it isn't over yet?"

He kissed the top of her head, easing both of them down until she was lying comfortably on the bed, still leaning against his shoulder. "Don't worry about it, my love. Try to rest and heal, and let tomorrow worry about itself."

She shook her head, feeling the weight of many unresolved things hanging over her, not the least of which was the hum of his thoughts and feelings in the back of her mind. It was something like always having a television on in the background, and while she was starting to get better at ignoring it, the implications were depressing.

"I don't know how to not worry about things," she sighed as he magically changed his armor for regular clothes, and she settled into against him. "Is this how courting always works?"

He laughed, "The emotional closeness, yes. The rest of it seems…unique to you."

She smiled with him and then sobered, "Are you sorry? That you ever met me? I wouldn't blame you if you were, I haven't done anything but cause you trouble."

He stroked her hair, "Never, Allie. I cannot imagine my life without you."

She resisted the urge to shake her head. Certainly he had changed her life for the better in many ways, but she couldn't see how she had done anything positive for him. She was exhausted and her ankle ached persistently, but despite herself she found her eyes growing heavy and closing. Allie had been afraid she would never be able to sleep again after the things she'd gone through in the last few hours, but with Jessilaen holding her, with his emotions swirling around her, she fell asleep quickly and slept without dreaming. She would deal with her worries about tomorrow when tomorrow came.

****

They'd gathered hastily as word had spread; everyone was agitated and the atmosphere of the small spare room was tense. The half dozen people talked in low voices among themselves, muttering and whispering as if they were afraid of being overheard. When the door finally opened and their leader strode in, the group's relief was obvious, although the tension was no less.

One of the young men standing against a wall spoke up immediately, "He failed. What do we do now?"

Silence reigned as they all waited for direction. "He failed because he didn't listen. He decided to go his own way, against the group."

The words fell like stones into a still pond. Everyone shifted uncomfortably, meeting the speaker's eyes and then looking away. "We can still succeed—will still succeed. But we have to stay together and stay strong as a group. We have to remain true to the cause."

Piercing eyes caught and held a frail woman's gaze, "Why are we doing this?"

"Because the Sundering is a sickness that has to be cured," the woman said, straightening as she spoke and pushing her brown hair behind her ears.

An older man across the room was next to be questioned. "What is our reward?"

The man's voice was confident, "The world will be returned to normal. We'll get our world back and send the elves and other creatures back from whence they came."

"And what is this worth?" The leader asked a middle aged woman hovering next to the man.

"Anything," she replied, her voice catching.

The woman next to her spoke without prompting, "Any sacrifice for the cause is worth making if it helps us ultimately succeed."

"That's right," The group's leader said, as several people began nodding. "Anything. Walters' failure is unfortunate but he did forward the cause, and he died without telling them anything about us. If he had listened to what he was told, he would not have failed, but even so, we can salvage the situation."

The last member of the group, a young man with a rose tattooed prominently on the side of his neck and was wearing a battered Bomber jacket, finally spoke.

"How?"

The leader met his eyes and he didn't look away as the others had. "Listen carefully. This is the new plan…"

Epilogue

"I don't understand" The hurt in Jess's voice cut at Allie's heart, but she knew she could not allow herself to relent. She sat on her bed, rubbing her bad ankle; it still ached although it was healed as much as it was likely to and she was learning to walk with her new limp without drawing too much attention to it. The weeks since the funeral and confrontation with Walters and the Dark elves had passed in a blur. The Guard and police had been unable to find any trace of the surviving Dark Elf or any proof of a conspiracy, despite searching Walters' apartment and house thoroughly. Jessilaen had come to tell her that the Guard was being withdrawn back to the Outpost and the case closed, and he had asked her to go with him.

"I can't go with you Jess. My life is here," she tried to keep her voice even.

"You do not love me then," he said sounding resigned.

"Of course I love you, you idiot." she said, angry and unable to hide it. She took a deep breath. "I love you. I don't know why, or how, and the Gods know I shouldn't. But I do, and I accept that I do, whether I want to or not."

She winced, "Sorry that didn't exactly come out right."

"No, I understand. That is how Elven emotions are," he sounded grimly amused.

"Well then I can see why you all work so hard to avoid them. It's a kind of madness, isn't it?" she quipped. "Besides thanks to this amplified soul-bond thing I gave us, you know how I feel. You can feel how I feel." She reached out and took his hand, letting her feelings wash over him even as his misery and worry flowed into her.

His breath caught. "Allie, please. You must come with me. I cannot stay here and I cannot bear the idea of living without you."

"No," she repeated.

He put his head in his hands and grabbed fistfuls of his hair, "Why? Why can you not?"

"Because," she repeated, literally feeling his frustration, "my whole life is here. Everything that isn't you. My home. My business, what's left of it anyway. My family, such as that is. My friends." She swallowed hard, "For Gods' sakes, I can't just drop everything and walk away because you want me to. How would you feel if I was asking you to do that? Leave the Guard, leave your family, your duty, everything, and come live in my life?"

He looked away, the muscles in his jaw working.

"Jess–I just buried my best friend. There is a part of me that wants to go with you because it would be easier to not deal with my life right now. But I'd regret it later. It would be me running away from my problems, not choosing you, do you understand that?"

He shook his head. "I cannot bear the thought of leaving you. What am I to do, if you will not go with me?"

"You are still stationed at the Outpost. You are still a Guard. Come and see me when you can," she said feeling her own sense of panic at the idea.

He shook his head again. "That will not be often. We will be apart almost all the time."

"We are never really apart anymore," she said, and he gave her a look that made it clear a freakish psychic bond was not enough for him. She tried again, "Maybe that will be the test of our relationship. We will see how we really feel and if we want to be together after we have had some time apart." She felt lame saying it, but didn't know what else to say.

He looked directly at her, then, and she flinched at the fury in his eyes. "I know how I really feel and I do not need to test anything. Or perhaps you are still considering another and it would be more convenient…"

"Don't drag him into this!" she raised her voice, surprising herself. She knew he was still upset after finding out that she had not denied Bleidd out of hand when he'd offered his court too. And she could not explain to him that no matter how much she loved him, she loved Bleidd too and she could not hurt him by pretending otherwise. She had chosen to be with Jess, but that wasn't enough for him, and now, with her refusal to run off with him, he was obviously looking to blame his rival.

Then, at a lower volume, but still angry she said, "This isn't about me trying to make time with two people and you know it. I don't see you promising not to sleep with anyone else."

She cut herself off, because the truth was that Elven culture didn't do monogamy outside of marriage, which was a highly contractual affair, and they were both free to sleep with whoever they chose even if they stayed a couple. It was, from an Elven point of view, a stupid thing to argue over. But coming from a human culture and knowing that thanks to her spell, she'd have to be a mental witness to any assignations he engaged in, Allie hated the idea of him with anyone else and didn't want to think about it.

"I would promise you as much if you would promise the same," he said.

"Don't offer a promise you can't keep," she felt her hands shaking as she spoke and clenched them into fists.

"I would keep my word, if I give it; it seems that you do not want to even offer such a promise," his voice was full of accusations and she felt her temper slip. Without thinking she hit him, her fist bouncing off his chest.

"You know damn well I have never slept with him, or anyone else. You think I'm just waiting for you to leave so I can fall into bed with him, as if I couldn't do that while you were still here if I wanted to? You're the one who is going to be surrounded by people who think of sex like eating and drinking–no big deal, and not something to refrain from," she wanted to hit him again, but managed to restrain herself.

"So then come with me," he said again, grabbing her hands and pulling her into him. She fought the urge to scream.

"I can't. I can't just drop everything like some ditzy maiden in an old ballad and run off with you. It would take me months to get things wrapped up so that I could go…" she trailed off as his arms tightened around her.

"Then do what you need to do, and say that you will join me as soon as you can," he begged shamelessly. She pressed her forehead into his chest wishing that her life could be simple. He seemed to sense that her resolve was wavering and he pressed, choosing a topic he knew still bothered her. "You are still in danger from the Dark Elf who fled during the fight. With me you would be safe."

"We don't know that he's still after me, he could have headed right back to wherever he came from. And even if he didn't, I can't live my whole life in fear," she said, trying to push her own anxiety at the thought away. She was still having nightmares about what she'd been through at the hands of the elf who had escaped and the idea of him coming back for her again was terrifying. Despite the constant concern she refused to let fear run her life, though, and she could not let Jess use her fear now to manipulate her into doing what he wanted either.

"This is impossible," he whispered, and she wanted to agree with him.

"Jess, please, for now, only for now accept that I cannot go with you," she said instead.

She felt his hope rising again. "Only for now though?"

"I will consider your offer and think about what it would mean, what I'd need to do. But for right now I can't go," she said firmly, trying not to feel like she was actually giving in.

He kissed her deeply, and she felt herself melting into him.

"As long as I have hope that you will join me soon, I can wait."

"And in the meantime," she hedged, "we will date like humans date, we'll see each other when we can, and spend our free time together."

He kissed her again, and without meaning to she reached out to his mind.

"*And I will always be just a thought away.*"

Made in the USA
Middletown, DE
07 February 2015